THE GIRL WHO LOVED CARAVAGGIO

THE GIRL WHO LOVED CARAVAGGIO

BELLE AMI

www.belleamiauthor.com

Published Internationally by Tema N. Merback
Calabasas, CA USA
belleamiauthor.com

PRINT ISBN 978-1-7322071-3-4
EBOOK ISBN 978-1-7322071-2-7

Editor: Joanna D'Angelo joannadangelo.com

The Girl Who Loved Caravaggio is dedicated to my friends and family—your encouragement and support on this life-changing journey have given me the strength to weather stormy seas and treasure calm waters. And to you, dear reader, I welcome you aboard. You are the wind in my sails.

ACKNOWLEDGMENTS

There are so many people who have touched my life and expanded my horizons. Thank you to my parents Dina & Leo, my husband Joe, my children Natasha & Benjamin, my siblings Sarah, Joel, and Josh, my other children Julianna & Mitch, and my brother-in-law Steve.

A special thank you to Joanna D'Angelo, my editor, advisor, coach, and dear friend, without you there would be no books. Thank you, Fiona Jayde for creating the cover for *The Girl Who Loved Caravaggio*—the second most beautiful cover I have ever seen—the first being *The Girl Who Knew da Vinci*, our first collaboration.

ALSO AVAILABLE

Out of Time Series
The Girl Who Knew da Vinci ~ Book 1 (#1 Amazon Bestseller)
The Girl Who Loved Caravaggio ~ Book 2
The Girl Who Adored Rembrandt ~ Book 3 (Coming Soon)

Tip of the Spear Series
Escape ~ Book 1
Vengeance ~ Book 2
Ransom ~ Book 3

The Only One Series
The One ~ Book 1
The One and More ~ Book 2
One More Time is Not Enough ~ Book 3

Holiday Ever After Anthology
The Christmas Encounter ~ Featured Short Story

Join Belle Ami's email list for exclusive sneak
peaks, contests, giveaways and more…

Click on: https://www.belleamiauthor.com/newslettersignup

I am always learning.

All works, no matter what or by whom painted, are nothing but bagatelles and childish trifles… unless they are made and painted from life, and there can be nothing better than to follow nature.

I bury my head in the pillow, and dream of my true love… I am rowing to you on the great, dark ocean.

Amor Vincit Omnia (Love conquers all).

Michelangelo Merisi da Caravaggio

CHAPTER 1

Rome, Italy
28 May, 1606

Michelangelo Merisi da Caravaggio sat up and glanced out the window. "*Merda!*" He had overslept. He was late. He didn't need a timepiece to know what hour of the day it was. The light streaming in through the open window had turned the walls a shade of ochre—evening was approaching. He leapt out of bed pulling the sheet with him.

"Painter, are you stealing my covers?"

"No, why?" Caravaggio smiled over his shoulder at the beautiful woman in bed.

Fillide Melandroni lay on her side, her long red curls tousled around her. Naked and still rosy from their lovemaking, she was the most beautiful woman in Rome. He bounded back to bed and nibbled her shoulder. She was delicious. His lips wandered down the length of her body to her full *culo*, the most perfect rump he'd ever seen. Unable to resist, he growled, pinching her ass before he delivered a sensuous love bite. "It is a sin to cover such a gift. Maybe I should paint you just like this, goddess, with your glorious *culo* preserved for all eternity. Botticelli had Simonetta Vespucci for his Venus, and you, Fillide, are mine."

She swatted him away. "Stop it! *Sei Pazzo!* You've painted me enough. I have something else in mind. Painting isn't your only talent, *il mio maestro.*"

He flipped her over to face him and claimed her lips. Her fingers feathered through his hair and she kissed him back. Then he felt her hand drop to his groin. He groaned, watching her luminous hazel eyes flame with desire.

"Do you want more, *amore mio*?" She fluttered her lashes at him. "Show me what kind of *stallone* you are."

His shaft hardened at the thought of her riding him like a stallion and for a moment he considered another round. But his friends were waiting

1

and there were serious matters to attend to, matters that took precedence over the pleasures of the bedroom. "Later, Fillide."

Her lush lips rounded into a pout. "You promised me you would ignore Ranuccio."

"I said I would, but it is unlikely I can," he said, rolling out of bed. "Ranuccio has profited off you enough, Fillide, and he's threatened to stop you from modeling for me. He's insulted my honor and this I cannot bear."

"Your honor? *Fanculo*, your honor. Men—" she hissed, "do you think honor matters when you are dead? Forget him, painter. *Per favore*, my second sight tells me nothing good will come of this."

"Don't start with your intuitions of the future. How can a prostitute understand a man's honor is everything?"

"*Testa di cazzo!*" Jumping out of bed, she grabbed a pewter tankard and hurled it at his head. He ducked just in time and it thumped against the wall.

Regretting his words, he spread his hands wide, pleading, "*Perdonami Madonna*. I would not hurt you for the world."

She ran at him with fists raised, but he caught her wrists and held her in check.

She writhed like a demon possessed, smoldering with rage. Not knowing what else to do, he pulled her against his chest and smothered her protests with a ferocious kiss. The goddess melted in his arms, appeased. For a moment his only thought was ramming his throbbing cock inside of her. Reminding himself that his friends were waiting he broke the kiss. "I have to go Fillide. Onorio and Paulo are waiting."

"Please, do not go. I have a bad feeling." She buried her face in his neck and wrapped her arms around him as if she could stop him from leaving. He gently broke free of her and pushed her away.

"There is nothing more to say about it."

"Humph." She grabbed the sheet off the floor and wrapped it around herself. "Caravaggio, don't think when he stabs you that you can come running to me to tend your wounds." She stomped back to bed. "You can bleed in the street for all I care."

He picked his clothes up off the floor and began to dress. As he hopped on one foot pulling his tights on, a cold wind whisked by him, sending a shiver skittering down his spine.

Forgive them Father, for they know not what they do…

Perhaps Fillide was right. Maybe he should put aside his vengeance… And then he remembered the *stronzo's* threats to Lena and Fillide. He shook his head and continued to dress. As he fastened his doublet, he heard a tearing sound. The once fine, black-velvet fabric was frayed and worn. It was a habit of his to wear out his clothes until they became so threadbare, they fell apart. He growled, annoyed at the prospect of having to buy new clothes. He hated taking time away from his work. *But perhaps it is a sign a new beginning is in order.*

He strapped his scabbard and sword around his waist and turned to bid farewell to Fillide, but she'd turned her back to him. He sighed, shaking his head. No matter how many women he painted and bedded, he would never completely understand the mysteries of the female sex.

Caravaggio shut the scarred wooden door, glancing up to the window, hoping she'd be there. She was not. Fillide's house was huddled in a narrow alleyway close to the Piazza del Popolo. He was late and hurried past the dingy rows of shop fronts with their cramped second and third story living quarters. Entering the Piazza del Popolo he glanced up at the Egyptian obelisk of Seti I that towered over the largest square in Rome. It had been brought to Rome by Octavius, who'd ended the reign of Cleopatra. He chuckled to himself. *Now there was a man who knew how to deal with a headstrong woman.*

"We need to make haste," Onorio Longhi called out to him. The hot-headed architect was perched on the edge of a fountain. Their other friend, tall and muscled Paulo Aldato, leaned toward the stream of water spouting from the stone cherub holding a pitcher. He cupped his hand and captured some of the cool liquid, slurping it down.

Caravaggio draped his cape over his shoulders. "Let the *bastardo* cool his heels waiting."

Paulo's one eye twitched—the other one lost in a battle. "We need to go. I promised Petronio I would get you there on time and I need to get back to the Castel Sant' Angelo for duty."

"You mercenaries from Bologna are always in a hurry to fight for the sake of fighting. Worry not, I will see you make it back to your watch on time. In short order I will teach Ranuccio Tomassino what it means to attack a man's honor. That *becco fottuto*, who moonlights as a *puttaniere*, deserves to have his balls shredded. Fillide and Lena must be free of this abusive pimp."

The full moon glowed in a blue-black sky casting a spotlight on the three men. Had his focus not been on the duel, Caravaggio would have been intrigued by the interplay of light and dark. Flickering shadows danced across Onorio and Paulo's faces, creating stark contrasts of chiaroscuro, much like in his renowned paintings. He pushed aside thoughts about work. There would be time enough for that later. He was on a mission. He reached beneath his cape and gripped the hilt of his sword that bumped against his leg. Filled with an inflated sense of righteousness, he strode through the narrow, cobbled streets and alleyways toward the Grand Duke of Tuscany's Palazzo Firenze.

Struggling to keep their voices hushed, the three men swaggered with confidence as they made their way to the Via di Pallacorda. Tennis Street was where the duel would be fought. Its open courts served as a venue where young men vented their frustrations competing and gambling raucously over games of tennis and fencing.

"The problem with Rome," declared Onorio, ever the philosopher, "is that it is teeming with men seeking Papal favor. They come from everywhere and live like rats, nursing their petty grievances and jealousies. The Bolognese hate the Tuscans, and everyone hates the Sicilians. Rome is a city of men with nothing to do but drink, fight, and fuck."

Paulo laughed. "At least you have things in their proper order."

"This is the way of the world," sighed Caravaggio. "Power is in the hands of the few, but that does not stop the hordes from seeking it."

"Ah, but what about the excitement of Rome? There is no city to match it." Onorio danced in a circle with his arms reaching to the heavens.

"Settle down, architect. Have you heard from the captain as to the agreed upon terms?" Caravaggio asked.

Onorio punched his arm. "It has been agreed, *amico mio*. Ranuccio's witnesses will be his brothers-in-law Ignacio and Federico Giugoli, and his brother Giovan Francisco will serve as his second." Onorio took an exaggerated bow, doffing his flat velvet cap to the ground. "Paulo and I will witness your victory over the pimp Ranuccio. Petronio will be your worthy second."

"And everyone knows the concocted story?" Caravaggio referred to the illegality of a duel. Dueling was a capital crime that carried a sentence of death.

"A spur of the moment argument between you and Ranuccio over a bet on a tennis match. Things heated up, got out of control, and a sword fight ensued."

"Let us hope everyone keeps their heads and repeats the same story or we'll end up with our entrails cut out of our bodies." Caravaggio pushed away the thought of being arrested by the *sbirri*, the papacy's police force, and possibly found guilty. A gruesome, degrading death would be their reward.

"You just focus on the swordfight, painter, and leave the explanations to Petronio and Giovan Francisco." Paolo squeezed his shoulder.

"Once and for all I will settle this score," Caravaggio snarled. The thought of killing Ranuccio filled him with a rush of adrenaline that fueled his bravado. "When I'm done with him, his days of pimping will be over. Both Fillide and Lena will be free of his tentacles." He grinned. "Better yet, they will be free of his testicles." All three men erupted in raucous laughter.

"Tentacles… testicles… that's very witty…" Paulo couldn't stop laughing as he repeated tentacles, testicles, tentacles, testicles, over and over.

"Besides," Caravaggio went on, "the most beautiful courtesans in Rome deserve a better protector, a man who will not take advantage of them. A fucked-over cuckold like Ranuccio who can't manage his own wife will not prevent me from painting the women I choose."

Onorio cupped his crotch and winced. "I'm glad it's not my testicles that are on the line."

Caravaggio grabbed his friend by the scruff of his neck affectionately. "Your jewels are safe for tonight, at least, *amico*."

Onorio slapped Caravaggio's hand away. "Settle down, painter. Do not jest about my testicles. Look, there's the captain in front of the courts."

The three men joined Petronio Toppa and shook hands. Caravaggio's eyes darted around. "Where are the Giugoli and Tomassino brothers?"

Petronio, a veteran warrior, spoke in a serious tone more in line with the gravity of the situation. "They should be here any minute. Once they arrive things will proceed quickly. The sooner this is over, the better. None will want to tarry once the outcome is decided."

Caravaggio hissed. "There can only be one outcome."

Petronio put his arm around Caravaggio's shoulder. "Your skill with the sword is great, *amico mio*, but it is better to be prepared for the unforeseen. Do not let your emotions get the better of you, keep your head on your shoulders. It is good to remember that blood is blood, we all bleed red when cut."

Caravaggio nodded. "Of course, you are right, Petronio. I will keep that in mind. I praise God you are my second."

From the end of the street Caravaggio heard voices approaching. The Giugoli brothers flanked Ranuccio with his brother Giovan bringing up the rear. The four men came to a stop and the seconds met in the middle of the tennis courts.

Petronio wasted no time getting down to business. "We all know why we are here and have agreed to the rules of engagement. The two combatants will fight until first blood and we, the seconds, will not interfere so long as the fight remains fair. The others will stand and bear witness to the duel and its outcome. When it is over, we will disperse, and the score will be settled. As for our stories, we have agreed this was an argument that got out of hand, a heated coming to blows over gambling and a tennis match."

Giovan stuck out his hand. "*Sì, è concordato.*" He turned to his brother and brothers-in-law and they nodded their agreement. Petronio turned to Caravaggio, Onorio, and Paulo and they all nodded in kind. Both Caravaggio and Ranuccio shed their cloaks and removed their leather scabbards. They had agreed to fight wearing usual attire, doublets and hose, to keep up the appearance of a chance encounter gone wrong.

Unsheathing his sword, Caravaggio flicked his rapier several times in the air accustoming his grip to the weight. The cold steel caught the moonlight and reflected a blinding flash of illumination. His sword tip was deadly sharp as was Ranuccio's and the reality that something might go wrong surged through his veins.

Only a fool isn't afraid of dying when going into battle.

His thoughts were spinning, and he couldn't think who'd said that to him. Maybe it was the captain, maybe it was his fencing master in Milan. Whoever said it was a wise man.

The six other men took their places forming a narrow row the length of the court. Only the seconds had drawn their swords, holding them with tips to the ground as a deterrent to any who thought to interfere in the duel.

Caravaggio raised his rapier in presentation, assuming a fighting stance. His heart thundered in his chest. Already his breath came quick as he prepared to engage. He barely heard Giovan say the command to begin "*Andare!*"

Ranuccio lunged and attacked with a shout of "*Culo stronzo!*"

The profane accusation of sodomy was like pouring oil on fire. Caravaggio parried the blow that landed with a jarring ring of steel upon steel. For a moment he gazed into the eyes of Ranuccio, his face only inches away. Through gritted teeth, Caravaggio hurled his own insult, calling Ranuccio *a becco fotutto*, a fucked-over cuckold. He pushed Ranuccio backward, riposted, and attacked, thrusting his rapier forward. He threw the full weight of his body behind his sword, doubling his efforts. His grunts and groans were punctuated by the clash of metal against metal as he drove Ranuccio a few steps backward.

Ranuccio parried hard, pushing Caravaggio back. Ranuccio tossed his head, beads of sweat flying off and landing on Caravaggio. He growled, "*Bastardo*." Backward and forward Caravaggio countered Ranuccio's thrusts, gaining ground and losing ground.

To Caravaggio it felt like hours had passed, though only minutes had passed. He sensed his opponent's fatigue. He knew his own strength was fading and he wouldn't be able to keep up much longer. His doublet was drenched in sweat. In a desperate attempt to finish it, he lunged and attacked, driving Ranuccio backward. Ranuccio struggled to hold his ground but was forced to retreat. When he stumbled on his own foot and fell, both Giovan and Petronio ran forward, but it was too late. Caravaggio saw his chance and lunged for Ranuccio's balls, yelling, "Without your testicles you'll be a threat to no woman!" The sword flashed in his hand and he struck but missed, slashing Ranuccio's thigh near the groin. Ranuccio screamed in anguish and blood spurted up like a fountain, soaking Caravaggio.

Horrified, but desperate to end the duel, Caravaggio raised his rapier to strike again. Exhausted, he failed to see Giovan leap at him, until it was too late. Giovan raised his own sword and brought it down on Caravaggio's head. The painter staggered back, tumbling to the ground. Caravaggio's eyes flickered open—his vision blurry from blood seeping from his head wound. Dazed, he watched as Giovan advanced with his sword raised, ready to finish him off. His lips moved in silent prayer, certain he was about to die.

"No!" Petronio pushed Giovan away and the two seconds clattered swords in combat. Everything happened so quickly it was almost impossible to follow, but somehow Giovan managed to land a severe blow and Petronio went down moaning, gripping his wounded arm.

Giovan turned to finish him. Caravaggio braced himself, awaiting the death blow.

"*Dio Santo!* Giovan, help us," the Giugoli brothers yelled.

Giovan cursed Caravaggio and abandoned the fight. He rushed to Ranuccio's side. The stricken brother appeared barely conscious. The Giugoli brothers were doing their best to staunch the gush of blood, removing their tunics and applying pressure to the wound. Reeling from his own injuries, Caravaggio was nauseous at the sight of Ranuccio's life draining from his body, painting the street red with blood.

Petronio's words echoed in Caravaggio's brain. 'Blood is blood. We all bleed red when cut.'

7

He moaned in pain as Onorio hefted him up, half-carrying him, half-dragging him away, while Paulo shouldered Petronio.

Glancing back, Caravaggio shuddered as he saw Giovan, Ignacio, and Federico carrying Ranuccio's lifeless body. The young man's legs trembled under the leaden weight of the dead man. "*O Dio!* What is to be done?" Their cries of despair echoed back to him.

The scene eerily replicated his painting, *The Entombment of Christ*. His eyes fluttered closed as he recalled his premonition earlier. Fillide had been right. What had begun as a matter of honor and a fight to first blood had ended in disaster. The least of his punishments would be exile from Rome. But if Ranuccio was dead, which he most surely was, there was no safe place for him. The Pope would issue a *band capitale,* which meant anyone in the papal states could kill him and receive a bounty. All that was needed to claim the bounty was his severed head. His hand flew to his throat. He was now a dead man walking.

He would have to flee his beloved Rome.

CHAPTER 2

Florence, Italy
Present day

She let out a piercing scream. She raked her nails down his cheeks, her fingernails catching in the bristly hair of his mustache and goatee. Rage flashed in his ebony eyes. All she could see was the angular face above hers, tanned skin stretched taut over high cheekbones. Around him hovered a thick fog. He grunted but didn't let go, his callused hands locked on her shoulders. A shock of black, wavy hair fell over his forehead with his effort to restrain her.

"Let go of me!" she cried. *You killed that man. I saw you do it!* She thrashed and bucked, kicking out with her legs. Desperate to be free of the killer.

"Angela, wake up! *Amore mio*, it's just a bad dream."

Angela Renatus blinked rapidly as the fog cleared and ebony eyes changed—one blue and one hazel—the mesmerizing eyes of her fiancé, Alex Caine.

"Alex! Oh my God. It's you." *It was just a bad dream.* Damp bed sheets knotted around their legs.

Confusion and worry flickered in his eyes.

"Alex?"

A trickle of blood ran down his cheek. Gently, she wiped the blood away with her fingers. "I'm sorry... I... I..." How could she have mistaken the man she'd loved through two different lifetimes—the same man who nearly died saving her life only a few short months ago—for the monster in her dream.

He gathered her into his arms and cradled her. "It's okay, Angela. You were having a nightmare, a real doozy from what I could tell."

"That's no excuse. I could have scratched your eye."

"*Amore mio*, I'm fine. This is nothing." He brushed her hair out of her eyes. "Do you remember anything from the dream?"

9

Dreams and nightmares. She thought they were behind her. For weeks now, she'd been free of them, after she and Alex had recovered the missing Leonardo da Vinci painting. Scordato was dead and his accomplice Enrico Fortuna was behind bars. Why now? She loved Alex. Why, when they were leaving in the morning for the States to announce their engagement and meet each other's parents, would the dreams start again? It terrified her to think about being pulled back into the past. "I remember a little. There was a swordfight, I think it was a duel. One of the men fell and the other stabbed him. He must have hit the femoral artery because there was so much blood everywhere…" She shook her head. "It was gruesome."

"That explains what you were shouting about."

"What did I say?"

"*Il sangue è sangue. Tutti sanguinano rosso quando tagliamo.*"

"What does that mean?" Her Italian was basic, and she was too upset to be able to decipher Alex's words.

"Blood is blood. We all bleed red when cut. Did you recognize either of the men?"

"No… I mean… not really." She couldn't bring herself to tell him that when she opened her eyes, she thought Alex was the killer. She couldn't bring herself to tell him he was in her nightmare. Why upset him when the whole episode was probably a hallucination? Not every dream meant something. Not every dream was real, and she couldn't imagine that this one was.

He was watching her intently. "Could you tell where it was, or the era?" She knew he must be as worried as she was. He'd watched her disappear into the past before. He'd been with her several times when the past pulled her back. He knew about her psychic ability. He also knew she struggled with it.

"Italy, but I'm not sure where. By their clothes I'd say Renaissance, give or take a hundred years."

"Always the Renaissance. Was Da Vinci there?"

"No, I haven't seen him since we visited the Louvre and I stood before the Mona Lisa. I haven't had any dreams or visions about my past life as Fioretta Gorini since we found the Leonardo. I think those ghosts are finally resting in peace."

Alex ran his hand through his hair, his eyes shadowed with exhaustion. She was robbing them of their sleep, they had an early flight. She caressed his face. "I insist you let me tend those scratches."

"Don't worry about it, I'll take care of it. Are you okay?"

"I'm fine. Now go and put some antibiotic on your face."

"Okay, Florence Nightingale. I'll be right back."

She sank into the pillows and stared at the ceiling. As a surprise for her, Alex had hired an artist to fresco the ceiling of their bedroom with a scene from the Sistine Chapel. He'd brought her into the bedroom blindfolded and she chuckled, thinking he had something kinky planned but when he pulled off her blindfold, she was speechless. In awe. For an art historian whose specialty was the Renaissance, seeing Michelangelo's masterpiece first thing in the morning and the last thing at night was a gift beyond measure. Above her head was *The Creation of Adam*—the outstretched hand of God reaching for the outstretched hand of Adam, imbuing him with life. When she'd protested the extravagance, he'd brushed it off saying, "What good is money if I can't use it to show the woman I love what she means to me?"

That was Alex. He loved her and didn't care what anyone else thought. How could she ever have confused him with a killer? She thought about the face of the man she'd seen when she opened her eyes. She'd seen his face before, she was sure of it. Closing her eyes, she tried to conjure up his features, but Alex exiting the bathroom distracted her. He must have thought she'd fallen asleep because he turned the light out and slipped beneath the sheets as quietly as he could.

"I'm not asleep." She turned and snuggled into his arms.

He breathed her in. "How did I ever sleep without you?"

She giggled. "I don't know. How did you? So much excitement and the added pleasure of never knowing when I might scratch your eyes out."

"Yeah, never a dull moment." He kissed her. "*Amore mio*, we need to get back to sleep before the alarm goes off." He pressed his body against her. "I think I know just how to make that happen."

"Hmm… and how is that?"

His lips answered for him as he claimed her mouth. When Alex made love to her nothing else in the world existed. Not even a madman with wild eyes who killed people in violent sword fights.

Angela's body was satiated from their lovemaking, but her mind wouldn't rest. Alex slept peacefully beside her, his chest rising and falling. She slipped from his embrace and tiptoed out of the room. Where do art historians go when they're troubled? To the library, of course. She made her way down the spiral staircase to the main level of the spacious apartment.

Alex had created a modern oasis with touches of old-world mystery and elegance.

She opened the massive carved wood doors and flicked on the lights. Alex's library never ceased to take her breath away. The Art Deco torchiere and the four-branch candelabras lit up, casting a warm glow on the floor-to-ceiling bookshelves that lined the walls. But the most arresting feature of the library was the massive picture window. She paused to gaze out at the magnificent view. A living, breathing painting whose colors shifted from gold and copper tints in the light of day, to a shadowy blue palette under the glow of the moon. At its center, the Duomo glittered like a jewel-encrusted crown. Filippo Brunelleschi's dome floated above the city of Florence in magnificent splendor.

A cold wind swept past her causing a shiver to scurry up her spine. She whirled around, a gasp escaping her lips.

"Who's there?"

Nothing. No one.

Stop it Angela. The dream has you on edge.

The dream had scared her to death. The pull of the past was beginning again. And with that would come more dreams and nightmares. She had to figure out the identity of the dark-eyed swordsman. Like a loose thread tempting to be pulled, she needed to unravel this mystery before her sense of foreboding took hold and nightmares became her norm.

She stared at the bookshelves, hoping for a clue.

Who are you? What do you want from me?

She ran her fingers lightly over the book jackets and came to a stop. The volumes were in chronological order. She closed her eyes, allowing the images from her dream to float to the surface of her mind. A high-necked, black doublet. The once fine fabric fraying at the seams. Buttons marching up the front, their golden color faded by time. Pantaloons with hose underneath. A dark flat cap with a long, pale feather... The sword fight had taken place either in the late Renaissance or early Baroque period. The large tome she pulled off the shelf was a catalogue raisonné of the Uffizi museum's most important holdings. Tucking her legs beneath her, she settled into the tufted burgundy leather chaise lounge Alex had recently purchased for her comfort. She began flipping through the pages. She thumbed past the Mannerist paintings and landed on a page in the Baroque period.

Her breath caught in her throat. Staring back at her from the page was the face of the killer.

Caravaggio!

How could she not have recognized him?

Probably because you were terrified of getting slashed by his sword?

She ignored her inner voice, reached behind her, and flicked on the reading lamp. The page flooded with an eerie light. Caravaggio's *Medusa* was one of the crown jewels of the Uffizi Gallery, depicting the moment after Perseus slew the Gorgon Medusa. The painter had mounted the canvas on a convex wood-like shield, the rounded shape of the canvas making the image of the decapitated head appear three dimensional. Caravaggio's blend of light and dark made the snakes in the dying monster's hair appear to be slithering, bringing the viewer's eye closer to the image.

Caravaggio had based his painting on Gaspare Murtola's poem about the Greek myth. But most historians agreed that in the painting Caravaggio knowingly placed himself in competition with Leonardo's lost painting *Medusa*.

Angela traced her fingers over Murtola's words, "*Flee, for if your eyes are petrified in amazement, she will turn you to stone.*" But it wasn't the poem that disturbed Angela, it was the horrified face of Medusa. It was Caravaggio's own face. The artist had chosen to paint a portrait of himself as a decapitated monster. Was it a metaphor for his own lurid deeds? The man she'd seen, the killer in the sword fight was Caravaggio. But why had she seen him morph into Alex? Was it merely the last vestiges of the dream playing with her mind, or was it something more?

In her recollection, Caravaggio was a volatile man driven by passions not normally attributed to artistic genius. She'd always considered him an anomaly, a personality unsuited for his aspirations. A flawed genius. History had painted him as a violent man with a terrible temper. Even though Angela appreciated the cinematic quality of his work, she had never felt emotionally connected to his paintings. His work was too dark, too bloody, too inflamed. Quite frankly, it frightened her.

On the other hand, she'd always been drawn to the work of Leonardo Da Vinci, which made sense after she discovered her past life as Fioretta Gorini, friend and muse of the maestro. Fioretta had secretly married Giuliano Medici and Leonardo had painted their wedding portrait. And, in her other tempestuous life as Caro, she'd found herself betrothed to Gerhard Jaeger, a German officer in World War II who rejected the Nazis and took a painting by the great master from the Nazi-controlled Uffizi Gallery in Florence.

Finding the missing Leonardo Da Vinci had solved the mystery and resolved those two star-crossed, past lives.

She and Alex were tied to each other by past incarnations. In a past life, Alex was Giuliano Medici, the love of Fioretta Gorini's life. When Alex and Angela met, it was literally love at first sight, even while Angela resisted the notion. But once they'd discovered the painting in a secret cave in Tuscany, it was over. Angela no longer felt the pull to the past. She stopped having disturbing dreams and visions that dragged her into her past lives. So, why did she have this dream about Caravaggio? An artist she had never been drawn to, as she had to Leonardo. Did she have a connection to him?

The last thing she wanted was to have to deal again with nightmares and visions of a past life. Setting the book on the side table, she got up and wandered back to the bookshelves, scanning the biography section. She found three books on Caravaggio's life by eminent scholars. Carrying the books back to the seating area, she set them on the side table and curled up on the chaise once more. It was going to be a long night of reading. She'd have to grab some sleep on the flight to Chicago. In the meantime, she felt a compelling need to delve into the artist's life.

Helmand Province, Afghanistan
May 22, 2012

The blood thrumming in his ears was so loud he wondered if his teammates in front and behind him could hear. Alex and his men were spread out in two lines on either side of the road. Their weapons drawn and their fingers trigger-ready. The mud-walled village no different than any other they'd cleared of Taliban weapons. A bad week. Three of their company had been killed and four wounded when their convoy had been ambushed while out on a routine patrol.

His buddy, Randy Charles, followed behind him. After signing up for a second tour of duty, Alex and Randy had both been transferred to Camp Leatherneck Marine Base in Helmand Province. Their daily routine focused on cutting off the supply lines of the Taliban and narcotraffickers and keeping Highway 1 open, the primary Afghanistan artery between Kabul and Kandahar.

"Just another day at the office," Randy joked.

"Yeah, the only difference is you might find yourself cashing in your chips because some bearded pot shot gets you in his sights," Alex shot back. Their shared sense of humor kept them sane. God knew the constant threat of landmines, booby-traps, and IEDs wasn't a laughing matter.

"Sometimes I think sitting behind a desk in a cushy leather chair beats another day in this hell-hole." Randy said.

"Who're you kidding? You fucking love it, macho man," Alex teased. Randy was always the first man in and last man out regardless of the danger. Randy had saved a soldier from being shot full of holes in the most recent ambush.

For today's gig they'd loaded up at base camp and Alex had driven the Humvee. They were followed by two more Humvees. The convoy headed out in the dead of night, arriving a couple of hours before dawn. Their destination was a village on the outskirts of Lashkar Gah, the provincial capital. They jumped out, surrounded by miniature tornadoes of swirling dust.

"Another day, another desert, and looky here another poppy field," Randy joked. "If all they grow is opium poppy, what the hell do they eat?"

Cutting a path through a newly planted poppy field, they marched forward, not worrying about IEDs. It wasn't a big stretch for the Taliban to figure out that killing the villagers with explosives wasn't a great idea. The Taliban needed the villagers to work the fields, otherwise good-bye to their heroin profits. Most of the tribal villagers were Taliban sympathizers anyway.

Tim, their company lieutenant, started in as they traipsed through fields of red, trying not to breathe too deeply. "I Googled *Helmand province* and guess what?" Tim had a habit of blowing off steam, rhyming off stats like a baseball announcer, when they were out in the field. Every soldier had a different way of dealing with the life-and-death situations they faced every day.

Randy grumbled, "I have a feeling you're going to tell us one way or the other."

"Look around you, guys. These fields represent ninety percent of the heroin supply in the world. We're talking four billion smackers. Can you believe that?"

"If Google says it's true, it must be." Randy shook his head.

"Hell, opium is Afghanistan's biggest export." When Tim started on a rant it was impossible to stop him. "We're screwed 'cause there's no way we're ever gonna be able to stop the drug trade. What the hell could they grow that could even come close to the kind of money they make from these damn poppies? The drug trade keeps them weaponized. It's all about the money, guys."

Screwed is putting it mildly, Alex thought.

As they walked through the village, word spread like wild fire that the Americans were there. The Afghani men began to emerge from their low, squat dwellings built of stone and concrete. Eyeing the lean, bearded men cautiously, Alex couldn't remember the last time he'd seen a woman in public. A few months back on a trek into another village he saw two women and a little boy, bustling along a dusty side-street. Alex tried to catch their eye, wanting to convey with his expression that he was there to help them. As they hurried past him, the young boy glanced up and his eyes widened. He smiled and opened his mouth to say something, but a windy swirl of dust kicked up and the taller of the two women pulled the little boy between her and the smaller woman. They kept their heads down and floated past him and his men like silent wraiths in their flowing black burqas.

Alex swallowed a lump in his throat. The boy had looked happy to see him. War always took the greatest toll on women and children. In this ancient tribal society, most women, particularly in the villages, had very few rights and only minimal education. Women married young and became mothers, raising their children and keeping the home. Afghani society had begun to shift after 2001, when the Taliban Regime was overthrown by the Northern Alliance. Thanks to the assistance of the United States military forces. But it was a long road to freedom, and the Taliban were lurking everywhere.

Tim stopped to question one of the villagers, asking when he'd last seen any Taliban. Animatedly, the man gestured, and spoke, pointing to the east and Pakistan. The translator related that the Taliban arrived every few nights on motorcycles demanding food and shelter. Broadcasting from the mosque, the villagers were threatened with beheading if they didn't cooperate.

"Yeah, I'll bet they have to twist their arms to get their cooperation," whispered Randy. "More likely they kiss their Taliban asses."

The team fanned out; rifles raised. The bomb experts went into the mud-walled mosque first, while Alex and the rest of the team waited outside. After the bomb squad cleared it, Alex and the rest of the team began their search. Inside a wall, they found a stash of rocket-propelled grenades, ammunition, rifles, and a wood coffin filled with everything you could wish for to make a bomb. Another coffin revealed a cache of rifles, ammo, a mortar, and communications gear.

"In a house of worship, no less," grunted Randy as he lifted an armload of rifles. "Did they think we'd just ease on down the road and not check?"

"Hiding in plain sight I guess." Alex shook his head with disgust. He hefted a shoulder missile launcher and added it to the pile.

"I sometimes wonder what the heck am I gonna do when my tour is over?" Randy drawled as he dumped an armload of rifles in a wheelbarrow.

"Don't you worry, southern boy, I've got plans for you." Alex squeezed his shoulder.

"Care to enlighten me?"

"Trust me. You're going to love what I have in mind. You'll be rolling in cash and beautiful women."

"You'd better deliver brother, or I'm going to kick your ass from here to Timbuktu."

Making a dozen trips, arms bulging with the loads of weapons they carried, they piled everything up a few hundred feet from the village. They were joined by other soldiers, hauling armloads and boxes of explosives and ammo.

One of the guys radioed Alex. "We found a bunch more of this shit in a barn with the goats." That too was added. Following protocol, all enemy munitions were to be destroyed, so Alex and Randy set the charges and the team took cover. With their fingers in their ears, they counted to ten and the explosives detonated with a boom that echoed throughout the valley.

"I hope those Taliban assholes heard it in those caves in Pakistan." Randy removed his helmet and wiped the sweat from his brow with his sleeve.

On their way out of town they handed out candy to the villagers.

"Why the hell do we hand out this candy anyway?" asked Randy.

Alex laughed. "Because, asshole, it's supposed to make them like us."

"Good luck with that, Shit-For-Brains," Randy guffawed.

"Well, it makes the kids happy at least," Tim said hooking his arms around Randy and Alex's necks. "Good day of work, wouldn't you say buds?"

"Can't think of anything I'd rather be doing," Alex replied with a roll of his eyes.

Randy began to sing Sonny and Cher's anthem, *I Got You Babe*.

Alex groaned when Joey and Tango joined in. They belted out in a tuneless chorus as they trudged back down the valley.

They were nearly through the poppy field when a mortar hit—they all ducked for cover.

"Shit!" yelled Tim as he scanned the direction of the mortar launch. "It's coming from that old truck by the side of the road. It wasn't there when we arrived."

The radio crackled, and Ray's gravelly voice came through. "I'm taking the mother out. Over." Ray was in charge of the rocket launcher.

"Don't talk about it, do it! Over!" Tim stuck his fingers in his ears.

The missile whizzed over their heads and hit pay dirt. The truck burst into the air, disintegrating into a thousand pieces of flaming metal.

"Let's move," Tim called out. "We need to reach transport now!"

Tim ran ahead with Alex close behind and Randy bringing up the rear. They'd been ambushed and were exposed, sitting ducks in a field of poppies. Alex spied their Humvees just a few yards ahead and breathed a sigh of relief.

An explosion came out of nowhere and blasted Alex off his feet. He must have been knocked unconscious because the next thing he knew, Randy and Joey were dragging him out of the field towards the Humvees.

Alex's head throbbed as if he'd been kicked by a mule. Warm blood oozed down one side of his face, blurring his vision. The field of poppies spun around him in a sea of red. When he tried to focus, he saw double. *Okay. Concussion. Shock.* He ran down a mental checklist. *Arms, legs, feet, fingers. Check.* "What the hell happened?" His words seemed to come from a distance. *It's the damned ringing in my ears.* "What the hell happened?" he repeated.

"Tim's bad. Doc's triaging him now. Stepped on an IED. You went down from the force and you've got some metal in you. But you'll live."

"Jesus. Anybody else?"

"Nicky got a shoulder wound, but Tim got the worst of it. Those bastards must have mined the field while we were in the village." Randy yelled over to one of the other guys, "Help me get Alex in the truck, I'll drive. Let's get the hell out of Dodge."

Alex ignored the ringing in his ears. "How bad is Tim?"

Randy glanced over at him as he shifted gears. The Humvees barreled down the road. "He's going home for sure. Both his legs are history."

Bile rose in Alex's throat. *This fucking war.* A thousand dead Taliban weren't worth Tim's legs.

"Hey guess what?" Randy said, laughing.

"What?"

"I got youuuuu, baaaaaabe."

"Shit," Alex groaned. "I don't know what's worse, your caterwauling or the ringing in my ears. At least you're muffled."

Randy turned to him, and mouthed the words —*I got you, babe.*

"What?" Alex yelled. "I can't hear you."

Randy leaned closer and belted the line, "They say we're young and we don't know…"

If you can't beat 'em, join 'em.

Alex added his tuneless voice, worse than the sound of nails scraping on a chalkboard.

That's what they did when the world fell apart. They sang and carried on. He tried not to think of Tim or the dozens of friends he'd lost.

Randy flashed him a toothy grin. It was the last thing he saw before the explosion blew the Humvee to pieces.

"Randy!" Alex woke up screaming. Randy's face hovered before him, blue eyes filled with mischief. *I Got You Babe*, ringing in his ears. Frantic, Alex bolted upright, his heart pounding in his chest, his body drenched in a cold sweat.

Where am I?

In a panic, his eyes whisked around the room. His frenetic mind registered the sliding glass doors. Moonlight glinting off his watch sitting on the dresser. Bathrobe draped over the back of a chair. Relieved at the familiar sights of his bedroom, he let out a breath in a whoosh and eased back against the pillows.

But the ringing in his ears continued. Pounding in his head. Nausea reared up. He closed his eyes and breathed deeply. In and out. In and out…

Why can't I let it go? Let Randy go?

How long was he going to blame himself for surviving? His war was over. He'd lost his best friend, and there was nothing he could do to change the past. Randy would want him to move on. PTSD was a bitch. He hadn't had an attack in a long time, at least six months. So why now?

His nausea under control, he glanced at the space next to him where Angela should have been sleeping. Panic reared again.

Where the hell is she?

He stumbled down the Corbusier spiral staircase, gripping the handrail. He found her in the library, sleeping. A book open, face down, on her lap. Easing her hand off the book, he picked it up. *Michelangelo Merisi da Caravaggio: The Man and His Art.* He noticed the other books piled on the floor beside the chaise. All about Caravaggio. Frowning, he flipped through the pages, his mind registering the bold colors and often gruesome depictions of the Baroque painter's style. A chill crept up his spine as his eyes landed on the agonized face of a beautiful young woman as she applied a blade to a man's neck, blood pouring from the open wound.

Randy! Oh God, no!

The explosion echoed in his mind and he dropped the book. It landed with a thud. A wave of nausea overcame him, and he began his breathing routine once more.

Judith Beheading Holofernes. He'd seen the painting several times in Rome, hanging in the Galleria Nazionale d'Arte Antica. But it had never had this impact on him.

The nightmare… First Angela and now me. Something is definitely going on…

"Alex?"

He turned at the sound of the sleep-softened voice. Smudges shadowed her deep, brown eyes, giving them a dark-purple cast.

Knowing how intuitive Angela was, he did his best to paste a rakish grin on his face and knelt down beside her. "*Buongiorno, amore mio.*" He planted a sweet kiss on her lush lips.

She sighed. "I love hearing you speak Italian to me."

He whispered another Italian phrase and grinned at the blush that bloomed on her cheeks. "Hey, have I suddenly started snoring in my sleep, is that why you're down here?"

She chuckled, stretching her arms above her head. He couldn't help it, his eyes wandered down to her full breasts straining against the tight white tee. "Nope. And even if you did snore, I'd just wear ear plugs."

"So, what's with the late-night study session?" he asked, gesturing to the pile of books.

"This…" She followed his gaze. "Just some research… I couldn't sleep so I decided to read."

"I guess I didn't tire you out enough. Maybe I need to do a better job." He wiggled his eyebrows in a mock lecherous look.

She laughed. "I think you more than fulfill your role of passionate lover."

He scratched the stubble on his face. "I don't know. A month ago, you could barely walk after a night of lovemaking. Now you're up all night, reading about a guy who's been dead for four hundred years. Could be I'm slipping."

"Come here, you." She put her arms around his neck and kissed him breathless. "I can assure you, Caravaggio has nothing on you. He was a bit of a scoundrel to tell you the truth."

"Well, according to every movie, book, and song—women love bad boys."

"Not this woman. At least not that kind of bad boy. I'm more into the badass-hero type." She ran her hands up and down his arms. "The kind that makes my body sing when he's batting for a home run and knocks one out of the park."

He grew hard at her touch. "That's good. Because I happen to know one."

"Really, who?"

He scooped her up into his arms. "Let me introduce you to him under a spigot of hot steamy water. I have a feeling you both have a lot in common."

She kicked her feet. "The books. I need to take them with me on the trip."

"You can pack the books after our shower, Little Miss Bookworm. Right now, I want my woman—bad." He carried her out of the room, determined to erase the last vestiges of the nightmares they'd both had the night before.

CHAPTER 3

Chicago, Illinois
Present day

Angela woke with a gasp of pain. Glancing down at her hand she realized Alex was squeezing it so tight her knuckles had turned white. She extricated her hand and rubbed the ache out of it. He mumbled in his sleep, his eyes moving beneath his lids as though he were following an action scene in a movie. She lay a hand on his damp forehead and he seemed to relax and settle back down into a more peaceful slumber.

The plane rattled and shook as if it might fall apart. Reaching for his hand once more she settled it on her lap and turned to the window, watching the swirl of thick black clouds for a few moments. She jumped in her seat as a flash of lightning blinded her. Now it was her turn to grip Alex's hand. Angela wasn't an experienced air traveler by any means, having only begun flying after she'd met Alex. But since then, they'd flown back and forth to France, England, and Italy. Now they were flying back home to the States, so Alex could meet her dad. She gulped as another flash of lightning illuminated the plane. At least she hoped they would reach home in one piece.

For a moment, Angela wished she had another kind of psychic ability—one that could illuminate the future. Instead she was drawn to the past. She bit her bottom lip in worry.

Is the Caravaggio dream connected to me in some way?

She still didn't know for sure, but she hoped it was just a one-off, triggered by something she'd read.

The plane shook with another wave of turbulence. This time the captain's droning voice came over the loud speaker reassuring them that it was just a storm cloud and they would be through it in a few moments. Alex began to mutter again—his other hand was wrapped like a claw around the armrest. It stunned her that this man who'd endured the horrors of war could be reduced to a trembling child by airplane turbulence.

He was Mister Cheery that morning, but something had flickered in his eyes. It was only a second, but it was there. Fear.

Why won't he open up to me?

"Alex, wake up," she said laying her hand against his cheek. "Alex."

He opened his eyes and looked at her in confusion.

"Alex, you were having a bad dream. You have my hand in a vice grip."

"I do…? I'm sorry, *amore mio.*" He loosened his grip and kissed her palm.

The plane dropped, and she felt her stomach drop with it. The cabin lights flicked off and back on. "Are you sure there isn't something else bothering you? What were you dreaming about?"

He stared ahead, his jaw taut. "I don't remember."

"Alex, I don't believe that for a minute. Please, tell me."

"Sometimes I get flashbacks."

"You must have seen some terrible things in Iraq and Afghanistan. You don't talk much about your time in the service."

"I don't like to think about it, and I sure as shit don't like to talk about it."

His rebuke hurt, but she bit her tongue and withdrew her hand from his. Soon they'd be in Chicago. This was supposed to be one of the best moments of her life. She'd never brought a boyfriend home to meet her father and it was a big deal for her.

He turned to her and the look in his eyes matched the storm raging outside. "Just let it go Angela. I can't talk about it right now. Please, just give it a rest?"

She glanced down at her hands clasped tightly in her lap. "Okay… but at some point, we have to talk about it." She looked up at him. "We're on the same team now. I love you."

The storm faded from his eyes. "It's just this damn turbulence. I'll be fine once we're on the ground." He took her hand back in his and pressed her knuckles to his lips. "You know how much I love you."

The warmth in his eyes eased the sting from his earlier words. "We should be landing in a few minutes." She smiled. "I can't wait for you and Dad to meet."

His smile crinkled the fine lines around his eyes. "Me too. I know your dad and I are going to be great friends. I want him to know how crazy I am about you."

She moved in close, her face inches from his. "Just you remember that. I got you, babe."

The color drained from his face.

"Alex, what is it? Did I say something wrong?"

"No… it's just that song. It-it reminds me of someone."

"Oh my God, Alex." Now she really felt like throwing up. "Does it remind you of an ex-girlfriend?" She knew he'd had a tumultuous relationship with an ambassador's daughter. Maybe somewhere deep in his heart he regretted losing her.

He grabbed her face between his hands. "No, Angela, there's no other woman. No one's ever came close to you."

Relief squeezed her heart. "You're not trying to dodge tying the knot, are you?" she said with an impish grin.

His answer was a fierce kiss.

Her reply was a deep sigh.

"When I put that ring on your finger, I made a solemn vow nothing would ever come between us." His lips quirked up in a smile. "However, when you meet my mother you might rue the day you agreed to marry me."

"Never."

He laughed. "We'll see. Faye can be very controlling. Nothing I do or have ever done meets with her approval. She cares about one thing and that's Crawford Oil—which she believes I should be running. She'll do anything to make that happen."

"Alex, I know you and your mom have issues, but I'm sure she loves you and means well. Why do you call her Faye?"

"Just to remind her she can't dictate my life." He winked. "Be ready, she's going to insist on a wedding extravaganza."

"Oh, ye of little faith. Don't you think I can handle your mother?"

Alex scrubbed his face in that habitual way he had when he was considering something. "I don't know, *amore mio*. But I'll be rooting for you, that's for sure."

"I've got this, Alex. You'll see."

~

Lake Bluff, Illinois
Present day

The way Angela looked when she introduced him to her father would remain with Alex all the days of his life. The love and pride in her eyes made him want to beat his chest and holler at the moon. He'd made some bad choices in his life, but Angela wasn't one of them. He couldn't think of one thing he'd change about her. Whatever the karma of their past lives, he must have done something right to win her in this one.

He was a little taken aback when he shook the hand of the man Angela called Daddy. She'd told him her father worked as a mechanic at the Lake Bluff Naval Base on Lake Michigan. He'd gotten the impression her dad was blue collar. But the imposing man standing before him was as far from a Midwest, working-class guy as you could get.

Oliver was about the same height as Alex, with the kind of build that looked more like an all-star quarterback, rather than a middle-aged dad. A salt-and-pepper buzz cut topped off an angular face, with a jaw that could definitely take a punch. Sharp, gray eyes regarded Alex with an assessing look. Alex was used to being around older, military tough-guys from his time as a SEAL. But this was different. This was Angela's dad. He hoped he passed muster.

"Daddy, did you pick up those things I asked for at the grocery store?"

"I sure did, baby doll, but since when do you cook?"

"Alex is cooking and you're in for a treat."

"Well, I'll be damned. Finally, someone who knows what to do in the kitchen." He winked at Alex.

Alex put his arm around Angela. "I'll have you know your daughter has become one hell of a sous chef. I suspect she'll surpass me one day," he shot back with a wink of his own. "In the kitchen that is."

"Ha-ha, I knew you two would get along," Angela said. "I don't mind being the brunt of your teasing. In fact, I enjoy it. It gives me the upper hand. Alex, you get the bags and I'll show you to your room."

He and Angela hadn't slept apart for nearly two months and the thought of not feeling her warmth against him for five days was going to be torture. He hoped her room was near his so he could sneak in and out.

Curious, Alex glanced around as Angela led the way to the bedrooms. Angela's childhood home was a classic Midwest split-level house. The cozy living room featured a distressed brown-leather sofa and matching recliners. A sturdy oak coffee table in the center could no doubt take the weight of two strapping men with big feet. The big-screen television was mounted above a red brick fireplace. Alex could imagine relaxing in front of a blazing fire, a beer in one hand and a sandwich in the other. *Football!* A sure-fire male bonding ritual. He prayed Oliver was a fan.

Alex glanced out the large picture window that opened to a view of juniper, bearberry, and pine trees. Through the branches he glimpsed the crystalline, blue water of Lake Michigan.

"Lake Michi-gami." Angela followed his gaze

"What?"

"The Indian Ojibwe tribe named it. It means 'great water'."

"This must have been a nice place to grow up."

"It was." She sighed. "But as I grew older it felt confined and small. I wanted to see what else was out there."

"I'm sure as hell happy you did."

She showed him to a spare room with a twin bed. While he put his bags down, she crossed her arms and leaned against the doorjamb. He scratched his head and did a three-sixty of the room.

"I know it's small Alex, but it's only for five days."

"Hey, it's fine. You forget I've slept in way-worse places. So, where's your room?"

"I was wondering how long it would take you to ask."

He picked up her bag. "Lead the way."

Her bedroom was basically across from his. He sighed with relief. For some reason he'd expected the room to be all girly and pink. What he found were lacquered red walls and dark-stained wood floors. Framed art prints decorated the room. He spotted Michelangelo, Leonardo, and Raphael, but the others, although familiar, he couldn't identify. He smiled when he saw the bed with its gold-satin duvet cover.

At least it's a double.

"Alex Caine, I know just what you're thinking. You are totally transparent."

"Me?"

She wrapped her arms around his neck and kissed him. "Yes, you."

"*Amore mio*, you know I'm going to sneak across the hall every chance I get."

"I certainly hope so. The look on your face was priceless when I said I'll show you to your room."

"It just never occurred to me we'd be sleeping apart. I can assure you at my mother's house this will not be happening. But I get it, once a daddy's girl, always a daddy's girl."

"It's more me than him, Alex. He just met you and just like that you're sleeping in my bed. It's all new to him and I want him to get used to us. We have our whole lives to be in the same bed. A few days won't kill us."

He kissed the tip of her nose. "You're right. It seems my military training to slip in and out of dangerous situations unseen is going to pay off."

Angela's stomach growled, and Alex cracked up. "Hungry, huh? Me too. Why don't we get dinner started?"

Angela opened her carry-on and pulled out a plastic bag and shook it. "Porcini," she sang. "I knew Dad would never find them, so I brought ours."

"Great move. Simple and delicious. Penne rigate, with porcini mushroom sauce, and a mixed green salad. Simple fare is always the best. Let's do this. But not before I get my surprise out of *my* bag."

"You're a damn good cook, Alex Caine." Oliver sat back and patted his stomach. "That pasta was delicious, and this wine…" He raised his glass. "This wine is something else. What did you say it was again?"

"It's a 2014 Barbaresco Costa Russi Gaja. And don't be shy, I brought us a half dozen bottles. Only the best for my girl." Alex raised his glass to Angela. "To the woman who changed my life. And to you Oliver for raising such an amazing and unique woman."

"I'll drink to that," Oliver said.

Angela's eyes narrowed. "What's all this toasting about?"

"We're celebrating, *amore.*"

"He's right. It's not often in today's world that a girl's suitor formally asks her father for her hand in marriage."

Angela turned to him. "You did that? Where was I?"

"You were unpacking and changing. I wanted this to be between Oliver and me."

"And did you say yes, Daddy?"

"Of course I said yes. I couldn't have asked for a finer young man as my daughter's future husband."

She reached for Alex's hand. He loved seeing her beam with happiness. Especially after all they'd been through. All those past-life nightmares were behind them. The ghosts of Fioretta Gorini and Giuliano Medici were at peace. Sophia Caro and Gerhard Jaeger had finally found each other again. And he and Angela were free to make a life for themselves without the haunting specter of the past. He wondered whether Leonardo da Vinci had an inkling his BFF, Fioretta, had finally found happiness, even if it had taken a few lifetimes.

For that matter, he couldn't believe a man as skeptical as himself now believed in reincarnation. If he hadn't witnessed everything with his own eyes, he'd have had his doubts. But what had occurred since he'd met Angela was all the proof he needed. He had to accept there were things beyond his perception.

"What are you thinking about?" Angela asked.

"Just musing... I still can't believe what a lucky guy I am."

She tilted her head, her gaze so penetrating that he wondered if she could read his mind, which he'd begun to suspect she could.

Oliver got up from the table and carried his dish to the sink. "You guys cooked, so I'm in charge of clean-up."

"We'll help, it'll get done faster," Angela said, standing.

"Great," Oliver said. "When we're done, we can play a game of Monopoly. I'll light the fireplace and we can play in the living room."

"Monopoly?" Alex laughed. "I haven't played Monopoly since I was a kid."

"Well, then you're in for a treat because Angela is a shark when it comes to Monopoly."

"Ah, you've been hiding something from me." He winked at Angela, who rolled her eyes. "A hidden talent. This I have to see."

The next four days flew by with good food, great conversation, and hilarious match-ups in Monopoly. Alex understood why Angela adored her dad. On Sunday, Alex got his wish for football. They were watching the Bears play the Raiders with their feet up on the coffee table and drinking beer. Their cheering reached such feverish heights that Angela excused herself, chuckling that she had a pair of earplugs that were calling her name.

"You okay, sweetie?" asked her dad.

She bent and kissed the top of his head. "Yes, Daddy, I'm fine, just a bit of a headache. I think I'll lie down and read for a bit. You guys enjoy yourselves."

"I'll check in on you when the game is over." Alex winked.

She blew Alex a kiss and left the room.

With Angela gone, Alex decided to ask Oliver a few things he'd been wondering about.

"So, are you looking forward to retirement sooner or later?"

Oliver turned to him, a heavy brow raised.

"It's just that Angela and I would be thrilled if you could plan a nice long visit with us—heck, maybe even move to Italy." Alex grinned.

Oliver took another sip of his beer before he replied. "Well, I must admit that does sound appealing."

"I'm curious about your work," Alex said, easing into his next question. "Angela said you work at the naval base? She probably told you, I'm a former SEAL. So, what kind of work do you do there?"

Oliver grabbed a handful of mixed nuts from the bowl on the coffee table. "Oh, a little of this, a little of that." He popped a few nuts in his mouth. "I'm kind of a jack-of-all-trades. I fill in wherever there's a need."

"Interesting, I've never heard of a position like that."

"That's what twenty-seven years gets you. It's called seniority," he said with a chuckle.

"Cheers to that." Alex raised his beer in a salute while he came up with another approach. "So, I'm sure Angela will want to start putting together a guest list for the wedding, but she hasn't mentioned any family other than you."

"There is none," he returned in a flat tone. "I was an only child and my parents are dead."

"What about your late wife's family?" Alex probed.

Oliver stared at the television screen. "Lost contact after her death."

"That's too bad… I thought it might be nice for Angela if—"

"It's just Angela and me," Oliver interrupted bluntly, the glance he threw at Alex was shuttered.

Something wasn't adding up. Alex considered everything he knew about Oliver and all he came up with was a big fat zero. There was one more thing he found odd. Nowhere in the house were there any photos of Natalie, Angela's mother. Granted, she died in childbirth and there wouldn't be any photos of her with Angela, but what about her pregnancy, or photos of Natalie with Oliver? Where were the wedding pics or the pics of two people in love?

Alex the detective couldn't lose the persistent suspicion that Oliver was hiding something, or the even weirder sensation that he was *in hiding*. Oliver's hoots brought Alex back to the game. The Bears scored a touchdown and Oliver slapped Alex's back. "You better get ready to hand over that Benjamin because those Raiders of yours are about to get their butts whipped."

When the game ended, Alex forked over a crisp, new, hundred-dollar bill.

Oliver pocketed it with a grin. "I just earned myself a nap."

"I think I'll check on Angela," Alex said.

"Good idea, son. She's probably tired of sharing you with her old man."

"Nah, she's perfect in every way except she doesn't understand the football thing."

"Yeah, I think I failed on that front."

Angela sank into the pillows, her eyelids growing heavy. Her temples throbbed and the book on her lap felt like a lead weight. The last thing she remembered as her lids fluttered shut was staring at the disconsolate face of Caravaggio. Drifting off, somewhere between waking and dreaming, a warm wind enveloped her, and the pages of the book fanned by invisible fingers, pulled her back in time...

Rome, Italy
20 June, 1595

Fillide wandered through the stalls of the marketplace, now and then pausing to pick up and smell a sun-ripened tomato or a honeyed peach. While the farmer turned his back to her, her gaze flitted through the crowd of shoppers before she stuffed the peach in her pocket. With a flounce of her skirt and a sway of her hips, she wandered on. A hand grabbed hold of her arm and stopped her. She turned, squinting up into the dark eyes of a brawny stranger. She sized him up, not impressed with what she saw. "*Toglimi la mano di dosso.* How dare you touch me." She was used to men accosting her wherever she went, but his amused grin sent her blood raging through her veins. "I will have you arrested if you persist." She turned and began to walk away.

"Maybe you should consider that ill-gotten peach in your pocket. I've been watching you."

Turning, she narrowed her eyes at him, deciding how best to rid herself of this nuisance. She moved closer, tilting her head to the side. "Would you harm a poor hungry girl who must rely on her wits to survive?"

A deep laugh rumbled through the barrel of his chest. "You're a sly one for sure. You could give the peach back."

"Why should I? Who are you to tell me what I should do?"

"I am no one to you, yet. But I have a proposition to make."

Of course, you do. Every man is the same. She fluttered her lashes at him. "And what might that be?"

"I want to paint you." He doffed his cap and with a sweep of his arm, he bowed. "I am Caravaggio, I'm sure you've heard mention of me."

Mama Mia, why does every man think I should have heard of them? She placed her finger in the dimple on her cheek. "Hmm, Caravaggio. No, I don't believe I've ever heard your name before."

His laughter resonated through the crowd, turning heads. "Well, that is perplexing. But I promise you I will make you famous. Come with me, *bella*, to my studio and I will show you my latest commission, so you can assess yourself if I have talent."

Fillide had lied. She'd heard word among the other prostitutes about this Caravaggio. She'd heard he was a magician with a brush and paid his models a decent wage. She was curious. "Lead the way. And mind you, no funny business."

His studio was like a theater, filled with costumes and props. A heavy canvas shrouded the one window. With a quick glance around Fillide saw a work space, with easels, brushes, pestles, mortars, jars of pigments and linseed oil, knives, palettes, and rags neatly arranged on a table. Lanterns hung from ropes in the ceiling. "It's so dark in here. Why don't you use the natural light from the window when you paint?"

He raised the canvas, flooding the room with light. "I prefer to arrange my lighting the way I want it. That way I can control the shadows." He pulled an easel into the center of the room and uncovered a painting. "I call it the *Penitent Magdalene*. What do you think?" He stood back and fiddled with the goatee on his chin, his gaze fixed in contemplative study.

Fillide considered the painting, which was unlike any she'd ever seen. Mary Magdalene seated on a low wooden stool stared at her folded hands. A single tear trailed down the side of her nose. Scattered about her were the jewels of her former life, for Caravaggio had chosen to paint the moment when she turned away from her life as a prostitute. For Fillide the emotional impact of the painting struck her like a bolt of lightning. It hit too close to the truth of her own existence.

She'd been forced into prostitution by her own mother and she had never forgiven her. After her father's death, the bereft family had moved to Rome from Siena seeking a cure for her ailing younger brother who suffered with rashes. But cures were costly and the teenaged Fillide had matured into a beauty. Her mother soon realized that selling her daughter's favors was the only way the family could survive. It didn't matter anymore, her mother and brother died a year later, victims of the plague. On her own, Fillide had nowhere to go, except the streets.

The painting had arrested Fillide's ability to speak. Before she could stop it, a lone tear escaped her eye and slid down her nose, mimicking Mary's tear in the painting.

The artist's hand caressed her cheek, capturing the tear. He stared at the dampness on his finger. "I hope this is a tear of joy."

Fillide sniffled and wiped her nose. "You have talent, Caravaggio. The painting is very beautiful."

"Then why do you weep, Fillide?"

"If you must know, this is not the life I dreamed of." She shrugged. "But it's the life I have been given. Your Mary has found her freedom. I have not." She squared her shoulders and stood tall. "I will model for you, Caravaggio."

He smiled and held out his hand. When she placed her hand in his, he bent and kissed it. "You're a fighter, Fillide, like me. You will never be confined by the opinions of others. Perhaps together we can improve our lot."

He wasn't handsome like a *cavaliere*, but he *was* dashing, and his words resonated within her. She smiled. "Have you a knife?"

His thick brow raised in question. The quirk of his lips betraying amusement. "Of course, I have a knife. I have a sword, too, in case you didn't notice."

"A sword would be overkill. I have a succulent peach to share with you." She was aware of the eroticism of her words and enjoyed the flush of color that filled his face.

"Any gift you wish to share I will be most pleased to taste."

She giggled. "A very good answer, painter. I think this could be the beginning of a beautiful friendship."

"I believe it is."

A warm wind blew through the window, tousling Fillide's hair. She heard a knock on the door and turned.

Lake Bluff, Illinois
Present Day

Alex rapped lightly on Angela's door and opened it. She was lying back against the headboard propped up by six or seven pillows. *Women and their love of pillows.* She was asleep, but her fluttering eyelids indicated she was dreaming.

"Angela, *amore mio,*" he whispered.

She bolted up, eyes wide, and the book slipped from her lap, landing with a thud on the floor. "Where am I?"

"I believe this is your childhood bedroom. The question is, where *were* you?"

"I… I don't remember. It was just a dream, nothing earthshaking."

"How's the headache?"

She smiled. "Nothing a couple of Excedrin couldn't quash." She rubbed her neck. "I never realized how soft this mattress was until you spoiled me with your bed, fit for a king."

"Here, lift your arms." He helped her off with her sweater. "Now lie on your stomach." He sank his strong fingers into her shoulders and back, kneading her muscles until she moaned. He leaned in and ran his tongue around the shell of her ear. "Your body smells like cookie dough and vanilla ice cream. Me thinks it's time for dessert."

"Dessert? Are you sure it's me you want, or is it a calorie-laden bowl of Häagen-Dazs? Are you after one of my famous hot-fudge sundaes?"

"You're famous for hot-fudge sundaes? How come I'm only finding out about this now?"

"Well, a girl has to have a few secrets up her sleeve."

There were definitely a few secrets to Angela, secrets he'd yet to discover, secrets she probably had no knowledge of either. "No, I'll take a rain check on the sundae. For the moment, everything I want is within reach."

"Then get your spoon and dig in lover boy."

He turned her over and gazed into her lovely eyes. "Don't mind if I do." He pressed his hardness against her and let instinct take over. Sleeping in another room was like being relegated to Siberia.

"Oh, Alex, don't ever stop loving me," she sighed.

"As if I ever could."

As the last rays of sunlight filtered through the blinds, Angela snuggled into his side, her breath steady and reassuring. Alex's thoughts strayed to Oliver and his growing suspicions about his future father-in-law. He kept rehashing the things Oliver said, or more importantly the things he didn't say. Angela had grown up in a regular, middle-class home without the frills and the accoutrements of wealth, but several times Oliver had slipped. Alex's gut was telling him there was nothing "regular" about Oliver.

Something that Oliver said that morning kept niggling at Alex. He seemed to have an appreciation and knowledge of the finer things that went beyond his supposed experience. He was incessantly curious about places Alex had traveled. Oliver's questions seemed more in line with someone who'd seen the world.

Alex had whipped up a few Monte Cristo sandwiches for breakfast and regaled them with a funny story about an art theft case that had taken him to Portugal a few years back. The perpetrator, who'd stolen two valuable coins from Vasco da Gama's 1502 Armada to India, had been obsessed with a particular restaurant that served an out-of-this world *francesinha*, a famous sandwich from the Porto area. Alex had tracked the thief to the restaurant and nabbed him just as he was about to tuck into his lunch. The thief was so disappointed at the prospect of not being able to savor his favorite meal that he invited Alex to join him and even paid for lunch.

Angela and Oliver were in stitches, laughing over the story. Angela had exclaimed over the laundry list of meats and other rich ingredients. "Sounds like they put everything from the deli counter in there," she chuckled. "Let me get this straight—steak, ham, sausage, chorizo, with an egg on top and smothered in tomato sauce?"

"You forgot the *Flemengo* cheese," Oliver quipped. "Which reminds me, I ordered a rump roast from Brockwell's Butchery for tonight's dinner."

"Daddy, are you going to make your famous pot roast?" Angela squealed in delight. She turned to Alex and told him her father's signature dish, the only dish he could make, had even won an award in a local cooking contest. Alex loved how excited Angela was as she turned back to her father and discussed the ingredients to his pot roast. But it was another ingredient that gave Alex pause.

Alex had only mentioned that cheese was part of the sandwich and yet Oliver had said *Flemengo*, which means *Flemish* in Portuguese. *Flemengo* is Portugal's version of Edam cheese and is often used in the *francesinha*. Alex couldn't get it out of his mind. Oliver wasn't a gourmet cook. Or was there something more to the man and his past? Something not even his daughter knew.

The next day, Angela was organizing the house and packing a few childhood pictures and mementos in her suitcase before they left for O'Hare. Oliver suggested he and Alex take a walk along the shore of the lake. The air was brisk, a storm was on its way. A rattling cry in the sky drew Alex's attention as a flock of cranes called to one another on their winter migratory journey south. It was now or never. Alex had to get to the truth.

He looked straight into Oliver's eyes. "It must have been hard raising a kid after losing your wife. Not that you didn't do an admirable job, but it definitely left an empty space in Angela's heart. I want to do everything I can to fill that space. Can you tell me anything about Natalie?"

Oliver stopped and gazed out at the lake. "Winter's coming." He heaved a deep sigh. "I always feel a sense of loss when summer and fall come to an end. I've spent twenty-seven years here, but it never gets any easier." He looked around and said, "Let's go sit over there." He nodded toward a picnic table under a grove of barren trees.

Alex didn't know why Oliver appeared so upset. The strain around his eyes or the way his shoulders sagged could mean he was sad his visit with his daughter was coming to an end, or it could mean something else.

The older man took out his pipe and began packing it with tobacco. "Alex, I'm about to tell you something only a few people know. Angela's mother is alive."

Oliver's revelation left him speechless.

"I'm sure you've been thinking that what Angela knows about me and her mother doesn't add up. But my daughter believes it, and that's all that matters. What I'm about to tell you must be kept between you and me. And *only* you and me. Angela has no inkling of it, and I'd like to keep it that way. She doesn't need all this long-dead shit in her life and she's safer if she doesn't know."

Alex swallowed the knot in his throat. "Safer?"

Oliver lit the pipe and puffed. A cloud of fragrant tobacco smoke wafted through the air. His eyes closed for a moment as though he were remembering a bittersweet memory. "I'm a former CIA operative. In 1991, I was stationed in London when I met Angela's mother at a cocktail party. She was breathtaking. Long black hair, dark eyes—like she'd just stepped out of an old Hollywood movie. I think, for me, it was love at first sight."

He opened his eyes and glanced at Alex. "Angela's mother's real name is Natalia Rozanova. At least I think it was. She'd been living in London for about two years on a student visa. She was studying painting at the Royal Academy of Arts." He turned back to gaze at the lake, his eyes wistful. "Angela looks a lot like her."

"What happened?"

"What happened? We started seeing each other and we fell madly in love. She just failed to tell me one small detail about herself. She was a spy for the KGB, today they call it the SVR."

"Shit."

"That's just about how I reacted. I figured she'd entrapped me. At least that part wasn't true. She was in just as deep as me. We were both headed for a fall. One that could end in our dismissal, our imprisonment, and maybe even our deaths. I pleaded with her to defect and I'd quit the spy game. We could live a low-key life. We were both trained operatives, what would be so difficult about disappearing from the world?

"We planned every detail and I called in a few favors from friends in high places. First came my change in identity to my mother's maiden name, Renatus. The rest was easy. New passport, social security card, etcetera. Natalia's name was changed to Natalie and we were married by a registrar. We traveled separately, taking planes, trains, boats, zigzagging around the world until we finally met up in Toronto. After we drove over the border and arrived in Niagara Falls, we could breathe again. We were in the clear. We'd done it. Natalia told me she was three months pregnant and I was ecstatic. We could live our life together, have a family. Be happy. We had new identities and I had a new job waiting for me in Lake Bluff. We'd covered our trail and expected to live happily ever after. Eventually the powers that be would forget about us."

"Did you live in the house you live in now?"

"Yes, for six months, throughout the remainder of Nat's pregnancy. Looking back on it, those were the happiest days of my life." Oliver puffed on his pipe.

The quiet felt excruciating. Alex had a million questions, but it was better to let Oliver unfold the story at his own pace.

"I thought Natalia was happy. I sure was. Boy, was I wrong. My CIA training short-circuited when it came to Nat. A few days after Angela was born, Natalia disappeared. She left a letter, but I burned it years ago. Burned it in anger. But I will never forget what was in it. She wrote that the SVR didn't take kindly to her desertion and had discovered our location. We'd never talked shop, but we were both hiding things. Natalia never said whether they had threatened her or not, but I assume they must have. There was no other reason she would just leave her newborn daughter and the man she professed to love more than life itself. I couldn't even contemplate any other reason why she would abandon us, other than to save her

37

daughter's life. I was smart enough to know the SVR has ways to carry out a threat. Even here, in this part of the world. She insisted it was better this way for Angela and me. She wrote 'Consider me dead.' Those were her final words in the letter."

If Alex had been on the receiving end of a letter like that with a newborn baby to take care of, he would have been devastated. He knew down to his soul Angela would never do what her mother did. It just wasn't in her DNA. And he should know, he had loved her through several lifetimes. "What did you do after the letter?" Alex asked, noting the faraway look in Oliver's eyes.

"I searched for her using whatever connections I had," Oliver replied. "But nothing ever turned up. She'd vanished. Disappeared without a trace. But I couldn't afford to wallow in self-pity. Nor could I go back to the CIA. I had a daughter to raise. A daughter who meant the world to me.

"I carried a grudge for years, but in the end, I didn't want to hurt Angela. I didn't want to tell her that her own mother had abandoned her a few days after giving birth to her. It was just easier to pretend she'd died in childbirth. I was careful not to draw any attention to Angela and myself. My friends protected my identity. My job at the Navy base provided an ample living. I probably should have moved when Angela was a baby, but the memories here are all I have left of Nat. In a sense, she *is* dead," he said, his voice cracking on the final words.

Alex blew out a breath. "This is a lot to take in. I appreciate that you told me the truth, but you could have kept up the pretense."

Oliver chuckled. "Alex, you're a shrewd guy. You knew there was something about me, didn't you? And besides, I'm not as sharp as I used to be when I was on active duty."

"Oh, I think you're plenty sharp, sir."

"God, please don't call me *sir*." Oliver gave an exaggerated groan. "It makes me feel old."

Alex laughed. "Oliver, why *did* you tell me the truth? You could have come up with another story, one just as plausible, while still keeping your secret."

"Natalia did disappear for many years, but recently I've heard a few whispers here and there from old and trusted friends. I suspect she's living in Europe. And since you and Angela live in Europe, and with the kind of work you do, I think it's only fair you should know the truth. I don't know what Natalia's relationship is with the SVR. But I sure as hell don't want my daughter in danger. I want you to protect her and you can't do it if you don't know there's a threat."

Alex considered what Oliver had told him. "I will protect Angela with every fiber of my being. But you've also put me in one hell of a position with the woman I love."

"I know, son. I know you love her."

"You had me checked out, didn't you?" Alex grinned.

"I sure as hell did." Oliver narrowed his eyes as he blew a smoke ring into the air. "I know you come from money and power and it didn't corrupt you. You're an honorable man who fought for your country and you're a damn fine detective, from what I found out."

"Thank you, sir...I mean...Oliver." They both chuckled at that.

"It's probably more than you bargained for," Oliver added, turning to look at Alex. "But I know how much you love her and the sooner she takes your name the happier I'll be. I know you'll keep my daughter safe. But Angela must never learn about my deceit... I lost Natalia, I can't lose Angela too. If she finds out, she might never forgive me."

Alex saw the stark fear in Oliver's eyes. "I have no intention of telling her. We both want the same thing, for Angela to be safe and happy."

Their gazes locked in mutual understanding—they both knew Angela would be devastated if she found out the truth. But Alex knew something Oliver didn't—Angela was a psychic.

Shit! She gets the ghosts and I get the secrets.

He would have to tread carefully. His fiancée already had enough to handle. Alex hoped Angela's extraordinary gift only connected her to her past lifetimes, and not her past in *this* lifetime.

CHAPTER 4

Tiberon, California
Present day

Alex drove the BMW rental car up to a massive iron gate and pressed the buzzer. A woman's voice came on the line. "Alex, is that you?"

"Yes, Mom, it's me and Angela."

"Why didn't you just punch in the code?"

"I wanted to hear your voice coming through the intercom."

"I suppose you think you're funny."

"Yup."

The gate slowly swung open and Alex raced the BMW up the long drive to the summit. Angela's jaw dropped. Based on what Alex had said she expected the house to be special, but the setting alone surpassed anything she'd imagined. It could easily have been a grand villa in Tuscany. With a red-tiled roof and creeping vines, it was nestled on a bluff surrounded by woodlands and towering pine and fir trees. A plethora of flowering gardens bloomed around the house and an emerald green lawn lined the stone walkway, leading to the red double front doors.

Angela stepped out of the car and Alex pulled her in for a quick kiss. "I haven't told my mother we're engaged. I wanted to do it in person. You don't mind, do you?"

"Not at all. I think it'll be fun to watch the fireworks."

"There'll be no fireworks. I think she's going to be gung-ho once she spends a little time with you." He pulled a velvet box from his pocket. "You're going to have to give me the ring back."

"You'll have to pry it from my cold, dead hand." She burst into laughter.

"I can see why you majored in art history and not stand-up." He chuckled. "I want to put it on your finger tonight in front of Faye. I want her to see how much I'm in love with you."

41

She planted a big kiss on his lips. "The feeling is mutual."

"I want you to relax and enjoy being the center of attention."

She tapped her chin with her finger. "Hmmm... No need to twist my arm." Glancing around, she sighed. "By the way, it's magical here."

Alex looked around as if seeing it in a different light. "Yeah, I suppose it is. My mother is very good at houses, she has enough of them."

He slipped his hand in hers and they walked to the door. Before they reached the top step, the door swung open and a slim, liveried, gray-haired man with a British accent greeted them.

"Master Alex, welcome home."

"Hi Johnny, how've you been?"

"I'm very well, young man." He held out his hand to Angela. "John Sterling at your service, miss. I'm very pleased to meet you in person. From our Skype chats I've already grown so fond of you."

"I know you hold a very special place in Alex's heart," Angela said clasping his hand warmly. "I look forward to knowing you better."

"The pleasure will be mine." They followed John in. Angela tugged on Alex's hand and whispered, "He's really the butler?"

He nodded.

"Alex, your mother is on the patio serving drinks," John said. "I suggest you make haste. She's quite anxious to see you. Your presence is greatly missed around here."

Alex grinned. "I'm sure it is." His hand on the small of her back, he guided Angela through the foyer and into the living room. He moved so quickly, Angela couldn't take it all in. Pitched wood beamed ceilings soared dramatically above elegant seating arrangements of white over-stuffed sofas and needlepoint chairs. In the corner, a Bösendorfer grand piano gleamed under a spotlight. She recognized the distinct brass plate from across the room. Brightly colored floral arrangements in sterling silver vases perfumed the air. Set between the windows was a stone, two-sided fireplace that opened to the outside patio.

"You can feast your eyes later when Faye gives you the grand tour, which I'm sure she'll do just to get you alone."

Angela sucked in a deep breath trying to calm her jittery nerves.

The sliding doors were open, and the next thing Angela knew she was looking at a spectacular view of the Bay. Across the water was the famous cityscape of San Francisco and the Golden Gate Bridge. Red-stoned patios and terraced gardens led to an infinity pool that hovered over a cliff. Angela was speechless. Everywhere her eyes alit, there was a picture-perfect, post-card view.

"The path over there leads down to the deck above the shoreline. Faye loves to throw big summer barbeques and parties there. The dock juts out from the deck. Too bad the yacht's not here right now, we could have escaped for a sail," Alex said.

A woman's voice rang out from the patio. "I'm so happy to see you." A perfectly coiffured, blonde-haired woman strolled toward them. "Darling, come give your mother a kiss. And who is this angelic looking young woman you've brought? What the hell is she doing with a scoundrel like you?" Her pale, blue eyes twinkled with humor.

"Now Faye, please don't scare Angela away, I'm madly in love with her," Alex said, turning to Angela. "Angela, meet the one and only Faye Crawford, my mother."

The smile on Faye's face froze.

Alex broke the awkward silence. "Mother?"

Faye took Angela's hand and shook it. "In love, did you say? Well, I can't blame you, of course, she's lovely."

"It's very nice to meet you, Mrs. Crawford."

"Crawford is my maiden name, but please call me Faye." She called over her shoulder, "Tom, Alex is here with his girlfriend." She turned to Angela. "My husband, Tom Harris, is Alex's step-father. I'm sure my son told you, his father Lance and I divorced years ago. Can I get you a cocktail?"

Tom Harris was a tall, lean man with a shock of snow-white hair and a ready smile. He strolled up to them, reaching for Alex's hand. "So glad you could join your mother and me. You know she misses you terribly. You need to make more time for her." His smile widened in his tanned face, deepening the lines around his striking gray eyes. "And who is this lovely young woman?"

"Angela Renatus, meet my stepfather, Tom Harris."

Angela shook his hand, it dwarfed hers in a strong grip. "Nice to meet you, Mr. Harris."

"My dear, just call me Tom."

"Better yet," interjected Alex, "call him Admiral like I do."

"Are you an admiral?"

He laughed. "Retired."

"Mom, excuse us for five minutes while I pick a bottle from the wine cellar. By the way I'll be shipping you a case of Casa del Sole, soon. The new Chianti vintage is a winner."

"Alex, your hobbies are very amusing. Navy SEAL. Detective. Vintner. What's next?"

"You know me, Mom, always restless. I'm thinking race car driver."

"Over my dead body, darling. Go take Angela to the cellar and help yourself."

He clasped Angela's hand and led her into the house. Alex growled under his breath. "Are you getting a clear picture of Mother yet? She turned into an ice sculpture when I said I was in love with you. Not to mention her snarky comment about my 'so-called hobbies'."

"Well, you did just spring that little tidbit on her. And I'm sure she considers anything other than running the family business a waste of time."

"Hey, aren't you supposed to be on my side?"

She rolled her eyes. "I'm just saying, her barbs are reasonable in her mind. It doesn't mean I agree with her."

"Sorry. She just gets under my skin."

"I have a feeling you and she are two peas in a pod. Too much of the same."

"You're killing me."

Angela decided it was best to let it drop for now. The Alex she was used to had begun to show some frayed edges when in the same vicinity as his mother.

Alex led her down a set of stone steps to the wine cellar and tasting room. Angela counted at least thirty vintages of wine displayed, with additional bottles in floor-to-ceiling wood racks flanking three walls. In the center of the room was a circular, high-top table surrounded by four bar stools. The remaining wall held glass-fronted wine refrigerators.

"If the temperature in this cellar is controlled, what are the refrigerators for?" Angela asked.

"White wines. It's better to keep them ten degrees cooler."

Alex ran his finger over the labels that were lined up across the wine rack. "Let's see what we have here. Might as well drink the best she's got…" He grinned. "And this one should do nicely. Chateau Petrus Pomerol 2010. I'll take two bottles just in case."

"Is that a good one?"

"Honey, it better be. It's worth four or five thousand a bottle."

Angela paled. "Dollars? We can't drink a bottle worth that much money, and certainly not two of them."

"And why not?"

"It's… it's immoral."

Alex roared with laughter. "Immoral? Not likely. Think of it this way, if we don't drink it, someone else will. It's the least I should get in return for putting up with my controlling mother. Who, by the way, is going to want to know everything about you. So, prepare yourself. Right now, she's probably deciding how best to approach this new wrinkle in her grand plan for her only son."

"Am I a wrinkle?"

"It's not you, *amore*, it's me. She wants to be the one in control of her scion. You represent a new challenger."

"Oh, Alex, she can't be that devious."

"Ha-ha, just wait and see. In the meantime, I plan to get soused on a very good wine and I suggest you do the same. This is going to be entertaining."

They rejoined Faye and Tom on the patio. The admiral had a witty sense of humor. "Did you empty the wine cellar, Alex? Not that I care, more a beer drinker myself. Never did get a taste for the fancy shit."

"No, Admiral, there's still a few bottles left."

Tom roared and slapped Alex on the back. "I imagine by the time you leave your mother will be bidding at the auctions again."

John poured the claret into large, crystal wine glasses and served Angela a glass of white wine and Alex the burgundy. Alex swirled the glass and sank his nose inside, inhaling the perfume of the wine. "Perfect." He raised his glass to toast. "To the woman who makes me happy, welcome to one of the family homesteads."

Faye raised an eyebrow and took a sip of her drink. "John, what fine wine did my son help himself to?

"The Petrus, Madam."

"Angela, my dear, a perfect example of how spoiled my son is. He picked the finest wine in the cellar. But that's okay, darling. I've only ever wanted the best for you."

Alex's smile could melt steel. "Thank you, 'Mommy Dearest.'"

Faye said nothing, and Angela wondered if Alex's reference to Joan Crawford and the movie that portrayed her as an abusive wire-hanger-toting monster bothered her.

"John, I'm famished, let's get some hors d'oeuvres out here pronto," Faye said.

"Yes, madam." John inclined his head and left.

Faye turned to Angela. "My dear, I'm dying to hear how you and Alex met."

"Alex was working a case and called a professor of mine at the University of Chicago, who suggested Alex get in touch with me about his questions.

We met in a bar for a drink. Crazy isn't it, the way things happen? He was very persistent for some reason and convinced me to help him out with the case he was working on. I never doubted his sincerity."

The way Alex looked at her made her tingle all over. She wanted him to touch her and she didn't care if his mother watched.

"I wasn't about to lose you, Angela. I knew immediately I needed you in my life." Alex put his arm around her waist and kissed her temple. "I just didn't know how much."

"I'm just curious, how long ago was that?" asked Faye.

"What?" He tilted Angela's chin up and kissed her again. "Nearly three months ago. It's been a whirlwind of a courtship. Full of surprises, intrigue, and adventure. Very exciting to say the least." Alex laughed, his eyes locked on her.

"I'll say." Faye's gaze flitted from Alex to Angela. "And you've been to Florence, Montefioralle, Rome, Paris, and now he's brought you here to meet his mother. Alex is certainly pulling out all the stops for you, Angela. He doesn't usually share so much with his girlfriends. You must be very special."

"Oh, and Chicago," Alex added. "We went there so I could meet Angela's dad."

Faye's eyes widened as she glanced at Angela. "Your dad… I… I didn't realize."

Alex drew Angela closer to his side. "Oliver Renatus is quite the guy. But I never expected less. I knew whomever had raised this woman had to be special."

The depth of Alex's love and how easily he expressed it never failed to amaze Angela. There were many things in this world she wasn't sure of, but Alex's love wasn't one of them.

John returned carrying a large tray loaded with an assortment of hors d'oeuvres. A silver dish with a mixture of olives, baby red potatoes topped with a dollop of silvery black caviar and crème fraiche, and an assortment of cheeses, pâté, and crackers. To top it off, a crystal tureen piled high with shrimp and a side of cocktail sauce.

"Johnny, my good man, this looks great. I'm starving."

"Well, we can't have that, now can we," the butler said dryly.

Alex had told her John had been more of a parental figure in his life than his mother and father. He couldn't remember a time before John, who had always traveled with them when Alex was growing up. It was usual for his parents to be out at various social engagements given Alex's father's diplomatic work. Alex had spent many a night hanging out in the kitchen with John watching sports on TV and munching on chocolate chip cookies, warm from the oven. Alex had told Angela it was John who had originally sparked his love of food and cooking.

"Shouldn't John be enjoying retirement by now?" Angela whispered to Alex as they filled their plates with a sampling of everything from the tray.

"He's gay. He's been with Maximillian, Faye's gardener, for the past five years. He's never been happier." Alex chuckled. "Besides, most of what he does now is for show. Mother has a top-notch kitchen and household staff. Trust me, Johnny's back there putting his feet up and watching the European Cup on the telly." Alex's eyes twinkled mischievously when he picked up a potato. "Open up." Not knowing what else to do, she opened her mouth and he popped the delectable baby potato in. She couldn't help the moan of pleasure that escaped her when the caviar exploded on her tongue.

He roared with laughter.

"What's so funny?" Faye asked strolling up to the bar with Tom.

"It's a private joke between Angela and me. Sorry, Mother."

Tom joined in Alex's laughter, having clearly witnessed the playful potato incident. "Now, that's a woman who isn't afraid to eat and enjoy. I admire that, Angela."

Alex patted his step-father on the back. "Exactly right, Tom. Everything about Angela is authentic. No subterfuge. What you see is what you get, and I want what I see."

Angela felt her cheeks heat as she cast a surreptitious glance at Faye, spying the older woman's pursed lips and crossed arms. She knew Alex was enjoying throwing his mother off balance. And she knew Alex's feelings for her were real. What she didn't want was Faye to feel threatened by her, or think she was a gold-digger. Angela was walking a narrow line between mother and son and she wasn't sure how to behave in front of Alex's mom.

Although, Faye was the furthest thing from a "mom" as you could get. Elegant. Regal. Refined would be better to describe the petite heiress whose cream silk blouse and dove-gray skirt whispered Chanel. Her blonde, chin-length bob had not one hair out of place.

Faye was right to question what seemed a whirlwind romance. Alex and Angela hadn't known each other very long.

If you only count this lifetime, her inner voice reminded her.

Angela took a sip of her *vinho verde*, savoring the green wine's light, sweet taste that blended beautifully with the shrimp. Musing about her past lives with Alex, she inwardly smiled. Indeed, she and Alex had known each other for centuries, through two great love affairs… Caravaggio's wild, dark eyes flashed through her mind, making her hand tremble and she almost spilled her wine. She tightened her hand around the globe of the wine glass, hoping she wouldn't break the delicate crystal.

She had gotten through the visit with her dad without any issues, so why was she having trouble now?

Oh, it's probably the fact that you can cut the tension here with the axe from The Shining.

Angela almost burst out laughing at the ridiculous notion. Nor would she share her thoughts with Alex, no matter how many curious glances he was throwing her way. Angela wondered what Faye would say if she told her about the past lives she shared with Alex. She set her glass down and focused on her plate, taking a bite of pâté and cracker, then dipping a shrimp in the cocktail sauce. She fought the urge to moan over the flavors that swept her taste buds.

"Hasn't my son been feeding you?" Faye's eyes were cool as she regarded Angela.

Darn! I'm not making a good impression at all.

Hoping to lighten the moment, Angela replied with a soft chuckle. "He spends a lot of time feeding me and educating me about world cuisine. Alex is an expert at balancing work and play."

"I'm afraid he got that from his father." There was no hint of amusement in Faye's voice.

"Touché, Mother."

Angela glanced between mother and son, at a loss as to how she could smooth things over between them. She was a motherless child and not the product of an ugly divorce. It was difficult for her to understand the undertone of animosity Faye had about Alex's father. Angela wished she could wrap her arms around Alex, the child, but she knew Alex the man had long ago become indifferent to his parents' never-ending feud.

Faye smiled as if she alone were privy to the future. "I suppose the next place he'll be taking you is London to meet Lance."

"Very good, Mother. You nailed it. We're going directly from here to London. It wouldn't be fair if we did otherwise."

"Fair? What has fairness to do with your father? He was never fair to me while we were married—" Faye seemed to bite her tongue at her statement.

"Dear, remember the past is in the past, isn't it?" Tom said, reaching for Faye's hand.

Faye glanced at her husband, her eyes flashed anger for a moment, then she turned to Angela and regarded her with what Angela sensed was the older woman's 'cool poise' trademark look. "Angela, are you and Alex working together?"

"Yes, Alex has asked me to work with him on future cases." Angela smiled. "I'm still considering his proposal."

"And here I thought you accepted my proposal." Alex's grin was playful.

"What is this case you're working on?" Faye said, clearly ignoring Alex's comment.

"We solved it, thanks to Angela," Alex said. "The painting is a Leonardo da Vinci that went missing during World War II. It's been returned to the Uffizi and Angela wrote a seminal paper on it."

"Really?" Faye's eyes widened at that. "What's your expertise, Angela?"

Angela swallowed, feeling nervous under Faye's scrutiny and patted her lips with a napkin. "The Renaissance. I'm a doctorate in Renaissance art history."

"I see… Not only beautiful, but smart as well. That in itself is different from his previous liaisons." Faye kept her eyes on Alex as she spoke, as if measuring his reactions to everything she said. Her gaze had warmed a bit as she turned back to Angela. Maybe finding out Angela was a PhD lessened Faye's worry that Angela was after Alex's money. "Would you like to see the rest of the house? I'd be delighted to show it to you." Faye gifted Angela with her first smile of the visit. Angela's return smile was quick and warm.

"I told you she'd want to take you on a tour. Go on, it'll be fun," Alex encouraged. "Tom and I always have plenty to chat about. Football, football, and more football."

Angela followed Faye into the living room. "The décor is so beautiful, Faye. I noticed the Bösendorfer piano. Do you play?"

Faye's eyes lit. "When I met Alex's father, I was studying to be a concert pianist. But I gave it up. Lance's position in the diplomatic corps had us moving every time we began to feel comfortable in a place. I couldn't very well pack up the Bösendorfer and stick it in a suitcase." She sighed. "I still play but not like I used to."

"I'm surprised Alex doesn't play. He's so accomplished in everything he does."

Faye laughed. "Believe me I tried, but I'm afraid my son doesn't have a musical bone in his body."

Angela sensed the tension easing between her and Faye. "Your home is so unique—did you have it custom-built?"

"Oh, yes, it was a major project. We spend as much time as possible here, but we have residences in other cities, including Houston where Crawford Oil is based. We divide our time between them. Tom and I enjoy traveling."

"The traveling bug must run in the family. Alex seems to spend a lot of time traveling, too."

"He spent his entire childhood being uprooted and dragged from one place to another." Faye sighed. "In many ways I regret that. It must have been very lonely for him. I should have done more to keep him in one place."

From everything Alex had told her about his mother, acknowledging personal failings was something Faye rarely did. She wasn't the kind of woman who ever allowed herself to come face to face with her imperfections. Was Faye beginning to trust Angela? She hoped so. She would do anything to heal the rift between mother and son.

"I think he turned out very well. He's hardworking, successful, and an honorable man. What more could a parent want?"

Faye frowned at the comment, making Angela wish she hadn't opened her mouth.

"Angela, you don't know Alex very well, but I appreciate your sentiment. However, Alex was groomed to run Crawford Oil & Gas and that's exactly what he should be doing. My family put everything into building that company and I'd prefer not to have strangers running it. Nothing Alex does is more important than continuing the legacy of his grandfather and my father."

Angela felt uncomfortable discussing what Alex should or shouldn't be doing with his mother. Particularly since she knew his feelings on the matter. "I really can't speak to your concerns. I think Alex has to do what he feels is right for him." She wanted to toss Faye a bone. "Perhaps one day he'll feel the desire to take up the reins of Crawford Oil."

"We'll see. The right woman for Alex will be the one who sees Crawford Oil as her children's legacy."

Angela didn't know what to say to that. Alex was entitled to—and quite capable of—deciding his own path in life. She would never betray his trust or try to steer him toward something he didn't want to do. It was best to make that clear from the start. "Faye, thank you for the tour. Your home is beautiful. Truth is, I've never been in one more beautiful. I'm a little overwhelmed."

"I can see what my son sees in you. I think you're a very clever girl to have captivated him the way you have. My son doesn't exactly live like an ascetic, foregoing life's pleasures. I think you know what I'm talking about. His lavish lifestyle isn't a secret by any means."

"Faye, I think you should know Alex and I are very serious about our relationship. I'm hoping you and I can become friends."

Faye looped her arm through Angela's. "My dear, I admire a woman who goes after what she wants. We'll say no more about it. Let's enjoy our visit. My son saw fit to introduce you to Tom and me, and that says more than you could possibly know. I'm certainly pleased he brought home someone of substance and not someone to give me sleepless nights."

They returned to the patio. Whatever discomfort Angela had been feeling was quick to vanish when she saw the huge grin on Alex's face. He put his arm around her waist and leaned in to whisper, "You know we haven't been apart much since we've met. How is it possible that you were out of my sight for only a few minutes and I missed you terribly?"

Damn it, don't cry. The smile she offered was hard-fought for. But she couldn't fool him. He'd developed an uncanny ability to read her. For the umpteenth time since meeting him she offered up a prayer. *Thank you, God.*

John carried in a tray of crystal flutes filled with bubbly, rosé champagne.

"What's this about, John?" Faye raised her brows in question. "I didn't call for any champagne."

"I did." Alex beamed as he handed everyone a glass, including John. John waved his hand as though to refuse. "I insist, Johnny. You're as much my family as anyone." He set his glass on the bar and knelt on one knee in front of Angela. Locking eyes with her, he took her hand.

Angela was having trouble breathing. This was the second time he'd gotten down on his knee to ask her to marry him. And she felt just as breathless as the first time. He pulled the velvet box from his pocket and opened it.

"Angela, I can't remember what life was like before you, and I can't imagine a life without you. You are my past, my present, and my future. Say you'll marry me and make me the happiest man on Earth."

She knelt to be eye-level with him. "I will marry you, Alex. You know how much I love you." Alex took the ring and slipped it on her finger. Of course, it fit like a glove. Then he got up, pulling her with him and kissed her as if there was no one else in the world but them.

When he broke the kiss, he continued to gaze into her eyes.

Alex couldn't see the shocked look in his mother's eyes, but Angela could.

Tom roared "Congratulations!" and grabbing Faye's elbow, led her over to them.

Faye quickly recovered. "Yes, darlings, congratulations." She wiped her eyes. "I'm sorry I was so slow to react. You just took me by surprise."

Alex turned to her. "Speechless, huh? That must be a new and unique feeling."

She slapped his arm. "Stop it, Alex. I'm just so overwhelmed. I'm really very happy for both of you." She wrapped her arms around Angela and hugged her. Tom handed her his handkerchief and she dabbed her eyes, wiping away the tears.

"Well done!" John hugged Alex and Angela. "Congratulations to you both."

"What are you thinking time-wise for the wedding?" Faye asked. "Spring would be lovely, and we could have it here."

Whatever trepidation Faye might be feeling, Angela was impressed with her ability to give ground when necessary. Instead of insisting, she'd asked Angela what *she* wanted, and Angela wanted to reciprocate. Angela glimpsed the ray of hope in Faye's eyes. She didn't have the heart to disappoint her. "That would be lovely. I'm sure my dad won't mind us not getting married in Chicago."

"Heavens no. We'll do it here. Angela, I hope you won't mind my help. Alex is my only child and—"

Angela took Faye's hands in hers. "Faye, my mother passed away when I was a baby, I'd be honored to have you plan the wedding."

Faye's eyes swam with tears. "Thank you, my dear."

Wiping her own eyes, Angela turned to Alex. "Don't you agree, honey? Having the wedding here will be perfect."

Alex placed his hands on her shoulders, his gaze searching hers. "You sure this is what you want, Angela?"

"Alex, of course, it's what Angela wants. Every girl wants a beautiful memory of the happiest day of her life." Faye tossed her head dismissing the notion.

"Mother, you really are something. The happiest day of her life is going to be what happens after the wedding." Alex pulled Angela into his side and winked at her.

Angela felt another blush heat her cheeks and shot him a warning look. She was trying to get along with Faye, not make her think she was some sort of floozy. She turned to Faye. "Something small and intimate would be lovely."

"Well Mother, you heard her. She doesn't want five hundred of your nearest and dearest. She wants it to be intimate and so do I. Agreed?"

"Whatever you both want will be perfectly wonderful."

"I'm going to hold you to that, Faye."

"Yes, yes, I understand, Alex. Excuse me for a few minutes." Without waiting for a reply Faye breezed past them.

"She's up to something," Alex whispered in her ear.

"Focus on me, Alex. I'm the girl you just asked to marry you," she whispered back.

"As usual, you're right, Ms. Renatus." He bent and stole a kiss.

A returning Faye interrupted. "I have a delightful surprise to share. I called Peter Argyle, one of my friends on the board of the Legion of Honor Art Museum. He's invited us to lunch tomorrow and a viewing of his Old Master's collection. If I remember correctly, I believe he has a Leonardo da Vinci drawing." She glanced at Alex and Angela, her face beaming.

Angela gasped with pleasure, reaching out to clasp Faye's hands. "I'd love to see a private collection of Renaissance art in a private home setting. I've never done that before." The older woman's smile gave Angela hope. Perhaps, she could affect some positive change in Alex's relationship with his mother, after all.

"Well, I guess that settles it then. Lunch with the well-heeled," Alex said, downing his champagne.

"Darling, Tom and I have a morning appointment," Faye said, bypassing Alex's quip. "We'll meet you and Angela there. Give you young ones a little privacy."

Angela was looking forward to viewing the collection, but she was also worried. A Leonard da Vinci? What if something happened? What if she had a vision and went into one of her trance-like states? It scared her to think they might start again but denying the truth would do nothing to stop them. The thought of coming face to face with a Leonardo made her pulse race. She swallowed the lump of fear stuck in her throat and prayed nothing would go wrong.

CHAPTER 5

San Francisco, California
Present day

Alex pulled the BMW to the curb in front of a sprawling Pacific Heights gothic-style manor.

Angela drew in her breath. "Wow. That's no house, that's a mansion."

"The rich, as a rule, keep friends with their own. My mother is a big proponent of that."

"Your mother is trying, Alex. She knows I'm not one of her own, but she's making an effort to accept me."

"That's because she knows you're the real deal for me, and if she alienates you, she alienates me."

Opening the passenger door, he offered her his hand. One of the qualities Angela loved about Alex—and there were many—was his gentlemanly manner. She got out of the car, her eyes taking in the red brick façade, the cornice-crowned eaves, and the arched windows of the Argyle residence.

"Don't worry, Angela, I'll protect you from the big, bad, rich people." He threaded his fingers through hers and they walked up the path to the door.

"I'm not worried. I'm excited to see the inside and especially the art."

Alex rang the doorbell and a petite, middle-aged woman of Hispanic descent, wearing a white blouse and a black skirt, answered. Smiling, she led them through a set of decorative wrought iron and glass double doors and then through a set of wide mahogany doors into an expansive foyer that featured a high, wood beamed ceiling with an antique chandelier that looked like it had been plucked from a French chateau. A glossy, parquet wood floor with an intricate star pattern extended up the elegant staircase to the second floor.

They followed the woman into a living room with a seating arrangement of tailored, cream-colored linen sofas and chairs with bent-wood frames surrounding a large, circular glass coffee table. In the corner was a grand piano displayed on a Tibetan rug. The housekeeper told them Mr. Argyle would join them shortly and welcomed them to sit and make themselves comfortable. She smiled once more, indicating a pitcher of lemonade and tall glasses set on a white-lacquered tray on the coffee table and left them in the beautiful room.

Angela spied a painting hanging above the fireplace and pulled Alex toward it, her body trembling with excitement.

"It's a Rembrandt self-portrait of the artist and his family," she whispered. "I heard it had changed hands a couple of years ago in a private sale. It's exquisite, isn't it?" Rembrandt had managed two completely different styles of paint application. In some parts of the painting he'd layered the paint thickly, his brush-work frenetic, while in other parts of the painting the application was polished and refined. The artist's features were barely discernible, hidden by shadow and the dip of his beret. Angela wondered about the family, unable to recall reading much about them.

"Maybe art collecting should become my next obsession. It would be justified, don't you think, considering I was once a member of one of the most prominent art patron families of all time?" Alex quipped.

Angela studied him. She knew it bothered him that their past lives continued to hover over them. "They're resting in peace now, remember?" she said softly.

He stared at the painting, nodding. "Why don't you give me my mandatory art lesson for today?"

She loved sharing her passion and life's work with Alex and appreciated his desire to know more. "Rembrandt was an art collector as well as being an artist, but unlike the Medici family, he ended up bankrupt and buried in a pauper's grave."

"So many masters never made a dime back then," Alex observed. "Pretty sad when you think of it."

Angela couldn't take her eyes off the painting. "When I look at this painting, I'm reminded of how different the Dutch Renaissance is from the Italian works from the same period. The northern work is dark and reflects the religious puritanism and practicality of its people, whereas the Italian works are bright with color and pageantry, somewhat like their Catholicism. One isn't better than the other, just different—" Angela stopped mid-sentence. The fine hairs on the back of her neck stood up. The air began to shift and thicken around her.

Something was very wrong.

A flash of light blinded her. She covered her eyes to block out its piercing brightness. A gust of wind swirled around her, so strong it propelled her forward and she stumbled and fell to the floor. She opened her eyes and gasped. The elegant room looked as if a tornado had swept through it. The furniture was overturned, broken glass littered the floor. From the corner of her eye she saw movement.

"No!"

Two men dressed in all black, wearing gas masks, were removing the painting from the fireplace.

The Rembrandt! "Stop!"

The men acted as though they couldn't hear her. They methodically cut the painting from its frame, wrapped the canvas in a foam sleeve, and slipped it into a heavy, black sack. One thief hefted the painting, as the other thief pulled out a gun and led the way out of the room.

Angela tried to go after them, but her legs were paralyzed—she couldn't get up from the floor. Then everything went dark, as though *she*, like the painting, was wrapped inside a heavy, black sac.

Alex! Alex, help me! But she could only hear the words inside her own mind. *Where's Alex? Why am I the only one here?*

A wave of dizziness overwhelmed her. She scrunched her eyes closed and her hands flew to her temples, to stop the spinning. She fought against losing consciousness, but it was no use. Everything went black...

Strong arms surrounded her. A comforting warmth washed over her. She knew. She knew who was holding her. She cracked open her eyes and gazed into the face of the man she loved. Alex's mouth was moving but she heard nothing, as though she were watching a video on mute. She focused on his lips, and as if from a great distance his words finally came to her...

"*Amore mio*, are you okay?"

"Yes," she whispered. She glanced around the room and everything was in order. No glass on the floor. No furniture overturned. No men dressed in Ninja clothes. The Rembrandt was still on the wall...

"Are you going to be all right to stay?" Alex smoothed his hand up and down her back. "We can leave if you're not. I'll just say you're not feeling well."

"N-no. I-I'm fine now. I'm sure it was nothing." She hated lying to Alex, but she didn't want to worry him. She wasn't fine. She wasn't fine at all. What she'd experienced wasn't a vision of the past—it was a premonition, a sight into the future. She didn't know how she knew, but she did. Dealing with the past was bad enough, but visions of the future…?

Something had shifted, and it scared her to the core.

Something was wrong, and it scared him.

Alex knew Angela was not fine. He also knew she'd just experienced a vision. He had half a mind to lift her in his arms and carry her away. Something had triggered this, and he would find out what it was. He helped Angela up, and enveloped her in his arms again. She was panting as though she couldn't catch her breath. Her heart thrummed against his chest. Alex stroked her hair and back, whispering soothing words in her ear. After a few moments her heart began to slow down to a regular rhythm and her breathing was calm once more.

"Welcome, Alex and Angela," a baritone voice reached them from the doorway. An older man approached with his hand extended to Angela. Average height, he moved with an energetic agility that belied his portly frame. Bald, with a white handle-bar moustache, he wore an open-necked, navy blue silk shirt and white chinos. "Peter Argyle, welcome to my home. I see you've spotted one of my treasures. I assume Angela, as an expert, you know the rarity of seeing a Rembrandt in a private collection," he said in a thick, New England accent.

"Lovely to meet you, Mr. Argyle." Angela took his hand and smiled.

Alex knew she was still suffering the effects of her latest episode, but she was a trooper, his Angela.

"Oh my, yes, I do agree with you, Mr. Argyle," Angela went on. "It is a rarity. And such a pleasure to see this particular Rembrandt. It's exquisite."

"Please call me Peter." His blue eyes glowed with pride. "I look forward to hearing your detailed opinion about it." He turned to Alex. "And you must be Alex. Your mother is effusive in her praise of you." The two men shook hands.

"Really?" Alex's lips quirked up in a smile. "Usually I'm the recipient of her complaints."

Argyle chuckled good-naturedly. "Parents don't always show their true feelings to their young. I'm sure my kids say the same thing about me." The doorbell chimed. "Ah, I'd guess that would be Faye and Tom. She must have sensed us talking about her. Prompt as usual."

A moment later, Faye entered with Tom in tow. His mother was dressed to the nines, as usual. Wearing a classic, checkered Chanel suit, an over-sized rope of pearls adorning her neck, she made a bee line for Angela and bussed her on both cheeks. "Angela, dear, you look lovely." Then she turned, patting Alex's face. "My darling, what a treat to see you, two days in a row."

He struggled not to roll his eyes at her dig. "Mother, happy to oblige and happy to be your ever-devoted son." He brushed his lips lightly on her cheek. For all her faults, Alex knew Faye loved him. He also knew she turned on the charm when she wanted to convince him to do something. And that something was heading up Crawford Oil. The last thing he wanted to do. He expected they'd be butting heads for years to come. Neither of them was willing to give an inch.

"Thank you, darling."

Without missing a beat, his mother turned to their host. "Peter, your invitation to lunch fulfilled a mother's wish." She took his hand and squeezed. "Thank you."

"It's hard to refuse you, Faye." He kissed her cheek and turned to Tom. "It's good to see you, old boy." Peter grasped Tom's hand, shaking it enthusiastically. "How about a drink? It's such a glorious day, we're serving lunch on the patio. My wife, Renée, should be down in a minute." He linked arms with Angela and Faye, leading them to the open French doors. The sheer, white curtains billowed from a gentle breeze coming off the patio. "Being the host means I'm lucky enough to escort you lovely ladies to the table."

Tom patted Alex on the back as they followed the trio outside. "Your mother's thrilled to spend the afternoon with you, son."

Sheesh, Mom's like a General on a campaign, she's got all her soldiers on the front line leading the charge.

"I'm glad," he said. He *was* glad to a certain extent, he wanted Faye and Tom to see how passionate and endearing Angela was when she talked about art. "I want you and Mother to get to know Angela better. I've found the woman of my dreams and I want her to feel part of the family."

"I'm all in for Angela," Tom said squeezing Alex's shoulder. "Your mother is too, don't you worry, Alex. Both Faye and I can see how Angela brings out the best in you."

"She *is* the best in me. Hell, she's the best thing that ever happened to me. I'm a lucky guy." He chuckled. "I'm going to make damn sure I live up to being worthy of her."

"Love does strange things to a man." Tom's gaze drifted adoringly toward Faye. Alex had to admit Tom was good for his mother. He shunned the spotlight and was delighted to give Faye center stage. But Alex knew behind every decision his mother made, Tom's quiet voice of reason could be heard. His mother had chosen well. He was certain Faye had had a late-night chat with Tom and he'd made any lingering doubts in her mind disappear.

Alex and Tom joined Peter, Faye, and Angela who were already seated at the glass table. A canary-yellow umbrella offered much welcomed shade. A large magnolia tree with bright pink flowers swayed in the breeze coming off the bay, and a shower of petals caught by the wind settled on the table. Even so close to winter, the temperate climate of San Francisco filled the garden with color. Flowerbeds of cone-bush and Scotch heather bordered the bright-green lawn.

Alex picked a purple-pink petal out of Angela's hair. He breathed in the scent of roses surrounding the patio and reached for Angela's hand. He was rewarded with her *I Love You Smile.* His favorite. He'd begun to notice the slight differences in her smiles a while ago. There was the *Oh, Yeah, Mister Smarty Pants Smile*, when one corner of her mouth lifted along with a sexy eyebrow, and then there was the *Let's Go to Bed Smile*, when her eyes got a hooded, sensual look. The *I Love You Smile* glowed in her eyes.

A few moments later a woman stepped out onto the patio to join them.

"Ah, here is my goddess now," Peter said smoothly as he stood and embraced the tall, willowy blonde wearing a flowing, yellow dress.

"Renée, you look as stunning as these flowers," Faye complimented, indicating the floral arrangement on the table. "These blue hydrangeas are so perfect they look as if they were painted by Monet."

"Thank you, Faye. Being an Easterner, they remind me of home."

Lunch was served amid lively conversation. Peter was an attorney-turned-investment-banker whose clientele included some of the biggest names in high-tech. He'd wisely invested in startups that grew into superstars on the stock exchanges. Renée was a model-turned-attorney who worked side-by-side with her husband. Their common interests had led them to become avid art collectors, but instead of pursuing highly sought-after impressionistic or modern works, they'd become enamored with the less populated Old Masters' market.

Renée recounted the tale about how they'd acquired the Rembrandt. "Peter and I had been tipped off that one of the aristocratic families in Britain was selling off bits and pieces of their collection. It was all very hush-hush, and our agent warned us we'd be held to a non-disclosure agreement."

Peter cut in. "Keep in mind, dear, it's still in effect."

"Oh, Peter, I'm well aware. I'm simply relating repeatable facts. Anyway, we set up a meeting and flew across the pond. We bought several pieces, saved a fortune on auction fees, and made it home by dinner, if you can believe that. After lunch you'll see the Leonardo da Vinci drawing we acquired."

After a delicious lunch of Dover sole and Pommes Château, a white chocolate mascarpone cake arrived. Alex couldn't stop himself from watching Angela gleefully tuck into the delectable dessert. Her eyelids fluttered closed in pleasure as she tasted her first bite.

When Renée mentioned the da Vinci, Angela's eyes flew open and her gaze met his. He reached out and laid his hand over hers, feeling her hand tremble, knowing she was both excited and wary to see the Leonardo.

"Alex, tell me about this case you just solved. Your mother dropped a few pearls, but nothing specific." Renée rested her chin on her hand.

"We discovered a painting that disappeared during the evacuation of Florence in 1944. A masterpiece by Leonardo da Vinci. It's a wedding portrait of Giuliano Medici and Fioretta Gorini. Seventy-four years ago, a young couple took it from the Uffizi and hid it in a cave in the Tuscan region. It was attributed to an artist of lesser standing and they were worried it might be plundered in the chaos of the German evacuation. Angela not only found the painting but corrected the historical record. Giuliano Medici and Fioretta Gorini had been secretly married and the portrait had been commissioned by Giuliano as a wedding gift to the woman he loved. We returned it to the Uffizi and Angela wrote the official paper on the history of the painting."

"Congratulations, Angela!" Renée said with a clap of her hands. "It sounds like you're making quite a name for yourself in the art world."

Angela blushed. "Alex is just as responsible for the recovery of the painting as I am. I'm happy the portrait is where it belongs and where it will be appreciated by the public."

Peter rose, indicating lunch was over. "Why don't we have our coffee in the library? I'm excited to show you our Leonardo, especially in light of the case you recently solved."

The wood-paneled library was like a sequestered museum room, with its lack of windows and the museum quality lighting that protected the precious books and drawings. The drawings were mounted in nooks built into the book shelves. Alex didn't know why, but the moment they entered, he felt a twinge of foreboding. There was a claustrophobic quality to the space, enhanced by the lack of natural light. Angela seemed fine though, so he shrugged off his discomfort.

They sat opposite each other on pearl gray, velvet sofas. Renée served from a silver coffee urn and placed a square of dark chocolate on each saucer. "I read that a piece of dark chocolate a day is healthier than an apple. For once, something we really want is being given a seal of approval. But, what's good and not good for you seems to change quicker than the weather." She chuckled. "Eat your chocolate, ladies, before the powers that be change their minds."

Angela nibbled on the chocolate, but her attention swung back and forth from the conversation to the drawings. Alex knew she was anxious to view the work up close. "Do you mind if Angela and I get a better look at the drawings?"

"No, of course not. Please, go ahead," Peter said. "I take it you don't need me to explain anything about what's what."

"No, enjoy your coffee. I'm certain Angela will school me in everything I need to know." Alex popped the chocolate in his mouth and took a last swig of coffee.

Angela jumped up on cue. He followed her to the first drawing.

She whispered to Alex. "This is an extraordinary collection. I want to take a moment to admire each one before getting to the Leonardo."

They paused at the first drawing on the wall. "This is an Albrecht Dürer," Angela said. They studied the drawing of the Madonna and child. "I love drawings, they offer a snapshot of the artist's mind in motion. They display the thinking process, often unresolved. The paintings are the finished products, but drawings hold the possibility of change. Dürer is the exception because he was a master draftsman. Many of his intensely detailed drawings and etchings stand on their own as complete artworks."

"I never thought of a drawing as being the 'artist's mind in motion'," Alex said. He loved how Angela's mind was also in motion. "But I can see by this drawing how much meaning a sketch can hold. I don't think I've ever seen a more beautiful Madonna."

Angela beamed, her face alive with excitement. She reached for his hand, and they moved on to a Michelangelo drawing.

"This is a study for the Sistine Chapel," she pointed out. "It's remarkable because in the finished fresco, Michelangelo changed it completely. It's a study for the Delphic Sibyl. I've always thought Michelangelo's drawings are masterpieces even though they were mostly created as working sketches for his frescoes, sculptures, and paintings. He probably never intended for them to be seen."

"Remarkable." He leaned in for a kiss. "As are you."

Her blush flooded her cheeks and neck. "Yes, very impressive," she agreed.

Alex was relieved that whatever had occurred in the room with the Rembrandt seemed forgotten. Even spending time with Faye hadn't been too bad.

They continued to examine each of the drawings, which included a Titian, Botticelli, Donatello, and Verrocchio. Every sketch was surrounded by books about the artist. Alex made a mental note to do something similar in his own library. "What do you think about the way the Argyle's have displayed the drawings?"

"I love it. For me it's the perfect scenario. To see the actual work surrounded by the books about the artist, kind of puts everything you need at your fingertips."

Alex followed Angela across the room. She stopped short, a few feet from the Leonardo. "Are you okay?" he whispered.

She began to tremble, and he slipped his arm around her waist. The drawing was of a beautiful young woman, with eyes that stared at the viewer. Signature Leonardo, he was certain. And then he realized it was Fioretta Gorini and Angela was probably being pulled into a past life remembrance. It must have been disconcerting to stare into the eyes of your past life. "Angela, come sit down. Let me get you a glass of water."

He guided her to the sofa and handed her a glass.

"Angela, are you all right?" asked Faye.

Angela sipped and nodded. "I'll be fine. I don't know what came over me. I sometimes react to small, confined spaces."

Renée nodded. "I have the same problem. Because of my allergies I often feel claustrophobic. Maybe you're allergic."

Seeing Angela return to herself calmed Alex. "Let's just hope you're not allergic to art," he teased.

Color returned to her cheeks when she laughed. "I better not be."

Peter's eyes lit with enthusiasm. "Angela, dear, now that you're feeling better can I prevail on you to give us your impressions of the Rembrandt?"

Alex felt Angela tense beside him. "I've got you, babe," he whispered, taking her hand.

Her hand relaxed in his. "Of course, I'd love to share some insights into your masterpiece."

Angela's hand trembled in his as they entered the living room. Above the mantle was the extraordinary Rembrandt, but instead of looking at it, Angela's gaze roamed the room. Everyone took a seat, their eyes intent on the painting. Angela hesitated and then moved closer to examine the portrait.

To Alex, her words seemed stilted. Missing was the excitement and enthusiasm that she usually displayed when she analyzed a painting. "Did you know, this work of art is the only one that includes Rembrandt's daughter? He never painted her, otherwise."

"Really," said Peter, "and why do you think that is?"

"Cornelia Rembrandt was born out of wedlock." Angela pointed at the beautiful golden-haired girl. "Rembrandt recognized her as his own, but regardless, the stain of being a bastard must have haunted her. Rembrandt painted this around 1666, just three years before his death. Cornelia was only twelve years old at the time. You can see from the portrait that she was strikingly beautiful. Ironically, he painted his son, Titus, dozens of times. Perhaps, he was protecting her from the wagging tongues of puritanical Dutch society.

"Tragically, the plague took Cornelia's mother, Hendrickje, and Titus, long before Rembrandt painted this family portrait. Sadly, this painting is a vision, or rather a dream, of a family that no longer existed—" Angela froze mid-sentence. Eyes wide with terror, her hands flew to her mouth. "I'm sorry—" Angela turned back to view the Rembrandt and screamed "No!"

Alex jumped up and grabbed hold of her, steadying her, shushing her. Her angry glare startled him and his grip on her lessened. She broke free of his hold and ran to the Argyles, pleading. "You have to do something."

Everyone gaped at her.

"Do you hear me?" she yelled. "You have to stop it!"

"Stop what?" Peter asked.

"The Rembrandt is going to be stolen. You have to protect it."

Peter's eyes narrowed. He focused like a laser on her. "What are you talking about? We have the most advanced security system in this house, young lady."

"It's not enough. I tell you they're going to steal it." Angela wrung her hands in agitation. Her cheeks were feverish, and her brow was damp.

Alex grabbed her shoulders and tried to draw her attention. "Stop, Angela! Don't say another word."

Her dilated eyes contracted and re-focused. "Alex, what's wrong?"

"It's okay, sweetheart." He couldn't say out loud that she'd been lost in a vision of some kind. He understood, but the others wouldn't. "You hardly slept last night. You're not used to jet lag and we drank a lot more than you're used to. I think I should take you home."

"Alex," his mother's voice trembled. "Does Angela have some kind of condition? Her behavior seems erratic. Please don't tell me she suffers from some form of mental disorder."

"I can assure you, she's saner than all of us." He turned to Peter and Renée. "I'm sorry about this. Angela and I appreciate the lovely lunch and tour, but as you can see, she's not herself."

Angela mumbled her thanks to the Argyles. Alex felt her weight against him. It was as if all her energy had dissolved. The sooner he got her out of there the better.

Peter rose. "I'll see you out," he said in a clipped tone.

"It's really not necessary."

"I'd prefer to."

On the doorstep, Alex shook Peter's hand and thanked him again. But the shine was off. Peter had become all business and Alex sensed his distrust. He hoped Peter didn't consider Angela a threat to the Rembrandt.

Alex helped Angela into the car, and they sped away from the mansion with a screech of tires. "Tell me what you saw *amore mio*."

Angela hugged herself tight and shivered. "I'm not sure, but I think I saw the Rembrandt being stolen."

"Wait. Is this why you fainted when we were looking at the Rembrandt? I knew you were having a vision—you should have told me."

"I'm sorry, I didn't want to ruin our afternoon."

"You had a vision about the future, didn't you?"

"Y-yes." Tears streamed down her face. He reached out and brushed his fingers on her cheek, wiping away her tears.

"I'm scared, Alex. This changes everything. Seeing the past is one thing, but the future? If I'm not insane now, I will be."

"We'll figure it out. We both know there's a reason for these visions. Just because you have one vision about the future doesn't mean you're going to become a Cassandra."

"Cassandra? I must not be thinking straight."

"In Greek mythology, Cassandra was a princess of Troy," Alex explained. "She was beautiful and could see the future, but no one believed her. Had they heeded her warnings, the Trojans might have saved Troy."

Angela hiccupped through her tears. "Oh no! Your mother thinks you're marrying someone mentally unstable."

"I don't give a damn what Faye thinks. Those that live in glass houses shouldn't throw stones. Believe me, my mother has plenty of issues of her own."

"Don't take this out on your mother, Alex. She didn't do anything other than worry aloud about her future daughter-in-law's mental stability." She pulled a tissue out of her purse and dabbed her eyes.

Alex had had enough. The sooner he took Angela to London and introduced her to his father, the sooner they could fly back to Florence. "I think we should leave tomorrow. I'll call the airline and change our departure. And we're not going to stay with my dad. I'll call him and tell him. I'd rather we have our privacy."

"It's probably for the best." Her listless gaze was fixed out the window.

He pulled over and grabbed her shoulders, turning her to face him. "You're the best. Understand? There is nothing wrong with you. And whatever happened was probably because you were over-tired." He kissed her fiercely and vowed to himself to keep her in his sight until they got back to Florence and they could piece together this mysterious vision.

CHAPTER 6

London, England
Claridge's Hotel
Present day

"I don't know about you, but I'm beat." Throwing himself on the bed, Alex kicked off his loafers.

"You're funny," Angela said, unzipping a suitcase. "We ate a lovely supper in the sky. You fell asleep in a very comfortable first-class bed, and awoke to fresh-squeezed orange juice, breakfast, and a hot towel. What's so tiring about that?"

"Packing, unpacking, my mother, crowds, security, airports, my mother. Did I mention my mother?"

Angela chuckled. "I hope your mother will forgive our sudden departure."

"She's used to it, it's not the first time I've up and run."

"It's different now, because I'm going to be her daughter-in-law and I can't get away with what you can. Especially after my behavior yesterday afternoon." She blew out a breath, worried about the odd impression she'd made on Faye and Tom.

Alex tugged her down beside him and tucked her under his arm. "I'll call her tomorrow and let her know everything is fine, and I'll plant some seeds for the wedding to get her busy planning."

"Thank you," she whispered cupping his face and giving him a soft, sweet kiss. She got back up and unzipped another suitcase. "And by the way, this suite is gorgeous. The colors remind me of your Florence apartment with its pale turquoise, beige, gray, and white palette. Very serene."

He folded his hands behind his head and stretched out on the bed, crossing his ankles. "You're right. The colors are the same. I've always been drawn to the Art Deco period. I've been staying at this hotel since I was a kid." His eyes followed her as she walked to the closet with a pair of his trousers. "Why don't you do that later and come back to bed for more kissing time?"

She slipped the pants onto a hanger and turned back to him with a cheeky grin. "We'll have plenty of time for kissing after I finish unpacking. Besides, I don't want wrinkles in my clothes."

"That's easily remedied, I can call for the butler and have everything pressed and brought back to the room in a snap. This is a very civilized hotel."

"Alex, you sound like a spoiled prince." She rolled her eyes.

"I'll have you know the princes of this realm are very nice chaps. And don't forget, I was Giuliano Medici in one of my past lives. He definitely qualifies as a prince."

"You actually know the princes?"

"Met them a time or two. I told you, Dad was a diplomat. I went to boarding school here."

"Speaking of your dad, when do we see him?"

"Tomorrow night." Alex's phone buzzed with an incoming text. His eyebrows drew together as he read it. "It's from Celestine Marchesi—she says she needs to talk to me ASAP. I better call her."

"I wonder what's up? It can't be about the Leonardo, she would have texted me." Angela hefted a stack of Caravaggio books and placed them on her nightstand.

"Celestine, it's Alex." He listened. "No, don't worry about the time change. I'm in London. Yes, she's here… I'll tell her." Angela looked at him, her eyebrows raised, and he mouthed—*she says hello.*

She mouthed back—*say hello back.*

"Angela says hello back."

Angela stepped into the bathroom and set out her cosmetics bag, Alex's shaving kit, and their other toiletries. She went back out to the bedroom and stopped in her tracks. Alex was sitting up, listening intently to Celestine. But it was the look in his eyes that set off alarm bells inside her.

"The da Vinci case was pretty grueling, and we were hoping for a little break. We just got engaged… Thank you, I'll tell her…" Alex continued to listen, a frown crossing his face. "Celestine, I'm not saying we won't take the case, but I need to discuss it with Angela." He listened again reaching out and picking up one of the Caravaggio books.

A frown swept Alex's forehead. "It's been missing since 1969, another few days isn't going to make a difference. *Parliamo domani.*" Hanging up, he dropped the phone on the bed.

"What's been missing since 1969?" Anxiety churned in her stomach as she waited for Alex to confirm what she already knew.

"A Caravaggio was stolen from a church in Palermo in 1969, cut from its frame…" He flipped through the book, his mouth thinned into a tight line. "Why are you suddenly interested in Caravaggio? Does it have something to do with the nightmare you had in Florence?"

She zipped up the now empty suitcases and placed them in the closet, wondering how to avoid telling him what she'd experienced until she had it all figured out, herself.

"You've been reading about him non-stop since you had that nightmare." His voice was laced with concern and frustration. "You're not leveling with me."

Stalling for time, she reached for her handbag and unzipped it. Pulling out her phone she pretended to check her messages. "Just some reading, that's all."

He set the book aside and went up to her, taking the phone from her hands. "You've been obsessed with Caravaggio since that nightmare in Florence," he said in a quiet voice. He tipped her chin up, capturing her gaze. "Talk to me, Angela. What's going on?"

She bit her lip. She trusted this man with everything in her being. But she feared where this could lead. "The man in the nightmare was Michelangelo Caravaggio. I wasn't sure at the time. Now, I'm sure. So yes, I've been obsessed trying to figure out why I dreamt about him." She searched his eyes. "What did Celestine ask of you?"

"She wants me to locate the painting. Or rather, she wants *us* to locate it. She got a tip through the grapevine that it's still in Sicily after all these years. Do you know anything about it?"

She nodded and stepped away from him. She moved to the window and gazed down on Brook Street and the bustle of Mayfair. "In 1606, Caravaggio killed a man in a duel. He went on the run for three years. After spending some time in Messina, Sicily, he went to Palermo in 1609. He was so fearful for his life he slept in his clothes with his dagger by his side. He probably needed money and took a commission for an altarpiece from a Franciscan confraternity. It was a large painting, six-by-nine feet, and known as the *Nativity with San Lorenzo and San Francesco*. For three-hundred-and-fifty years it hung above the altar in the Oratory of San Lorenzo in Palermo until a stormy night in October of 1969, when it was stolen, supposedly by the Mafia. It's considered to be one of the greatest art thefts in history and is number two on the FBI's list of art crimes." She finished her tale and turned back to Alex.

"I don't want to take this case," he said bluntly.

"Why?" she asked softly. She didn't want him to take the case either, but perhaps they didn't have a choice, especially if these nightmares and visions continued.

"Are you serious?" He raised his hand and counted off the reasons. "The nightmares have already started. Have you forgotten how you disappeared into the past in Florence and Montefioralle? Jeez, I was scared shitless of losing you forever."

"How could I forget any of it, Alex?" she whispered.

"Caravaggio's art gives me the creeps. But my biggest issue is the *Cosa Nostra*, the Sicilian Mafia. I've gone up against some bad dudes over the years, but the idea of stepping into the original mafia's territory isn't exactly on my bucket list."

"The recovery of this painting would be huge," she mused. "Caravaggio died when he was only thirty-eight years old. All told, there are only about seventy works of his art accounted for. You're talking about the most important artist of the seventeenth century. He's considered one of the top ten artists who ever lived. You would become world famous, Alex."

He snorted. "Being famous kinda cramps my style." He joined her at the window and gathered her in his arms. "Why are you having nightmares about Caravaggio? Do you think it's a harbinger?"

"I'm not sure," she said with a lift of her shoulders. "Maybe we should talk to Celestine and get more details before we make a final decision?"

He touched his forehead to hers. "Okay, tomorrow we'll conference call with Celestine and find out what this is all about. But right now, I'd like to take a nap and cuddle with my girl. Then we can go out and grab some Indian food. I've got a hankering for curry and I know just the restaurant. How does that sound?"

"Mmmm… curry." She slipped her hands around his neck and kissed him. "And before we call Celestine tomorrow, would you mind going with me to the National Gallery? They have three important paintings by Caravaggio that we should see."

He ran his lips up her neck to her ear. "That's one of the things I love most about you."

She closed her eyes and tilted her head to give him better access. "What's one of the things you love most?"

"You say 'mmmm' every time I mention food." He chuckled. "But there's another thing I love about you."

"What's that?" Her voice sounded breathless to her ears as his lips nipped at her bra strap.

"I love how you respond to me. Each time we kiss, it feels like the first time."

"That's because it is," she breathed out a sigh. "It's the first time for this kiss." She claimed his lips. "And the first time for this one." She kissed him again. His chest rumbled with laughter. "And this one," she went in for round three.

"Damn, I love you, woman. You set me on fire. Okay, I'll go see the Caravaggios tomorrow, if you spend tonight putting out the blaze you've just started."

She ran her fingers over the front of his pants, loving the groan that vibrated in his throat. "Fire Marshall Renatus, reporting for duty." She giggled as he picked her up with a growl and carried her to bed.

She pushed away her worries about Caravaggio and the investigation. Tomorrow would come soon enough. Tonight, she would lose herself with the man she loved.

CHAPTER 7

London, England
National Gallery
Present day

The three Caravaggio paintings hanging in gallery thirty-two were magnificent. But you wouldn't know it by looking at Alex—arms crossed over his chest, right foot tapping impatiently—the only thing missing was an eye roll. Angela was determined to get to the bottom of Alex's disdain for what were some of the most engaging and transformational works ever created.

Alex's interest perked up only after she began relating the history of the painting. "*Boy Bitten by a Lizard*, is one of Caravaggio's earliest works, painted soon after he arrived in Rome," she said, as she entwined her fingers with his. "He already showed great promise in his exploration of human nature and the difficulties of life, by his use of symbolism. The boy in the painting is reaching for the cherries and is bitten by a lizard. Caravaggio juxtaposes the fruit—symbolic of love—with the pain of love scorned, represented by the lizard's bite."

Angela watched Alex's face as he scanned the painting. He arched a brow. "It's very homoerotic," he said. "I guess he liked boys."

"I'm sure he did. But if you look at his entire oeuvre, you'll see he was just as drawn to—and passionate about—women."

She tugged him along to the next painting, stopping in front of *Salome Receives the Head of John the Baptist*. "This is one of Caravaggio's final paintings and really shows his maturity, how at ease he was with his style," she explained. "It also shows his obsession with death and his fear of dying."

"Now I see why you call him the father of cinematography," Alex said. "The lighting, shadow, and contrast is like a still from a movie. It's gruesome, but captivating. Each character embodies a different emotion in reaction to the action in the painting. There's no background, he's done away with everything but the awe factor."

"I couldn't have said it better myself. He condenses the figures so tightly into the shot it forces the viewer's participation. Caravaggio broke all the rules when it came to perspective. He changed art and influenced artists for generations to come." She squeezed his arm and smiled up at him, relieved he was showing more interest in the paintings.

But why is Alex so repulsed by Caravaggio?

She paused, scanning the canvas. "He was wanted, with a price on his head. This was when he began to paint the severed heads, symbolic of his own predicament," she added in a quiet voice. "But even faced with adversity, he remained true to his vision. His early work catapulted him to success, but tastes were beginning to change. The Church wanted idyllic altarpieces, but Caravaggio was all about gritty realism. Eventually, he would fall out of favor."

"C'mon—he was a thug who happened to be able to paint," Alex said with a snort.

"I disagree. Most of his biographers were jealous of him and hated him," Angela replied, jumping to Caravaggio's defense. "I'm not saying he didn't attract trouble or even go looking for it, but after so many centuries, what is truth and what is hyperbole? Think of what happens when you whisper a secret in someone's ear and they tell the next person, and so on and so forth. As time passes, the story bears no resemblance to the truth. History can be altered, fashioned, and molded to reflect the teller's personal bias."

"Because of your visions, we can find out the truth," Alex said.

"I hope so."

They moved on to the last Caravaggio painting in the gallery. "*The Supper at Emmaus* was painted in Rome before all hell broke loose in his life," Angela said. "He's captured the moment when two of the apostles invite a stranger to dine with them in a tavern. It's the exact moment when realization dawns on the apostles that the stranger is the resurrected Christ, and they are witnessing a miracle.

"Caravaggio dared to transform the Biblical icons of the Church into the peasant class—beggars, street people, and prostitutes. This is why he was such a hero to the poor. He showed them in a different light."

Alex's phone buzzed—he pulled it out of his pocket and glanced at the screen. "Dad just texted me with a change of plans. We're going to meet him at a cocktail party at the U.S. Ambassador's residence and from there we'll go on to dinner."

Angela's face turned fifty shades of crimson. "The ambassador's house? Alex, I didn't bring anything appropriate to wear. Maybe we should just meet your dad at the restaurant."

"Nope. I've never been to Winfield House and I'd like to see it." He bent his head and kissed the tip of her nose. "I'll take you shopping. I bet that's one sentence a guy doesn't say very often."

"It makes me uncomfortable when you buy me things."

"Get used to it. It's time to let that bullshit go. You fell in love with a guy with money. So what? Has it occurred to you you're depriving me of pleasure, because that's what I get when I buy things for you. It pleases me."

"Okay, okay. You made your point Prince Charming. Go ahead and spoil your Cinderella. You better hope she doesn't turn into a pumpkin at midnight though."

He drew her into his embrace. "I'll promise not to turn into a lizard like the dude in the Caravaggio painting, if you promise not to run away at midnight. As for the spoiling part, you're too stubborn to let that happen." He grinned as she shook her finger at him.

Before they left the Gallery, Angela took a last, long look at the paintings. Now she knew what she was up against. Convincing Alex to take the case was going to require a lot more inveigling on her part. After seeing Caravaggio's work first-hand, she was convinced she and Alex had to find and return the stolen painting to the world.

Alex was having trouble keeping his eyes off Angela. He'd had to overcome her protestations of excess with every purchase, but the result was worth every penny. The red, floral-patterned, lace cocktail dress with capped sleeves and cinched waistline made her look both demure and alluring at the same time. He'd arranged for the hotel to send a top-notch hair and make-up person to their suite. The stylist had swept Angela's dark hair into an up-do that gave her an Audrey Hepburn *Breakfast at Tiffany's* sophistication. It was the first time she let him go all out, and he couldn't wait to see his dad's reaction.

Angela drew the line at the bejeweled high heels. When she'd seen the price of the shoes, she nearly fainted. "Alex, you could buy a car for what these heels cost."

"A used car at best. Besides, it makes me happy to buy them for you." In the end she'd acquiesced. Angela never argued about things that didn't matter. She saved her ammunition for the important battles, and he sensed she was preparing for combat over the Caravaggio case.

In honor of the occasion he bought himself a royal blue velvet blazer, gray slacks, and white-pleated shirt and tie. She jokingly quipped, "Standing together we look like either the Union Jack or Old Glory. Since we live in Italy, shouldn't we be wearing the *Il tricolore*—green, white, and red?"

"I'm very comfortable straddling different countries, thank you. Not to mention our outfits are made in Italy. Now that I have you on my arm, I need to step it up."

When they walked through Claridge's to the car he couldn't fail to notice the admiring glances. Angela was a femme fatale, even if she didn't have a clue about her power. The fact that she had beauty and brains only made her more appealing.

The drive from the hotel to Regent's Park took only a few minutes. When they arrived at the fifteen-foot-tall iron gates, Angela scooted to the edge of her seat. Alex nearly burst out laughing. The girl who hadn't wanted to attend was practically bouncing with excitement.

The Bentley followed a line of cars and limousines to the front of the red brick Georgian-style manor. When they'd passed through security, they entered the large reception hall through a pair of matching white marble Doric columns. The hall itself ran the depth of the house, to tall French doors that opened to what Alex assumed must be the terrace and lawns beyond. The oak parquet floors were polished and shone like glass, reflecting the crystal chandelier overhead that had once hung in a palace in India. He knew this because Google had told him so, and he always wanted to be prepared for Angela's inquisitive mind. The walls were adorned with 18th Century French paneling that neatly absorbed the conversation and laughter emanating from the richly dressed guests. The grandeur of the ballroom harkened back to another time.

The reception hall was filled with all manner of attendees, their conversation punctuated by the occasional burst of laughter. Diplomats, members of the aristocracy, and men and women in military dress uniform, their jackets laden with medals, ribbons, and badges, mingled with turbaned and robed officials from the Middle East, India, and Africa. Several well-known celebrities, journalists, and actors were thrown into the mix, as well. Alex pointed out a few of the glitterati to Angela. He always found it strange seeing an actor in person. He couldn't help looking for quirks in their personalities that resembled their on-screen personas.

Serving staff dressed in white and black, moved seamlessly through the crowd with silver trays bearing hors d'oeuvres and tall flutes of champagne. Alex snatched two glasses for them and handed one to Angela. "What do you think?"

"It's magnificent. Very stately and beautifully decorated. I almost feel like I belong," she giggled.

Alex scanned the room. "This residence was a gift from American heiress Barbara Hutton, who purchased it in the 1930s. She gave it to the United States in the 1950s for a dollar. Generous to a fault, she died pretty much penniless."

"How tragic," Angela said. "Wasn't she married to Cary Grant at one point?"

Alex nodded as he sipped his champagne. "He was one of seven husbands. The press dubbed her 'poor little rich girl'. Hers is a story of wealth gone wrong. Pretty sad, but a lesson for sure. Money can't buy happiness."

Angela took his hand. "It never does."

"Alex, son," his father's voice boomed, turning heads.

"Dad." A tall, silver-haired man wearing a gray suit and a silk, red paisley ascot cravat joined them. Ignoring protocol, he grabbed Alex in a bear hug.

Stepping back, he squeezed Alex on the shoulder. "So good to see you, son. It's been too long." Lance's eyes darted back and forth from Angela to him. "Are you going to introduce me to this young woman?"

"Dad, this is Angela."

Alex's father took Angela's hand in his and patted it. "So, this is the brilliant academic who stole my son's heart." He threw a grin at Alex. "You didn't tell me she was smashingly gorgeous."

"Nice to meet you Mr. Caine, and thank you for the compliment," Angela said, her cheeks turning crimson. She playfully punched Alex's arm. "How could you fail to mention what a great beauty I am?"

"Trust me, I mentioned it. He's just trying to score points with you."

"What's this 'Mr. Caine' business? Call me Lance." Lance's arms encircled her in a warm hug, and he kissed her on both cheeks. "Please, indulge an elder statesman. Not to mention, it can't hurt for all these boors to see me making time with the younger set. It's good for the gossip mill to have something to talk about."

"Sir, if you're the example of getting on in years, then I can't wait for Alex to grow older since he looks so much like you."

"Okay, you two, I don't appreciate you discussing me as if I'm part of the decor."

"I like this girl, Alex. She's clever and funny, as well as beautiful."

"I knew you would, Dad. You've always had a keen eye for the ladies." Alex regretted his barb immediately but his father, who was in good humor, ignored it. Angela, however, threw him a quick glance, her eyes warning him to behave. He knew she was nervous about Faye accepting her, but she had nothing to fear from Lance. Alex knew his dad would love her on sight, and he was right.

"Angela, have you seen the gardens yet?" Lance asked.

"No, we just got here only a few minutes ago and I've been taking in this beautiful room."

"Perfect. You're going to be in for a treat." Lance tucked her arm into his and turned to his son. "I'll bring her back soon, Alex. I'd like to spend a few minutes alone with the girl who reined you in, without you hovering over us like a mother hen."

"Just bring her back before midnight," he quipped.

Angela giggled and promised not to turn into a pumpkin. Alex almost hooted with laughter as his dad's loud voice echoed above the chatter, "What's this about a pumpkin? Don't you start worrying about your figure, dear. Enjoy your desserts, just make sure you take a brisk walk every morning..."

Alex grinned as he observed his charming father introduce Angela to various people on their way to the gardens. A flash of movement from the corner of his eye caught his attention. An older woman was staring at Angela and his father as if spellbound. *A former flame of Dad's?* She seemed familiar, and yet her face sparked no memory and no name.

Alex had to admit his father had good taste. The woman was beautifully dressed in an amber-brocaded suit that accentuated her halo of curly, red hair and large blue eyes. The pearls around her neck were the size of quail eggs. Lance was famous for his wandering eye—it had ruined his marriage to Faye.

Alex's childhood had been a never-ending tennis match—his parents the opponents, and he the ball. He couldn't fathom ever wreaking that kind of turmoil on his future family. When Alex reached the age of majority and was free of his parents' machinations, he swore to himself, if he ever found the right woman, he'd remain loyal to her. Angela was the right woman and he had every intention of devoting himself to her happiness.

Alex made his way to the open bar to order a Scotch.

"Are you, perchance, Lancelot Caine's son?"

Alex turned at the sound of the lilting Eastern European accent. He schooled his face into a placid smile as he came face to face with the woman who'd been watching Lance and Angela. "Yes, I am." He inclined his head with a polite nod of greeting. "I'm Alex Caine, and who do I have the pleasure of addressing?"

"Anastasia Dolya, I'm a friend of your father's."

"Really? What sort of friend?"

"How very direct you are, young Mr. Caine." She gave a throaty chuckle. "I see you haven't inherited the art of diplomacy from your father."

He smiled, blandly. "I leave that to my father, it's in his blood."

"So, it is not true what you Americans say about the apple falling close to the tree? In your case, perhaps the apple rolled far away?" She made a spinning motion with her finger as she flashed him a sly smile.

"Close, but no cigar," Alex said. "*The apple never falls far from the stem*, is the correct saying. It was first coined by Ralph Waldo Emerson." Alex paused at his own nerdiness as he saw an odd expression pass over her face. "But you didn't come up to me to discuss American proverbs, did you?"

She threw her head back and laughed, drawing curious glances in their direction. "Lancelot indicated you were a rebel. He keeps me informed on your activities."

"I guess that answers my question as to what sort of *friend* you are."

"I wouldn't flatter yourself to think you're the main topic of our discourse," she replied, with a slight flare of her nostrils.

"I should hope not, I'm sure you have so many other interesting things to talk about."

"Indulge my curiosity, Mr. Caine. What precious masterpiece have you recently recovered?"

She doesn't miss a beat, this one. "I see your pillow talk with Lance *does* go beyond your favorite scene in *Casablanca*, and how you take your morning coffee."

"Touché, Mr. Caine." She inclined her head. "Your father did mention in passing that you are a private investigator who specializes in retrieving stolen and lost artwork. He is very proud of you."

"I don't need to hear how my father feels about me from one of his *friends*," Alex said bluntly. "But, since you asked so nicely, and it's public record, it was a Leonardo da Vinci that disappeared in World War II—" Alex paused at the gleam of awareness that flashed in her eyes. "I see from your expression you've heard of the painting."

"I read about it." She gave him a non-committal smile. "What a feather in your cap."

"It was a team effort."

"Ah, could the other member of your team be the beautiful, young woman I saw you with? Your fiancée, perhaps?"

Alex's eyes narrowed slightly at her probing question. *How does she know Angela is my fiancée, unless she was eavesdropping on us?*

"Alex." Alex turned as Angela and Lance approached them.

"How was the tour of the gardens?" He smiled at Angela's glowing face. He was almost certain she'd taken snapshots with her iPhone of the statues throughout the garden to look up later.

"One word: Stunning." Angela cast a curious glance at the older woman.

Lance kissed the redhead on both cheeks, greeting her with a whispered growl in her ear then in a louder voice. "Anastasia, my darling, so good to see you here."

Alex wanted to hurl. He wished his dad would stop shooting for "stud of the year", and finally settle down with a nice woman.

"I see you've met Anastasia. Anastasia, my dear, meet Angela, Alex's girlfriend."

Anastasia reached for Angela's hand and clasped it in both of hers. "Anastasia Dolya. It is a pleasure to meet you."

Angela smiled. "Nice to meet you, Anastasia."

Anastasia held up Angela's hand—the diamond engagement ring twinkled under the glittering chandeliers. "Hmm… a lovely ring. I'd say by the setting, circa 1920s, and this could only be Mellerio dits Meller—the oldest, privately owned jeweler in the world. You are in good company my dear. Mellerio dits Meller is the jeweler of queens, Marie de Medici and Marie Antoinette, to name a couple. Congratulations."

"Anastasia, what are you talking about?" Lance arched a gray brow. "Do you know something I don't?"

"Dad, you've always been a bit of an absent-minded professor." Alex forced a laugh to cover his irritation at Anastasia's boldness. "This was Grandma's ring. Angela and I just got engaged. I was going to tell you tonight, but Anastasia seems to have beaten me to it." Alex tugged Angela's hand from the redhead's grip and gently pulled her to his side.

Lance slapped Alex on the back. "That's jolly good news, son. I couldn't be more pleased, it's about time you settled down." He leaned down and kissed Angela on both cheeks. "Congratulations, my dear." He rubbed his hands together. "We are definitely going to celebrate tonight. Anastasia, join us for dinner. I snagged a devilishly hard-to-get reservation at The Ledbury."

"I wouldn't want to intrude."

"Don't be ridiculous. It's a bloody table for four, all they need to do is throw down another place setting."

"Oh, please," said Angela warmly. "We'd love it, wouldn't we Alex?"

Alex hesitated. There was something about Anastasia that set off warning bells. She hadn't taken her eyes off Angela, and her reaction to the da Vinci painting was unsettling. *She's cagey this one. What is she after?* Alex had come across plenty of con artists in his line of work. Anastasia didn't strike him as a grifter—but she was hiding something. "Ah, yes, of course, please do join us."

Lance looked pleased as punch. "Good, it's settled then." He glanced at his watch. "We'll fly in thirty minutes. I have a driver and car tonight. A little perk from the office. Let me freshen your cocktail, my dear." He took Angela's glass. "Oh look, there's the prince!"

"Which one?" Angela's eyes widened.

"The ginger." Lance winked. "He's alone tonight. Pity, his wife is adorable. Come along Angela, let me introduce you. Alex do come with, it's been years since you've seen each other." He turned to Anastasia. "Are you coming, darling?"

"I'll meet you at the entrance in thirty minutes," she said, giving Lance a quick peck on the cheek. "I need to say hello to a few acquaintances before we head out."

"Yes, yes. You go, my dear." Lance took Angela's elbow and steered her toward a boisterous group surrounding Prince Harry. Alex threw a hooded glance in Anastasia's direction, catching her staring intently at Angela before she turned and disappeared into the crowd.

CHAPTER 8

The Ledbury
Notting Hill, London
Present day

The dining room, with its understated elegance, promised a special meal. The Ledbury was the first Michelin-starred restaurant Angela had ever been to and it didn't disappoint. When she bit into the finger-sized Scottish langoustine, wrapped in shiitake slices with cauliflower purée, her moan of pleasure elicited laughter around the table.

"My goodness, Alex, I see you've found a fellow 'foodie' to be your roommate," Lance chuckled.

Alex grinned. "Feeding my girl is one of my greatest pleasures in life."

Angela blushed. "I don't know what all the fuss is about. When food tastes this good it should be acknowledged. Not to mention this room is totally Zen. I love that the ambience isn't at war with the cuisine. The food is the star, and I for one, have no trouble oohing and ahhing over it."

"Hear, hear, my dear," Lance said. "Alex was always a good eater. His mother and I took him to many of the best restaurants in the world. Speaking of your mother, Alex, how is she?"

"Faye is Faye, always grabbing the wheel whether or not she's in the driver's seat. Angela's given her a job that should occupy her for a time though. She's the official wedding planner."

"And when will that be? I need to plan my calendar as much in advance as possible."

Angela took a sip of the Chablis Alex had ordered for her. "Spring—April I think. The wedding will be in Tiburon. Hopefully in the garden with the Pacific as the backdrop." Angela took another bite of the langoustine and managed to refrain from moaning.

"Where are you from, Angela?" Anastasia asked. "Your parents must be very excited for you and Alex."

"I'm from just outside of Chicago, a quaint, little town called Lake Bluff on Lake Michigan. My father still lives in the house I was raised in."

"Sounds like a lovely place," Anastasia said. "You mentioned your father—does your mother still live there as well?"

Angela's smile dimmed. "My mother died giving birth to me."

"I'm sorry about your mother, Angela. That must have been very hard on your father and you."

"Thank you, but I had the best father a girl could wish for. As for a mother, I guess I missed the little things when I saw other girls with their moms. But as I grew older, my father more than made up for the loss. I came to the realization you can't miss what you never had." Angela felt Alex's arm go around her and she leaned into his side.

"And now you have your wonderful fiancé," Anastasia said with a smile, glancing at Alex. "And you live in Florence…"

"Ah, one of my favorite cities in the world," Lance piped up.

"Mine as well…" Anastasia echoed as she lay her hand over his on the table.

"Your accent is interesting," Alex said. "Russian?"

"No," Anastasia answered smoothly. "I'm from Kiev, it's the capital of Ukraine. I grew up on the banks of the Dnieper River. My parents are no longer alive and my ties to the city have diminished. I haven't been back in years. London's my home now."

"You lived there during the Soviet years I presume," Alex said.

"I left as a young woman and came to London to attend art school here. I married an Italian architect and lived in Florence until the marriage fell apart. I moved back to London ten years ago and started an art consulting firm. That's why I knew about the Leonardo you and Angela recovered."

"No children?" Alex asked.

"Sadly, no." Her gaze dropped to her wine glass.

"We have something in common." Angela laid her hand over Anastasia's. "I have no mother, and you have no children."

Alex refilled Angela's wine glass and his own. "Sounds like the start of a good spy novel. Beautiful young artist trained by the KGB is sent to school in London and becomes an agent right under the nose of MI5."

Anastasia smiled. "You have a vivid imagination, Alex. If it were true, I'd be the greatest spy ever. Thirty years without detection. Quite a feat I'd say."

"Oh, I'm sure there are plenty of spies walking around out there, with pretend lives, trading in secrets…"

"I hate to disappoint you, but I've never had any relationships with anyone in the government before your father, and we were introduced by dear friends. I assure you—your father's pillow talk has never been about state secrets."

"Ah, but the bedroom is where spies do their best work—"

"Alex, what the hell are you about?" Lance interrupted. "You think every Eastern European living in London is a spy? You've been watching too many James Bond movies, son."

Angela felt Alex stiffen beside her. What had gotten into him?

"Sorry. I was just having a bit of fun," Alex said. "No harm intended."

"Well, I'd jolly well appreciate it if your fun didn't include my sex life."

Angela knew Alex hadn't been jesting, he was interrogating Anastasia. She seemed like a perfectly lovely woman. Did Alex still harbor negative feelings about his parents' divorce? Feelings he hadn't shared with her? No, that couldn't be it. He'd told her everything about his parents. It had to be something else.

Alex had been acting strange ever since the night he'd woken from the nightmare about Afghanistan. Angela wanted to do everything she could to help the man she loved. Maybe what Alex needed was a case to take his mind off his painful memories. Taking on the stolen Caravaggio case might be just the ticket to focus his energies in a positive manner. Tomorrow, she and Celestine would convince him. Tonight, she had other plans for her bad boy. The way he looked in the blue velvet jacket made her want to jump in his lap and cuddle against him like a kitten.

Claridge's Hotel
London, England
Present day

The drive home from the restaurant was quiet. Alex had insisted on taking a cab instead of allowing Lance and Anastasia to drop them off. Not one more minute with Anastasia. He shut the door to their suite, slid the security chain in place, and breathed a sigh of relief. "I think that went as well as could be expected."

Angela slipped off the jeweled stilettos. She walked to the bedroom and plopped down on the bed, stretching and curling her toes. "Really? Do you think your father appreciated you attacking his girlfriend with that preposterous hypothesis that she's a spy?"

"I know I get carried away sometimes. But my father is privy to a lot of top-secret stuff. He should be more careful about who he dates. Particularly, mysterious women from Russia."

"Your father is a lovely man who was thoroughly happy for you tonight. Happy to see you in love. And Anastasia is not Russian, she's Ukrainian."

"Ukrainian—Russian, same difference. My father's always happy when he's got a beautiful woman on his arm. He spent a lifetime choosing personal gratification over his family. I will never do to you or our children what he did to my mother and me." He knelt in front of her and began massaging her feet. "Besides, you know I have issues with my parents. I carry a shitload of baggage I'd rather forget. It doesn't mean I don't love my mother and father, but I can only take them in small doses before I blow a fuse."

"Maybe you need to see someone professionally, to work some of your anger out."

"*Amore mio*, it would take several lifetimes for that to happen." He pulled her forward to the edge of the bed and wrapped his arms around her. "What I need is to make love with the woman I love."

Her hands cupped his face. "That's interesting, because what I need is to make love with the man I love."

"Hmm… must be a psychic connection." He ran his hands up and down her back. His yearning grew stronger with every touch. He pulled her to her feet and unzipped her dress, slipping it off her shoulders and down her body to the floor. "I've been wanting to do this all night," he breathed in her ear. Underneath the dress she wore the red lace teddy he'd bought her. "You're like a fantasy come true."

She chuckled and undid his tie, tossing it with a flourish on the couch. Then she kissed him and began to unbutton his shirt. She raked her nails lightly down his chest and flicked her tongue against his lips. "Aren't you going to help me?"

"No way. I'm having too much fun with you in the lead."

"Ah, so you like it when I'm in charge, do you?"

"I love everything about you, *amore mio*."

"Hmmm. Well, I love your Italian endearments…" She proceeded to kiss her way down his chest, unbuckling his belt as she went. "And I love you…"

"Don't stop, *amore mio*. Don't ever stop."

Angela yawned. She'd tried to fall asleep. But even after their fiery lovemaking, she found herself staring at the ceiling. Alex's arm rested around her waist, and the rise and fall of his chest pressed against her back. He slept soundly as she carefully slipped from his embrace.

She sat on the couch, tucking her feet under her, and opened a book about Caravaggio's life. Four hundred years of rumors and innuendo made it difficult to separate truth from fiction. So much of the artist's life was hidden from view and most of it was filtered through unreliable sources. Everything she'd read pointed to a deeply troubled man.

He'd been labeled a homosexual, and yet it was evident in the sensual way he painted women he was attracted to them. He could have been bisexual, but whatever his sexual preferences, the facts were so scant that it was difficult to construct who he really was.

Everything about him seemed contrary to his genius. The only artist atelier he apprenticed at in Milan was run by Simone Peterzano, a painter of biblical scenes whose work was mediocre at best. In comparing the two artists' paintings, the best Caravaggio could have learned from Peterzano is how to mix paints.

Caravaggio was historical proof genius is born, and also proof genius is not without flaw. Because as flawed as the man was, the genius managed to invent an explosive, raw, realistic, symbolistic school of painting. In order to do so, he had to break with tradition and invent his own methodology. Angela was fascinated with his method that was so distinct from all other painters of his time. Most artists sketched and blocked out their paintings, but Caravaggio, in a complete reversal of common practice, painted from life without preparative drawings. He dispensed with this time-consuming preparation. His genius inspired him to compose a painting in his mind and carry out that mental vision as he applied brush to canvas. For continuity, he cleverly made small incisions in the under-paint after each session, to recall the positions of his models when he resumed painting.

These short-cuts sped up the process, and yet Angela found it astounding that even using the modern technology of infrared imaging and X-rays, only a few of Caravaggio's paintings showed a glimmer of pentimento, a visible repainting beneath layers of paint. It was extraordinary—once he took up his brush and began to apply paint, he rarely erred or questioned his direction.

Flipping the pages of the book, Angela landed on a painting of Fillide Melandroni, the model he painted more than any other. From what she'd read, Fillide was a fiery, red-headed prostitute who'd had several run-ins with the law. The most notable was an attack on another prostitute whom she found in bed with Ranuccio Tomassino, her alleged pimp. The same Ranuccio who Caravaggio stabbed and killed in a swordfight, a tragedy that would lead to Caravaggio's downward spiral, ending in his death just shy of his thirty-ninth birthday.

Angela raised her reading glasses and pinched her nose. It was impossible not to draw a conclusion that Fillide and Caravaggio were more than painter and model. Were they lovers? Was Ranuccio an abusive pimp? Did the swordfight between Ranuccio and Caravaggio have anything to do with Fillide? These questions had been addressed in a happenstance manner for centuries, but no concrete evidence could be found.

Jealous rivals had painted a picture of Caravaggio as an arrogant, vengeful man who was driven by uncontrolled emotions and a propensity to strike at anyone who opposed or questioned his honor. Those same rivals belittled his talent and his output. Few acknowledged his indisputable genius.

If she and Alex were going to find a stolen Caravaggio, she needed to understand the man who painted this lost treasure. She was being thrown down the rabbit's hole for a reason.

Angela continued to read long into the night, until her eyelids grew heavy, and sleep finally claimed her.

Rome, Italy
28 May, 1606

The pounding on her door sent her heart into a thunderous gallop. *Cara Madre di Dio*, nothing good ever came of being out after curfew. Fillide crossed herself, invoking the Virgin's protection, as she rose from her bed and lit a candle. She crept to the window. The full moon lit the street with silvery beams revealing two men holding another man between them. She ran down the wooden steps to the door. "Who bothers a woman in the safety of her home so late at night?"

She could just make out the garbled words. "Fillide, *amore mio*, for the love of God open the door."

"Caravaggio!" She threw open the door. The bruised and battered man shaking on her doorstep bore little resemblance to the swaggering painter who'd left her bed only a few hours ago. She held her candle higher, illuminating the ravaged man, his head caked with dried blood. His doublet looked as if it had been painted red by the artist himself. His eyes were wide with terror as if he'd witnessed his own demise.

She hurriedly whisked the men inside, casting a quick glance up and down the street before shutting and locking the door. "Upstairs." They half-dragged, half-carried Caravaggio up the stairs and deposited him on the bed. He closed his eyes and drew a breath of relief. His chest rose shallowly, and he winced.

"What in God's name happened?" Fillide asked as she fetched a basin of water and cloth.

"A duel between Caravaggio and Ranuccio. Caravaggio drove the *bastardo* to the ground and went to cut his testicles off, but Ranuccio moved and Caravaggio missed and stabbed him near the groin. He must have sliced deep, because he bled like a stuck pig. His brother and brothers-in-law carried Ranuccio's body from the tennis courts. He is a dead man for certain."

Caravaggio moaned as Fillide gently washed the blood from his face and head, careful not to disturb the deep line of gruesome stitches. "If Ranuccio was injured, how did the painter get this wound on his head?" she asked, dipping the cloth into the basin and wringing it out to continue her ministrations.

Onorio's words tumbled from him. "Ranuccio's brother Giovan Francisco retaliated and clubbed Caravaggio with his sword. Then the captain joined the skirmish to stop Giovan from killing Caravaggio. Giovan and the captain fought and Petronio was badly wounded. We all fled before the *sbirri* showed up and arrested us. Paulo and I took Caravaggio and Petronio to the barber surgeon, Pompeo Navagna. He stitched up Caravaggio and Toppa, but Toppa was too badly injured to be moved and we had to leave him. It is certain the *sbirri*, those bastards of the papal constabulary, will arrest him and take him to the Tor di Nona. If he survives that hellhole of a prison, it will be a miracle."

"What were you fools thinking?" She wanted to slap silly each of these boys who pretended to be men. "What will happen next?"

"The capital crime of dueling comes with a death sentence and we are all in danger," Onorio said. "By tomorrow, the Guigoli brothers, Giovan Francisco, and everyone except poor Toppa will have fled Rome."

Paulo was pacing. "We need to go Onorio, we need to leave Rome now!"

Onorio grabbed the agitated Paulo, halting his nervous pacing. "*Si, si,* I know, Paulo." He turned to Fillide. "Can you get Caravaggio to the Marchesa Costanza Colonna? He needs to leave Rome for he is sure to be arrested. She has always protected him and pray to God she doesn't desert him now, or he's a dead man."

Fillide examined the feverish face of the painter. She wanted to kill him herself for leaving her bed when she'd pleaded for him to stay. By right, she should toss him in the street or better yet, call the *poliziotti.* It would serve him right. But in her heart, she knew she could never cause him harm. He'd killed Ranuccio for *her*, to free her from the abusive pimp.

She loved him.

She'd been in love with him since that fateful day at the market when he caught her stealing a peach.

Caravaggio was her kindred spirit—passionate and fiery—refusing to accept the plate of bitter herbs life had served him. Caravaggio had always reached beyond his fate. And in so doing, he'd reached beyond hers. He'd seen into her soul and had painted her on numerous occasions. If the critics were to be believed, he'd immortalized her.

No one better than Caravaggio understood the loss of a father. He understood her harsh loneliness—growing up without the anchor of a family. A mother who forced her into prostitution, instead of protecting her. Even as she crossed herself for thinking ill of the dead, Fillide could not bury that long-ago betrayal.

Gazing at the man who—like her—struggled to conquer his demons, she made up her mind. "Leave. I will see to him."

Onorio grabbed her hands and kissed them. "Thank you. I will go to Milan and my family in Lombardy. Pray the Pope will grant us all forgiveness and allow us to return to Rome."

"You're sure the Marchesa will help him?"

"She's like a guardian angel to him. Their ties go back to his mother and aunt. The aunt was a wet nurse to the Sforza Colonna's children. It is doubtful she will turn her back on him in his hour of need."

"Go. I will get him to the Villa Colonna and pray the Marchesa sees fit to save him."

With the two men gone, she heated a bowl of beef broth and spoon-fed Caravaggio. "This time you've gone too far, painter. How will you see your way clear of this disaster?"

"In the Church's eyes I'm damned and I fear I will never find salvation in God's eyes. But I do not regret ending the life of that *bastardo*." He sipped a spoonful of the fortifying soup. His eyes mellowed and warmed. "Who would think that a whore would be my dearest friend."

It rankled her to be called a whore, but she could not argue with the truth of his words. "I don't know why I agreed to help you."

"Could it be I hold a special place in your heart?"

"And even if it were true, what good does it do me? You will leave Rome and never give me another thought."

"You know that is not true, *amore mio*. Is it not fate that puts certain people in our paths? Even a painter and whore have hearts that yearn for more from this life. Are we not entitled to love and to be loved?"

She smiled and brushed a wayward lock from his brow. "Love has never been in the cards for you or me. We service the powerful and bow to their wishes." She bent to kiss him. "I wish it were true the possibility of love, but now it is too late."

He snarled. "It has always been too late for me. What others take for granted, I've fought my whole life to win."

"Anger will not make it so, nor will it change anything. Both you and I are too quick to anger. A bit more temperance would serve us well. God gave you a talent greater than any man I know." She laid her head on his chest. "Painter, I do not want to lose you. It breaks my heart to think I may never see you again." She looked up and gazed imploringly at him. "What if I came with you?"

"I cannot allow you to ruin your life. Your patron Giulio Strozzi is a good man who will see to your security. You don't need a pimp when you are the exclusive lover of an aristocrat. You have a chance to live in comfort and you must take it, Fillide."

She wiped his damp brow with the cloth. "I know you are right, and it seemed like a good arrangement so long as I had you, too, but now you will be gone. There will no longer be anyone to share my feelings with. No one who truly understands me."

Picking up the bowl she spooned the last of the broth into his mouth. He gazed at her intently. "I will return to Rome, I promise you Fillide. I will not attempt another painting with you as my heroine until I do. Once

I return, we will find a way to be together and you will once more become my muse."

She smiled through her tears. "Promise me you will return to me."

"I swear it."

"Hold me for a minute or two and then we'll go." Climbing into the bed, she rested in his strong embrace. Why had they waited so long to lay out their hearts to each other?

Draped in his *ferraiuolo*, his black cape, Caravaggio leaned heavily against Fillide as they crept through the streets of a still slumbering Rome. They stopped first at his lodgings in the home of the lawyer Andrea Ruffetti so he could pack some clothing, art supplies, and most importantly his money. His ever-faithful assistant, Cecco, insisted on going into exile with him.

It was the dead of night when the three arrived at the imposing Palazzo Colonna. They waited several minutes after awakening the watch for the majordomo to arrive. The man recognized Caravaggio at once and showed the three in. They waited in the entry. Fillide had never seen anything so grand. The palazzo was elaborate in design and furnishings. Gilded frames of gold held paintings of the venerable Colonna family that hung on brocaded walls, lit by chandeliers of the finest Murano glass. Never had she felt so lowly and out of place as she did at that moment in this monument to wealth and power.

The Marchesa herself wrapped in a silk robe descended the stairway. She appraised the motley crew that stood before her. Fillide shrank beneath her eagle-eyed gaze. "What have you gotten yourself into now, Michelangelo?"

Caravaggio dropped to his knees and grabbed his protectress's hand, pressing his lips to it. "Madonna, I beg your forgiveness for this intrusion, but I had nowhere else to turn." And then the whole sordid business poured from him, all of it, the duel, and the accidental death of Ranuccio.

The Marchesa's gaze wavered from Caravaggio to Fillide. "And who is this woman and man you have brought to my home?"

Fillide knew Caravaggio would not be foolish enough to lie to the Marchesa. "A courtesan and friend who kindly helped me. I am indebted to her. And this is Cecco, my assistant. Forgive me for troubling you, but I had nowhere else to turn." He wept and threw himself at the mercy of his benefactress.

Costanza gripped the stair railing and listened, her hand absently finger-
ing his disorderly hair. "Say goodbye to your friend, Caravaggio." She turned
to Fillide and there was a softening in her eyes. "I recognize you from his
painting of you as *St Katherine*. If he saw fit to see you as a saint, the least I
can do is thank you. This intrepid painter has known my protection and will
continue to know it, for as long as I live. He is like a black-sheep son to me.
Thank you for helping him." The Marchesa turned and ascended the stairs.
She called over her shoulder. "Clean up and get some sleep, Michelangelo.
In the morning we will see to getting you out of Rome."

"Cecco, help me see Fillide safely from here."

"Maestro, is it necessary? You would be better cleaning up and resting.
The morning will soon be upon us."

"Fillide is more important than any of that. I will not see her for some
time, and it will be a great loss to me."

Caravaggio supported by Cecco, walked Fillide outside the palazzo.

She kissed his cheek. "Everything that needs to be said has been said.
Come back to me, painter."

He grabbed her, crushing her to his chest and whispered in her ear. "I
promise, Fillide, I will return to you. No matter what happens, I will return."

Her eyes brimmed with tears as she scampered down the stairs and
path to the gates. She looked back once and waved to the painter who
watched her go.

In the early hours of the morning she returned to the palazzo and from
a short distance she saw a coach drawn by four horses leave the stables. The
coach with its insignia of the house of Colonna had the drapes drawn over
the windows. For a moment she could have sworn she saw a hand part the
drapes and a face in shadow smile at her. She would hold that image in her
mind for years to come.

CHAPTER 9

Claridge's Hotel
London, England
Present day

A shout wrenched Angela awake.

Oh, my God! I know the truth!

Everything was clear, now... That first nightmare when Alex's face had transformed into Caravaggio... The dream about Caravaggio and Fillide arguing over the duel with Ranuccio... The dream about the first time Fillide and Caravaggio met, at the market... And now, the dream about Fillide tenderly tending Caravaggio's wounds and taking him to the Marchesa Colonna's palazzo.

They loved each other.

Of course, how could she have missed it?

Alex is Caravaggio. And I'm Fillide.

"Once the door is opened, it is impossible to close..." Prophetic words. Maria, their housekeeper in Montefioralle, called it *al saselea simt*, sixth-sense. The Romanian woman was not only wise, she had an uncanny ability to read Angela's mind. Angela believed Maria had ESP, extra-sensory perception. Maria encouraged Angela to accept her ability as a unique gift.

She was right. Angela's psychic ability was here to stay. Her visions of the past were not a fluke. She had them for a reason. Caravaggio was a test.

She had to respect the visions that came to her. Her visions were a revelation of another past life, connected to the Caravaggio painting stolen in 1969. The past was calling to her again, and she needed to listen, and follow where the visions led.

A crash and breaking glass shocked her out of her musings. A scream turned her blood cold.

Alex!

She ran into the bedroom and flipped the light switch. The lamp from Alex's nightstand lay in pieces on the carpet. Alex was twisting and moaning on the bed, as if in agony. "Alex, wake up." She gently squeezed his shoulder.

He snarled and grabbed her, throwing her onto the bed, pinning her beneath him.

"Alex!"

His eyes flew open. "My God!" He tumbled back on the bed, his eyes horrified. "What have I done?" he said, brokenly. He sat up slowly, one hand reaching out, but not touching her. His tortured gaze filled with tears. "Please tell me I didn't hurt you."

Angela sat up and slid closer to him. "I'm fine, you did nothing wrong." She reached out and clasped his hand. They pulled each other in, their arms entwining,

holding tight. "You were having a bad dream," she whispered. "Do you remember anything?"

"I saw… Tim and Randy…" he said, his voice cracking. "When does it stop, Angela? When will I be free?"

She wished her love could erase the nightmares of war… "When we get home, I'll go with you. I'll see a therapist with you. We can do this together."

"I've done all that, Angela. I was in therapy for years after… after I went home. I was doing well. I haven't had a PTSD episode in a long time… Just don't give up on me… Please."

"Give up on you. Are you crazy—?" Her breath caught. "I'm sorry, I didn't mean it that way. You're not crazy."

He buried his face in her hair. "It's okay. I *am* crazy about you."

"That kind of crazy works for me." She planted gentle kisses on the side of his neck. "Why don't you take a shower and let's order up some breakfast? By the way, you're not the only one who had a dream last night."

Alex leaned back, his face awash in concern. "I'm so damned selfish. What happened?"

"Shower first, then I'll tell you over breakfast. You're always saying how much you love to watch me eat. Now's your chance—apparently dreams are hard work. I'm starving."

Do you recognize this woman?

Alex hit send and hopped in the shower. He squirted the shampoo onto his palm and lathered his scalp. The audacity of that woman to sit across from her own daughter and pretend they'd only just met! Angela had taken an instant liking to Anastasia, and Alex had snapped a few pics of them, sending them to Oliver. He didn't expect to hear back from him until sometime later as it was the middle of the night in Lake Bluff.

Being held to silence by his future father-in-law had put him in a terrible situation. Telling Angela that Anastasia might be her mother would devastate her; but not telling her was wrong. Alex knew from his parents that keeping secrets could poison a marriage. If he held onto this secret, he'd risk losing Angela's trust. And what about her trust in her dad? Angela adored Oliver and finding out the truth might destroy her relationship with him. Alex scrubbed his scalp as if he could remove his turbulent thoughts, or better yet, wash Anastasia down the drain.

He needed to find a way out. If need be, he'd convince Anastasia to forever hold her peace. It was too late for a mother-and-daughter relationship. Friendship or nothing... but what if Anastasia resisted? After all these years, she might think a reunion was ordained... and what about Angela's psychic ability? If Angela spent more time with Anastasia, she'd figure it out.

He dried his hair with a towel, mulling over the options. The other problem was his dad. If Anastasia was still affiliated with the SVR, Lance's career was in peril. In Alex's mind, Anastasia was an enemy combatant, and eventually he'd have to deal with her. One thing was certain—he was taking Angela home ASAP. The call of Florence had never been so strong. If he had to take the Caravaggio case to get Angela back to Italy and away from Anastasia, so be it.

CHAPTER 10

Florence, Italy
Present day

Angela put the last of the breakfast dishes into the dishwasher and glanced out the window. It was a partly cloudy day, one of those days when light and shadow brought everything into focus. They planned on walking to the Uffizi to meet with Celestine Marchesi. Angela had been surprised how easy it was to convince Alex to take on the case—since he'd been so negative about it. She wasn't sure why he'd had a sudden change of heart, but she suspected that after his debilitating PTSD attack, he'd realized that immersing himself in a new case was just what the doctor ordered.

They'd returned from London on Saturday, a day earlier than scheduled. Alex seemed to have a thing about leaving early when he visited his parents. He'd assured her that if they were lying on a beach in St. Tropez—where he promised to take her on their honeymoon—he'd be far more likely to extend their vacation than cut it short. But, as she'd learned, Alex was impulsive, and used to his world spinning in the direction he chose.

At least they'd had a lovely farewell breakfast with Lance and Anastasia before departing, and Alex had surprised her by inviting his father to visit Montefioralle for Christmas. Excited for their first Christmas together, Angela had invited Anastasia as well. A frown had shadowed Alex's face for a moment before he gave Anastasia a stiff smile and echoed Angela's invitation. Angela couldn't understand his aversion to Anastasia. The only explanation could be he'd dislike any girlfriend of his father's. After all, it was Lance's cheating which had caused the biggest crack in his marriage to Faye.

An idea occurred to her that she might ask her father to fly over and spend the holidays with them too. Perhaps with her own father there, the tension Alex felt toward Anastasia would be muted. Alex and her dad had bonded so well, she couldn't imagine anything better than all three men together at Montefioralle. She decided to keep the idea a secret, and surprise Alex the way he often surprised her. It never occurred to her that her father and Lance might not get along. In fact, she felt certain they would become fast friends, and she was sure her father would love Anastasia.

Her only concern was disappointing Alex's mother. It seemed reasonable to assume she might be upset if they didn't show up for Christmas. And she'd already made a fool of herself at the Argyle's home when she'd had that strange vision of the Rembrandt being stolen. Faye had been beside herself with worry, asking Alex if Angela had a mental illness. She certainly didn't want to offend Faye and Tom—then again, Alex had made a point of telling Faye they'd be flying stateside for the Super Bowl. He'd already purchased tickets and hired a private jet for him and Admiral Tom to attend the big game in Miami.

When he mentioned the Super Bowl to Angela, she begged off, even though flying in a private jet was more than a little tempting. He'd laughed and admitted he wasn't bothered in the least. A little separation was good for them and a few days without him and Tom underfoot would give her and Faye a chance to get things finalized for the wedding. Alex had made it clear he would be hands-off when it came to planning the wedding, but he would pay for whatever Angela wanted. When Angela suggested her father could contribute, Alex chuckled and informed her Faye would be insulted if he or Oliver even suggested spending a dime on the reception. His mother wasn't one to share the glory and her idea of a small and intimate gathering would fill half a Super Bowl stadium.

Alex had insisted on buying Angela's wedding gown and all the fripperies that went along with it. While a part of Angela was touched with Alex's romantic gesture, another part worried about the extravagance. In London, Alex had snuck out one afternoon, while she was reading, and dropped a bundle on clothes, shoes, accessories, and fancy underwear. He'd even had all the labels and price tags removed, the cheeky devil! Then to celebrate having pulled one over on her, he'd ordered up fish and chips and Guinness. He plopped himself on the sofa and grinned from ear to ear. That was it. She threw her hands up in the air and gave in. He cajoled her into giving him a private fashion show. So, she decided to go all out—pirouetting down the makeshift runway from the bedroom to the living room. He applauded and whistled with each wardrobe change.

Angela understood Alex's propensity for acquiring new toys, but he was already so generous with her. She lived in his home, or rather, homes.

He paid all their expenses, including flights. It was important for her to contribute to their marriage. Angela had been paid for her paper on the discovery of the Leonardo. At least there was that. And he valued her insight.

She sighed as she poured herself another cup of coffee. Making him happy was so much fun, she found it hard to refuse him. Truthfully, she found it hard to refuse him anything. Having found the perfect guy, it seemed foolish to try and change him.

Alex and Angela strolled from the condo in the Palazzo Rucellai to the Uffizi Gallery. With plenty of time to spare, they enjoyed the scenic views from the Lungarno Corsini, the river walk along the Arno. It was impossible not to be drawn into the beauty of greenery, sky, and architecture reflected in the serene, blue water.

"I want to show you something." He sidetracked down a narrow street and pulled her into a stone-and-brick building with massive, red double-doors, surrounded by variegated gray-and-white marble. One of the things Angela loved about Alex was his appreciation of art, history, and architecture. It was something they shared to their very cores and it assured their future together would be a life of adventure and discovery. As if it could be anything else when they were now partners in the search for missing art works.

"I actually planned on showing this to you today, so I did a little research, *Professoressa*." Alex opened the doors and grinned when she shrieked in delight. "I wanted to impress my girl. This is the Church of Santo Stefano al Ponte and it's one of the oldest churches in Florence. It was built in the eleventh and twelfth centuries with a polychrome marble façade similar to the Duomo. Sadly, what you saw surrounding the arches over the exterior doors is all that's left of the façade. In the fourteenth century, they renovated the interiors and removed the three separate aisles creating a hall. What you see before you is an acoustically perfect room, where classical concerts and opera are performed."

Angela turned in a slow circle, amazed at the beauty. "Oh, Alex, it's incredible, a seamless melding of Romanesque, Gothic, and Baroque architecture. I can't believe how many treasures are here in Florence that I never knew existed."

"I knew you'd love it, wait until you see it at night with colored lights. It comes alive in a thoroughly modern way. They perform several operas here during the year."

"I've never been to the opera."

"I want you to attend your first opera in this intimate space. I think *La Traviata* is coming up in December." His eyebrow lifted mischievously. "What do you think sweetheart? Am I tempting you?"

She looped her arm through his and gazed into his eyes. "You've got yourself a date." Sometimes she wanted to pinch herself just to make sure she wasn't dreaming. Her first opera in Florence with the man she loved, it just didn't seem real.

Angela's pulse accelerated when they entered the Uffizi Gallery. The last time she'd been there she'd experienced two visions, one from her past life as Fioretta Gorini, who'd secretly been married to Giuliano Medici. The other from her past life as Sophia Caro, who'd fallen in love with a German officer, Gerhard Jaeger. Gerhard and Sophia had removed the da Vinci masterpiece from the Uffizi and hid the painting during the German evacuation of Florence. Just being amid the Medici collection and the setting of her past life with Alex made the hairs rise on her arms.

Celestine rose from her desk and greeted them. Dressed in a tailored, forest-green suit and matching paisley pashmina, she managed to exude both femininity and power. Angela was glad she'd worn the navy knit dress Alex had suggested. Celestine wore her dark hair in her customary, classic French roll, and high heels that Angela couldn't imagine wearing all day.

Angela felt honored Celestine had agreed to let her write the seminal academic paper about the Leonardo. Celestine could have given the privilege to a more eminent scholar. Angela was grateful to the directress for believing in her. Her admiration was even greater knowing what it must have taken for a woman to rise to the pinnacle of the art world and become the head of one of the most revered museums in the world. Celestine had shattered the glass ceiling, and her sponsorship meant the world to Angela.

"I want to congratulate you both on your engagement. I couldn't be happier, you're so well-suited to each other." Celestine bussed Angela on both cheeks. "Have you set a date yet?"

"Thank you, Celestine," Angela said. "We're planning for a spring wedding and we'd be delighted to see you in San Francisco for the celebration."

"I promise you, I'm going to move heaven and earth to attend. To miss out on such a happy occasion of friends would be very un-Italian."

"We won't take no for an answer, Celestine," Alex joined in. "Maybe you can combine a working trip with a little pleasure. Faye's friends have a brilliant, Old Masters collection—I'm sure they'd be delighted to show you."

"Oh, yes," said Angela, "they have a masterpiece by Rembrandt rarely seen in a private collection, and their drawings include Botticelli, Leonardo, and Michelangelo."

"I'd love to see it." She clapped her hands. "But I'd be even more inclined if you would take the case and find the stolen Caravaggio first." It was a bit of blackmail tossed out in jest. But beneath the jest lay Celestine's hunger for the painting, and the acclaim that would go with it. Caravaggio's stolen masterpiece belonged in an Italian museum. It would be a coup for the Uffizi.

Celestine indicated the two Barcelona chairs in front of her intricately carved desk. "Please sit and let's discuss the painting in question and then I'd like to show you the Sala del Caravaggio. We've opened a new wing dedicated to the seventeenth century. I'd like you to see our three Caravaggio holdings."

"I'm sure Angela will be thrilled to see it, but I'm wondering why you think this cold case can be solved now? Investigators have been searching for this painting for nearly fifty years. Why now? And why Angela and me?"

"That's exactly why I want to enlist your help," Celestine said. "Fifty years of failure. The case needs fresh eyes, Alex. And let me be direct, I know Angela has some kind of psychic ability besides being an art historian. If she could unearth the whereabouts of the Leonardo, maybe she can do the same with Caravaggio's *Nativity*."

"You know?" Angela gripped the arms of the chair.

"Of course, I know." Celestine waved her hand dismissively. "People don't usually talk about Leonardo da Vinci as if he were their best friend, nor do they know where the hidden entrance to the Vasari corridor is in this museum…but *you* did."

Alex crossed his arms over his chest. "Well, so much for our secret."

Celestine shrugged. "Angela's secret is safe with me. I have no intention of sharing it with anyone. If she can use her ability to find the Caravaggio, why not?"

Alex scratched his stubble. "Angela is already determined to find it, anyway. She had a dream about Caravaggio more than a week ago and she's been studying him like a bloodhound ever since."

The glamorous directress's gaze locked on Angela. "Really? Can I ask what you saw in the dream?"

"I'm not ready to talk about it right now, but suffice it to say, we'll take the case." Angela read the disappointment on Celestine's face. She hadn't told Alex the truth yet, how could she tell Celestine.

"*Va bene*, I accept that. Now, moving forward, I've arranged for you to meet with the head of the Division for the Protection of Cultural Heritage. He's agreed to share everything he has on the case with you."

"I know Salvatore Spinelli. I wouldn't call my relationship with the TPC totally amicable. He's never shared much with me before. I guess he considers me a rival in the art recovery world."

"I assure you Alex, he'll be completely cooperative. I made it clear I will accept nothing less. The Oratorio de San Lorenzo from where the painting was stolen is owned by the Franciscan order. They understand the painting, if found, can no longer safely be kept in the church. They have a beautiful reproduction hanging above the altar where the painting once hung. The Friars have agreed the original *Nativity* would be much safer here at the Uffizi." Celestine's eyes flashed with triumph when she stood. "Let us see the Caravaggios."

He couldn't catch his breath… His heart had begun to pound.

Alex followed Celestine and Angela into the Medici red-walled Caravaggio salon. As he watched their lips move, the pulsing in his ears drowned out their words. He hoped they didn't notice his anxiety, but one look at Angela told him otherwise.

"Alex, are you all right?" she asked.

No, he wasn't all right. He wasn't even a little all right. He was having trouble breathing, his brow was damp, and his palms were definitely sweaty. This was a hell of a time to experience a PTSD episode.

"Alex, what's wrong?"

"I'm sorry… I…" His words froze when his gaze landed on the glass-enclosed object. He sucked in his breath, the rush of blood in his ears accelerating. The painting of Medusa with writhing, dying, snakes making his head spin. But it was the face frozen in contorted agony that arrested his ability to complete his sentence.

Mounted on a wooden ceremonial parade shield, the painting was rendered three-dimensional. The scream emanating from the tragic face resounded in his ears—growing so loud he had to cover them. But no matter how hard he tried, the agonized scream tore through the fabric of his sanity. The face on the shield was Caravaggio, but the scream was buried inside of him and in some bizarre way it was his own.

Above the din of the scream, Angela's voice called to him and he grabbed hold of the lifeline she threw him. Wading through the madness of PTSD and the darkness in his past, she did not let go.

Alex had always considered himself a tough guy, the last man standing, regardless of the challenge. He was the man who'd rescued his comrades in arms, dragging them to safety at whatever cost, only to find himself helpless as he watched the light fade from their eyes. He'd buried those losses in his soul. In silence, he blamed himself for surviving when his best friend Randy didn't. The military had taught him how to fight, but it never taught him how to forgive himself.

But Angela had changed all of that. She saw beneath the façade of tough-guy-playboy who acquired things instead of love. She had a tenaciousness that went far beyond physical strength. She was like a willow tree that bends in the face of gale force winds and then rebounds stronger and more determined than before. She would never abandon him, not in this lifetime. Not in any lifetime, future or past. The past was an open book to her. The veil had been lifted and she'd seen vivid visions where the past was revealed. She knew the beginning and the end. And though it scared her, she'd learned to control her fear, and that was just one of the things that amazed him about her.

The soft touch of her hand caressing his face led him back from the abyss. He opened his eyes and his sanity returned. Staring into Angela's compassionate gaze, he glimpsed his past and his future. In that instant he knew what it truly meant to be loved. She, who had loved him through two previous lifetimes, would love him always. For the first time he understood what the word soulmate meant. Angela was his future just as she was his past.

Her love brought him back. It would always bring him back.

"Alex, come back to me."

The haunting scream faded away… "*Amore mio*, I'm sorry."

She smiled. "There's no need to be sorry. We were just worried about you. You left us, but now you're back."

"We?" He turned and saw Celestine quietly observing. The only emotion written in her expression was concern.

"Yes, Alex—Celestine and me. Do you remember anything?"

"No… I mean, yes. I'm fine now, but I'm not sure what happened. The painting must have triggered something inside of me. I have to be honest, Celestine, I've been hiding my PTSD from you, from Angela, and from myself."

"I think facing up to it is the first step to recovery, my friend," said Celestine.

"I'll put it to you straight, Celestine. Do you still want Angela and me, *me* being the one in question, to investigate and find the Caravaggio? I can't blame you if you've changed your mind after seeing me go unhinged."

"More than ever. May I remind you, this is not the first time our art tour has been interrupted by a strange occurrence. Last time, it was Angela's reaction to Sandro Botticelli's *Birth of Venus*. '*La mia amica, Simonetta. O Dio, Sandro l'adorava, la sua morte lo ha distrutto.*' Your exact words, Angela. 'My friend, Simonetta. O God, Sandro adored her, her death destroyed him.' Angela had a connection to the painting and to da Vinci. By your reaction to the *Medusa*, I believe you and Caravaggio share something. I believe finding the Caravaggio is as important to you as it is to me."

He nodded and took Angela's hand. Just touching her imbued him with courage. "I need to see the other two Caravaggios in the collection. Lead on, directress."

CHAPTER 11

The short commuter flight from Florence to Rome was a snap. The concierge made sure everything went smoothly from the moment they were picked up in the Hassler's navy blue Rolls Royce until they were installed in the Medici Villa suite, where they'd stayed on their last trip to Rome when they were searching for the Leonardo wedding portrait. However, as much as Angela would have liked to lounge around on the luxurious upholstered red suede furniture and gape at the bird's eye views of the Eternal City, she was even more excited to get to the headquarters of the Carabinieri Command for the Protection of Italy's Cultural Heritage, otherwise known as the TPC.

Their driver dropped them in the old, working-class neighborhood of Trastevere at the Piazza Sant' Ignazio. Angela's first glimpse of the charming square reminded her of a movie set. The tangerine-colored plastered Rococo buildings seemed more like illusions, where you open the door to walk in and realize there's nothing there, just a façade with supportive scaffolding. The early eighteenth-century apartment buildings fit together like a jigsaw puzzle whose pieces were constantly being rearranged by stagehands. Originally built as small palaces, they'd long ago been converted into apartments. Some of the apartment house facades were curved, while those on the sides resembled bookends holding them up. All of them offered a view of the piazza and an opportunity to people-watch, a pastime Romans were particularly fond of doing.

Angela's imagination couldn't help but wander. She pictured a hot summer's night and a window being thrown open by a sultry-eyed Sophia Loren dressed in nothing but a silky robe. Sophia, disheveled, and looking like every school-boy's dream, leaned over the balcony displaying her magnificent cleavage to the camera. Catching sight of her departing lover, a flustered Marcello Mastroianni, she would have no problem calling down to scold him and throwing her slipper at him as her neighbors watched in 'I-told-you-so' delight. The entire neighborhood spellbound as the scene unfolded, all because Marcello dared to sneak away without promising to marry her after compromising her virtue. It was a captivating image and one Angela was loath to turn her attention from. Alex, however, had other plans, and he took her elbow and steered her toward the building where Lieutenant Salvatore Spinelli awaited them. Her daydream of Sophia and Marcello faded like the end of a movie.

The building itself looked more like a diplomatic embassy with its official flags and uniformed guards. It seemed an odd place for one of the most elite police forces in the world to call home, but this was Italy and she'd begun to understand the Italian attitude to life, *que sera sera*, 'what will be will be'. If a palazzo was where they wished to headquarter, who was she to question their wisdom. Italians didn't stress the small things. Whenever she found herself in a conundrum as to why the pace of living was so much slower in Italy than anywhere else, she reminded herself this was the land of *la Dolce vita*, 'the sweet life'.

The lieutenant, silver-haired, with a youthful, unlined face, was dressed in brown corduroys and a sweater—he stood to greet them when they entered his office. To Angela, the man appeared more like a college professor than a detective, but plain, everyday clothes made an investigator more accessible and easier for the public to trust. Alex and Lieutenant Spinelli had met before and shook hands familiarly.

"Salvatore Spinelli, may I introduce my fiancée and partner Angela Renatus."

"My pleasure to meet you." Spinelli's handshake was firm, and she appreciated his businesslike approach. He indicated they should take a seat.

Angela glanced around the office. Spinelli seemed a true admirer of art. Behind his desk was a floor-to-ceiling shelf displaying ancient pottery and small statues. To the left of the desk was a window, offering a view of the Piazza Sant'Ignazio. Italy was definitely a country of art and art lovers. She wondered if he too enjoyed people watching from his lofty perch.

"*Signorina*, let me thank you on behalf of a grateful nation on finding the da Vinci and returning it to the Uffizi," he said.

Angela appreciated his speaking English. Her Italian was coming along, but she was barely above high school student level on a summer immersion program, certainly not proficient enough to communicate complex sentences, let alone complex thoughts.

"You've secured a formidable friend in Celestine Marchesi," Salvatore continued. "Can I offer you both an espresso?"

"Espresso would be great. Angela?" Alex leaned back in the easy chair. "Yes, please."

Salvatore attended to the *Barista Express* espresso-maker behind his desk, while he chatted amiably, directing his questions to Angela and her impressions of Rome. He moved with precision and efficiency, and in minutes they were all holding demitasse cups of steaming espresso.

"Salvatore, would you mind summarizing a little about the TPC for Angela, and the changes that have come about since its inception?"

"*Piacere mio*, my pleasure. Let me start by saying I'd be lying, *signorina*, if I didn't admit that the TPC was founded following the outrage that occurred after the theft of Caravaggio's *Nativity* in 1969. The time was ripe, art theft was at an all-time high, and Italy's patrimony was at stake. The populace expressed their indignation that a religious painting could be cut from its frame in a church and the government responded by establishing an elite unit.

"Our officers are trained in archaeology, antiquities, art history, and restoration, in addition to criminal detective work. As you might know, trafficking in stolen artworks is a multi-billion-dollar industry. Since the establishment of the TPC we have recovered more than one hundred and fifty thousand artworks worth well over five hundred million dollars." He sipped his espresso and heaved a deep sigh. "However, the one painting we are most anxious to find is Caravaggio's *Nativity*. We've come close to finding it in the past, but it has always eluded us."

"I know you're not exactly thrilled about sharing this case with us," said Alex. "But we're after the same thing, Salvatore, retrieving a priceless masterpiece and returning it to its rightful owner, the people of Italy. For the benefit of all, it would behoove us to cooperate."

"I'm more than willing to bury my misgivings about you, Alex. I have considered art detectives to be self-serving treasure hunters, but Celestine has convinced me otherwise. I now believe, for several reasons, which I will tell you after you've reviewed the case files, that a government agency won't be able to penetrate the veil." He leaned forward and *sotto voce* said, "We fear the painting may be in the hands of powerful individuals who are closely connected to top officials in our own government. Bringing an investigation to their doorstep would be nearly impossible. The TPC functions under the auspices of the government and the push-back would be enormous."

Angela glanced at Alex and saw the tell-tale tic in his jaw. Alex had a way of exuding calm in a professional situation, but clearly this was something that gave him pause. "Are you saying there are those in powerful positions that would somehow stop you from investigating? This sounds worse than the Mafia."

"I'm saying precisely that, but let's not get ahead of ourselves."

Angela now understood. Alex had to be calculating the potential risk.

"Angela, you may have heard of our database. We call it Leonardo. It is the most comprehensive database of its kind in the world, with over six million registered artworks. Of those, one and a half million of them are missing. The vast majority were either stolen or illegally excavated. The stolen-art black market finances drug cartels, arms deals, and an indecent amount of criminal activity. After our espresso I will show you Leonardo in action and then I want you to see the bunker where we store tens of thousands of recovered artworks. That is, if you'd like?"

"I'd like it very much, Salvatore," Angela replied. "As for the case itself, will we be allowed to have a copy of everything you've compiled in the investigation to date? I'm certain we couldn't possibly get through all of it during our stay in Rome."

"I've had everything uploaded to a secure flash drive and I will be providing you with a special computer that cannot be tampered with. The flash drive will only work on this laptop and the technology will require authentication. It will respond to your retinas." He smiled. "I take it you two work closely together."

Alex chuckled and reached for Angela's hand. "We work so well together that now we're engaged. A working hazard of close proximity, I suppose, but a welcome one."

Salvatore smiled. "*L'amore trova la strada.*"

Alex nodded. "Love will find a way."

Salvatore continued. "I will also be providing you with secure cell phones with tracking technology, and you will have codes to access the Leonardo database. Do you have any idea where you intend to start?"

Angela hadn't shared what she'd been planning with Alex, but now seemed to be as good a time as ever to reveal her idea. "I think it's imperative we follow Caravaggio's journey after the sword fight with Ranuccio Tomassino. Beginning here in Rome with the Colonna Palace."

"But why? After all, what happened to Caravaggio has nothing to do with what happened to his *Nativity*."

"It's how I work. It's a form of immersion." She hesitated, allowing the words to formulate in her mind. "The artist and the painting are forever one. Caravaggio will lead us to his painting."

Lieutenant Spinelli's brows furrowed together. "I'm not sure I understand."

From the corner of her eye, Angela could see Alex frowning. Alex wasn't keen on anyone knowing about her psychic talent. Celestine had figured it out, but she was a close friend. It seemed impossible for her not to share the truth with Lieutenant Spinelli. The window had opened to such an extent, that based on what had happened in San Francisco, it seemed she could under certain circumstances see into the future as well. She took a deep breath, knowing what she was about to say might seem crazy to the lieutenant. "Whether you believe makes no difference to me, but I am psychic. I have visions and dreams. That's how I found the Leonardo. I've already begun to have dreams about Caravaggio." She stopped short of telling him about her past lives with Alex, that was personal.

Salvatore arched a thick, salt-and-pepper eyebrow. "As a *carabiniere* of more than twenty years, I rely on forensics, bank accounts, wire taps, and as you Americans say, good old-fashioned detective work. Over the years we have had many people contact us who claim to know where the *Nativity* is. They claim to have the second sight. From elderly Nonnas to defrocked priests." He leaned forward and continued. "But there is something about you, Angela. You accomplished an amazing feat in retrieving the lost da Vinci. I am willing to suspend my usual inclinations to support whatever method you choose. Every day that passes makes it less likely we will ever recover the *Nativity*. I'm at your service, *signorina*."

By the time Alex and Angela left the Palazzo Sant'Ignazio it was two o'clock and they were hungry for lunch.

They had spent two hours behind an armored door in the basement of Palazzo Sant'Ignazio. Lieutenant Spinelli had led them through the storage rooms where thousands of retrieved artworks were kept. The shelves were lined with wooden crucifixes, marble busts, bronze statues, and hundreds of paintings. These were the spoils that had been rescued by the TPC. Salvatore explained that they remained in custody until their country of origin and legal ownership could be determined. The TPC conservationists carefully restored the damaged works. The vault contained a state-of-the-art scientific laboratory with all of the latest technology. Salvatore mentioned their close relationships with universities and experts throughout the world, who assisted in areas such as carbon dating.

In the innocuous gray case that hung from Alex's shoulder was the new laptop and the flash drive. Both he and Angela were in possession of their new cell phones, but for the moment Alex had only one thing on his mind—food.

A Mercedes sent from the Hassler was waiting outside the palazzo headquarters when they exited. From an app on his phone, Alex made a reservation at a restaurant that was only a mile away on the outskirts of Trastevere. Of course, with Rome's gridlock it still took about twenty minutes to go the distance.

It was a mild day and Alex suggested they sit outside as the old Roman restaurants could be stuffy. There were no tourists in sight. It was a good sign they would enjoy their lunch in relative quiet.

His fingers drummed the table as they waited for their Antinori Castello della Sala Cervaro to be served. He was in the mood for a crisp, white wine with body. "I was surprised when you told Salvatore about being psychic." In fact, he was more than surprised, he was concerned. If word got out among the world's art thieves, it might make Angela a target. Some secrets were better kept under wraps.

Angela didn't answer immediately—she was too busy dipping a chunk of freshly baked bread in olive oil. "Hmm... good. I'm so hungry."

Even with his stomach growling its complaint, Alex couldn't help but smile at the look of sheer bliss on Angela's face. Watching her eat sent a spark to his groin. He almost imagined passing on eating and heading straight for their bed. Almost.

She dabbed her lips with her napkin. "There was no way to explain my unorthodox approach to finding the painting. He promised not to tell anyone that I'm psychic."

"Yeah, but this kind of information has a way of leaking out. We now have three people who know you're psychic."

"Three?"

"Celestine, Salvatore, and that dirt-bag cousin of Scordato's, Enrico Fortuna, who's in prison."

"I'm not sure he's smart enough to have understood I'm psychic."

"Never underestimate the enemy, *amore mio*. People talk, and Italy's prisons are filled with thugs hoping to find some information that might be worth something to the higher-ups."

"I can't allow what-ifs to hinder our investigation. Besides, I have G.I. Joe to protect me." She gave him an impish grin. "I trust my future husband is going to keep me safe."

He couldn't help but grin back. Who'd have ever thought that the man who didn't trust women would willingly place his heart in the hands of a woman barely out of college, and never look back. The way he felt about her was a bigger mystery to him than finding the Caravaggio. But then again, their karmic connection went back at least five hundred years.

Did I really just think that?

Everything about his life had changed when Angela had sat down at the *Bistro Prossima Volta bar in Los Angeles. Looking back, he had to admit it was love at first sight for him. It had taken her a little longer, given their working relationship. But as Salvatore said, 'L'amore trova la strada'.* True love can never be denied.

The waiter returned to the table, opened the wine and poured, informing them their meal would be right up.

Alex raised his glass. "*Salute!*"

"*Cin cin!*"

Angela leaned in for a kiss.

The wine is good, but the kiss is better.

Alex wanted to get back to the hotel as soon as possible so he could indulge his romantic inclinations in that suite made for love.

The waiter returned with a platter heaping with three types of pasta. Angela sat up waving the aromatic steam toward her face. "Oh, my God, it smells divine."

"When in Rome, these are the three pastas Roma is known for," Alex explained, happy to indulge his foodie inclination for the time being.

"What are they?" Angela interjected, pushing her plate forward.

Alex held up a hand. "I'm going to get to that, *amore mio*. Patience. I want to explain first."

Angela grinned, sat up straight, and clasped her hands in front of her on the tabletop.

Alex chuckled at her eagerness. He pointed to the pastas. "These three are variations of the same pasta, plus or minus an ingredient or two. The key ingredient is *guanciali*, cured pork jowl. And the biggest secret is sautéing it while the pasta cooks, and then throwing in some of the starchy water, which allows the *guanciali* to render its fat but remain juicy."

Angela's eyes gleamed as she listened attentively. "You talk about food in the same way I talk about art—with passion. Positively swoon-worthy, detective."

"If you keep looking at me with those bedroom eyes, I'll be forced to show you my notion of 'swoon-worthy'." Alex wiggled his eyebrows. "Besides, I haven't finished my lecture." He cleared his throat in exaggeration, making Angela giggle, then heaped a sample of each pasta on their plates.

"As you know, Italy's unification was fairly recent, historically speaking," he went on. "The Italian states were uniquely different in their culture, architecture, music, even language. But perhaps, the greatest differences can be found in Italian cuisine. Romans favor *alla carbonera*, spaghetti with eggs, goat cheese, pepper, olive oil, and of course freshly grated Pecorino Romano made from sheep's milk. The second in this Roman pasta triumvirate is *buccatini all'Amatriciana*, which is nearly the same recipe, but made with tomatoes and sans egg. The last is the simplest of the three, *Cacio e Pepe*, Rome's answer to mac and cheese." Alex spoke, while expertly swirling the spaghetti with fork and spoon, serving first Angela and then himself. "Dig in, *amore*."

He waited while she tasted it, watching her expression. She leaned forward and closed her eyes. "Mmm, this is better than anything I've ever tasted."

Alex laughed. "You say that at nearly every meal, *amore*. I always feel like I'm in a competition with your last meal."

"I do it to keep you on your toes, lover boy."

"Well, consider me on my toes. I'm always working hard to coax that same response from you in the bedroom. Woe is me if I ever fail."

"My money's on you, soldier." She popped another bite in her mouth and uttered another rapturous moan.

Alex pretended her moan hadn't traveled the length of his body. A change of topic was in order, so he could at least get through lunch. "So, what's your plan… I'm talking Caravaggio."

"I think we should go to Montefioralle for a few days and plan our itinerary and study the case file. I'm missing the dogs and the vineyard. I need a little rest from visiting our parents." She rolled her eyes. "And tracking Caravaggio's final years is going to be an arduous journey crisscrossing much of Italy."

"I'll book our flight back to Florence for tomorrow. How about we cuddle up in our suite tonight and order whatever you desire. Then hopefully you'll leave a little desire left for me." He quirked a smile.

Angela covered his hand with hers. "Alex, you do know the food passion comes second to you."

"And I intend to keep it that way. Besides, you did say it keeps me on my toes. But before I indulge in the sweetness of your body, is there anything in Rome we need to do?"

"I think we should take Salvatore up on his offer and see the Palazzo Colonna this afternoon. I'm determined to follow the painter's trail, starting with the last night he spent in Rome."

Alex grabbed his phone from his pocket and thumbed a quick text. "Your wish is my command."

Salvatore Spinelli arranged a private tour of the Palazzo Colonna for them immediately following the close of public hours. Their driver dropped them at the palace entrance on the Via della Pilotta. The elaborate Roman Baroque building encompassed a city block and was built like a fortress around an inner garden at the foot of the Quirinal Hill. Angela gaped at the enormity of the structure as they were led inside. She whispered. "It's like a mini-Versailles."

Gabriella D'Angelo, the docent, met them and explained she would be directing them on their tour. "The Colonna family was one of the most powerful in Rome." Short and plump, with dark hair fashioned in a 1950s hair style, she welcomed them warmly. Spinelli told them Gabriella had been a docent for more than twenty-five years and knew more about the Palazzo than anyone else. "Twenty generations have occupied this house since the thirteenth century," Gabriella said, her hazel eyes twinkling with good humor. "Lieutenant Spinelli explained you were particularly interested in the time period when Costanza Colonna occupied the palace."

Alex only heard part of what Gabriella said before it began again. The eerie, free-falling sensation, like he was on an elevator with a snapped cable. Heart palpations followed, then a cold sweat. He wiped his brow, hoping Angela wouldn't notice this time. Too late, his intuitive angel glanced at him. Worry flickered in her eyes. He gritted his teeth and nodded, trying with all his might to keep his knees from buckling. Smoothly, she looped her arm through his, and leaned into his side. Her touch, her warmth enfolded him.

"Yes, we're doing research on Michelangelo Caravaggio and the last few years of his life," Angela said as she rubbed circles on Alex's palm with the pad of her thumb.

Her voice echoed to him as though from the end of a long tunnel. *Breathe...*

"Costanza and her brothers Fabrizio and Duke Marzio Colonna were his friends and protectors," Angela went on. "It makes sense to start where his downward spiral began. After the swordfight and death of Ranuccio, he sought refuge with the Colonna family. This is where he spent his last night in Rome."

"Caravaggio and the Colonna family shared a peculiar relationship," Gabriella said, her lips quirked in a quintessential Mona Lisa half-smile. "It has always been a mystery to the family why the Marchesa held such a deep and abiding devotion to the painter. She was his sponsor and protector, yet she never became a patron. She never commissioned a single work. As you know, there are no Caravaggios in the collection."

"Maybe she didn't like his paintings, but she cared about the man," Alex rasped. His voice sounded odd to his own ears. Angela continued swirling circles with the pad of her thumb on his palm. He tried to focus on Gabriella's explanation.

"Yes, she most certainly secured him patrons and collectors," Gabriella went on, pointing a finger in the air. "Much like an agent or manager might today. But you could be right. The Marchesa was a prolific writer who found her artistic voice through letter-writing and not through the fine art disciplines. She maintained a fondness for the Renaissance and the philosophical explorations of the mind. Caravaggio's work might have been too crude and realistic for her sensibilities."

"I take it there's no evidence of Caravaggio's visits here at the palace or of the last night he spent here before leaving Rome?" Angela asked.

"No, none I'm afraid. There is a suite of rooms on the top floor where the visiting guests' servants were housed. It's most likely Caravaggio slept there. At the time the furnishings would have been modest but comfortable." Gabriella gave a little shrug. "Most of those rooms have been cleaned and emptied. It's the part of the palace no longer used, except for storage… I would be happy to show them to you if you think it would help you in your investigation?"

"Yes, please, lead the way," Angela replied.

"*Va bene*… But first, allow me to show you something magnificent, one of the crown jewels of the palazzo, the Galleria Colonna." Gabriella gestured for them to follow her as she picked up her pace, her ballet flats tapping on the marble floor.

"Hey, how are you holding up?" Angela whispered pulling away to look at him.

"Just barely." Alex lifted her hand and kissed it. "Thank you for helping me. You always seem to know what I need and when I need it."

"I love you. It's part of the job description." She threaded her fingers through his as they followed Gabriella to a hall as long as a football field.

Angela caught her breath as they entered the hall. The frescoed ceilings soared several stories above them. Two-tiered crystal chandeliers ran the length of the hall, illuminating the paintings that filled every open space on the walls. Marble busts rested on ornately carved Baroque console tables and Roman statues stood on pedestals between rows of tall windows that opened out to the gardens. The floor, polished to a sparkling shine, was designed with repetitive squares of inlaid colored marble that drew the eye down the full length of the hall. At either end of the hall, massive marble columns supported a carved lintel crown that bordered the perimeter. Below the lintel on one side, open windows emanated natural light, joining with the glow of the chandeliers. It was easy to see why the Galleria had been compared to the Hall of Mirrors at Versailles.

Angela and Alex craned their necks to gaze at the frescoed ceiling. Above their head was a war galleon being welcomed into heaven by angels and the Holy Mother Mary.

"The Galleria was built in dedication to Costanza's father, Marcantonio II, the hero of Lepanto who led the Papal fleet against the Turks in triumph on October 7, 1571," Gabriella explained. "He saved not only the Papacy, but the entire European continent and was regarded as a great hero," Gabriella continued. "After his victory, he rode into Rome with the same pageantry afforded Caesar. Undoubtedly, the Colonnas must have considered Caravaggio's birth to be auspicious, as he was born just a week before on the feast of Sant' Michael, September 29, 1571."

"That could explain their devotion to him, but I wouldn't exactly call his life lucky, I'd call it cursed," Alex blurted in a harsh tone.

Gabriella's eyes widened at his remark. Angela looked at him in concern.

Shit! Get a grip on yourself, Caine. "My apologies Gabriella, this investigation is proving to be a tricky one. What I meant to say is, from what we've read of Caravaggio, his talent and rise to fame parallels the depths of his inner torment."

Angela squeezed Alex's hand. "Genius isn't always a reward," she added. "Sometimes it's a curse. For an artist, the act of painting was as dangerous as marching into battle for a soldier. The paints themselves were toxic. Some artists were more susceptible than others to the lead and mercury. We may assume that Caravaggio was affected, which would explain his increasing volatility over the years."

Gabriella nodded, her eyes reflecting sorrow. "Before we are born, an angel shows us what our lives will be like. She tells us there will be both happiness and sorrow, but there will also be the unknown. If we choose that life, it will serve a purpose that we cannot comprehend until after we die… and then all will be revealed to us…" The light streaming in from the window misted around her, forming a nimbus, and she smiled that half-smile once more. "Shall we continue on our way?"

They climbed a darkened stairway to a floor that had none of the majesty of the rest of the palazzo. The hallway was damp and musty with wall sconces that flickered on and off, offering an eerie light. Alex had the odd sensation that no one had trodden the worn, threadbare runners in several hundred years, which he knew couldn't be true.

A series of pings emanated from Gabriella's pocket. She pulled her phone out and swiped the screen. A frown crossed her face. "My apologies, would you mind investigating the rooms on your own, I have an urgent call to take. I'll meet you downstairs in the Galleria if you don't mind."

"No, go ahead, we shouldn't be long," said Angela with a warm smile. "Thank you for the illuminating tour."

CHAPTER 12

Rome, Italy
Palazzo Colonna
Present day

Alex wandered down the hall aimlessly.

Angela followed him, close behind.

Something is definitely wrong with him... It's not only PTSD, it must be connected to Caravaggio as well.

Should she tell him her revelation? She hated keeping secrets from him. It was no way to start a marriage. But she was worried about what it might do to him, given his PTSD and his escalating nightmares.

When Alex got to the end of the hall, he stopped. He stood still as if listening— waiting for someone to tell him what to do.

"Alex, what are you doing?"

He turned, beads of sweat pouring down his face. "I know where he slept. I've been here before."

She tried to keep her voice calm. "When? Alex, you told me earlier you've never been here before."

His eyes clouded with confusion. "I told you that?"

"Yes, at lunch. You specifically mentioned you'd never been to the Colonna Palazzo."

"Maybe I just didn't remember, but now I do. I'll show you." He hurried past her, and stopped at one of the doors that lined the hallway. His hand shook when he placed it on the knob. "Do you hear that?"

"Hear what? I don't hear anything."

"Someone's talking. Someone's in there." He threw open the door. In the center of the room was a carved wooden bed with a red velvet canopy and a crucifix hanging above the headboard. A side table held a basin and jug for washing and a stack of white embroidered linen towels beside it. Large

119

bronze candlesticks with honeycomb candles stood on the end tables, casting a golden glow around the bed. The red velvet drapery was pulled closed, it hung in thick pleats to the floor. Alex stumbled to the bed resting his hands on the coverlet. He looked as if he might collapse and Angela ran to him. "Alex, what's wrong?"

"Cecco, what have I done?" The gravelly voice, quivering with emotion, sounded nothing like Alex. He turned and grabbed her shoulders. She gasped in shock. His eyes were dilated and dark as if his blue and hazel irises had been swallowed by a storm. His mesmerizing gaze dragged her into the depths of his despair.

Alex's hands were planted on her shoulders, anchoring her, and yet the room began to spin—or perhaps she was spinning, she couldn't tell the difference. She closed her eyes against the dizziness and when she opened them, she was no longer looking at Alex, she was looking out into the room.

Her head throbbed painfully, and she lifted her fingers and touched a bandage. It was sticky and damp and when she took her fingers away, she could see the red imprint of blood.

Oh, my God, I can see what he sees!

The physical touch of his hands on her shoulders must have triggered a vision and allowed her to see into Alex's mind… Into the mind of Caravaggio.

"We are doomed, Cecco. How will I ever find forgiveness from the Pope, from God?" A deep, mournful cry erupted from Caravaggio. "I have taken a life, and for me awaits only Hell."

"Rome is not the only city on Earth," Cecco replied. Angela heard the echo of his voice in her mind. "You can work no matter where you are. The Marchesa will see to your future. Do not fear, Maestro. If you paint and offer penance in your paintings to the Pope's nephew, Scipione, you may earn his forgiveness and he will help you gain pardon from the Borghese Pope."

"But what of Fillide? Maybe I should have let her accompany us. Her presence soothes me, and I trust her."

"You've done the right thing by Fillide. To join you in banishment would be impossible. Write to her. Let her know you haven't forgotten her."

"Yes, yes, you're right, Cecco, there is hope. Costanza and Fabrizio will never abandon me. I will secretly correspond with Fillide and then tell her to burn my letters after she reads them, and I will burn her letters for both of our safety."

Caravaggio's gaze shifted to the windows, moonlight threading through the heavy drapes. "It will be light soon… we must rest, my friend… tomorrow promises to be an arduous journey. Costanza will most likely send us to the Colonna estate in the Alban Hills, where no one will think to seek us. I will immerse myself in painting. *Si*, I will paint myself out of this disaster..."

Caravaggio let go of Angela's shoulders and ran to the window, pulling back the drapes, breaking the connection to Angela's vision. He pressed his hands to the glass. "Fillide, are you waiting down there watching, waiting for a sign that I have not forgotten you? Will God grant me my wish to see you again?"

Angela's heart broke at the sorrow in his voice. She followed him to the window and wrapped her arms around him, pressing her cheek to his back.

"Fillide, is it you?" He turned, cupped her face, and drew her lips to his. He murmured, "*Amore mio*, you've come back to me."

Angela's eyes filled with tears as she kissed him. This time, his touch did not propel her into his vision. This time, she was struck by another bolt of awareness. The reason she'd dreamt about Caravaggio was a premonition of what was to come, but more importantly, an illumination.

Caravaggio and Fillide were star-crossed lovers, their souls meant to be together, but tragically torn apart just like Giuliano and Fioretta, and Gerhard and Sophia... Now she knew, finding the *Nativity* would free Caravaggio and Fillide... But what about Alex?

My visions about the Leonardo nearly tore me apart. Finding that painting healed me. Will finding the Nativity release Alex from his torment?

"I never left you." She twined her arms around his neck and pressed her lips to his, pouring all her love into the kiss. When she pulled back, she watched the darkness fade from his eyes. Once more she was staring into the most incredible eyes she had ever seen—one hazel and the other a pale blue—Alex had come back to her.

"Not that I don't mind, but an empty, musty old room isn't exactly a romantic spot for a make-out session," he said with a half-smile.

She looked around, and her breath caught in her throat. The room was bare, no bed, no candlesticks, no velvet drapery...

"Come on, let's get out of here. This place gives me the creeps," he said.

Were identical visions possible? She remembered the vision, whereas Alex could not. But just like with the Leonardo wedding portrait of Fioretta and Giuliano, she and Alex were being led by unexplainable forces. Not only were they seeking a stolen masterpiece, they were seeking the truth of a man much maligned by history—and reuniting the Master and the Muse.

It was time.

Safely ensconced in their hotel room, Angela had to tell Alex the truth. He needed to know that in his past life he was the artist Caravaggio. It explained so many things about him, and about her. In every one of their past lives, art had played a key role, and in every past life, love had been snatched from them. The fear of losing Alex resurfaced. Would her visions enable her to stop this trajectory once again? She couldn't bear losing Alex, not now, not when they were about to embark on a life together as husband and wife.

Whatever was at work here, whatever the reasons for her visions, the hand of fate was righting the wrongs of the past. In this life, she and Alex had been given the chance to fulfill their destinies and finally live a happy life. She had to believe that. She refused to give in to her fears—refused to be haunted by the tragedies that snuffed out the lives of Fioretta and Giuliano and Sophia and Gerhard. This second sight was a gift from out of time— a key that could unlock the past and be used for good.

Caravaggio had loved Fillide and had been loved in return. This truth was unknown to history. They must find that missing painting, so the past could be laid to rest. She and Alex had been given this duty and they would honor it. The past continued to grip them in its foggy mist, but Angela refused to let it take hold. No, this was not history repeating itself. It was not about re-writing history—it was about seeking the truth.

She needed Alex to understand. But Alex was in an amorous mood… He locked the door and turned toward her—the fire in his eyes said it all. Nothing short of World War III could keep him from her.

She'd never imagined that she could kindle unquenchable desire in a man. Nor had she expected anyone to ever ignite her passion the way Alex did. When he touched her, the girl who'd spent her entire life burying herself in history and art metamorphosed into the goddess of love.

Love is a powerful force, but to have loved the same man through three— no, correction—four different lifetimes took her breath away.

"*Amore mio*, it's been a long day; all I want is to love you. What do you think about joining me in a steamy shower?"

Amore mio! It all makes sense now.

Alex had used the endearment at the Palazzo Colonna. Caravaggio had called Fillide '*amore mio.*' Alex had been calling her *amore mio* for several weeks now. Before either of them had begun having visions and dreams, Caravaggio was already making his presence known.

Tell him. Tell him now.

Alex pulled her into his embrace and began trailing kisses down her neck. "I promise to give you a scalp massage…" he whispered in her ear.

Just the thought of him pressing her against the cold-marble wall and hot water streaming down over them made her forget everything else in the world. The heat of his touch made her fears vanish…

Caravaggio can wait.

"What woman in her right mind could resist that offer?" She shivered with anticipation as she pulled him toward the bathroom.

An hour later, Angela sat on the sofa with her legs crossed, and lifted a slice of pizza, biting into the cheesy taste of heaven. After marathon man's love-making she was always crazy with hunger. "Is there anything better than pizza?"

"Yeah, dessert." He rolled up a slice and took a sizeable bite. They chewed silently for a minute. Alex took a swig of champagne and cleared his throat. "Something happened to me at the Colonna Palazzo. I think I had a PTSD attack or something. That poor woman, Gabriella, must have thought I was fit for a straitjacket."

"She thought nothing of the sort," Angela answered, reaching for another slice. "I texted her to thank her for the tour. She was lovely, and so knowledgeable."

"That was nice of you." He grinned. "But then again, you're a nice lady."

"Nice lady? What am I, your great aunt?"

Alex chuckled and raised his champagne flute to her. "Well, you have been around a very long time, a couple of lifetimes, in fact…" He sipped and set his glass down. "So, are you going to share your thoughts with me? I know something happened in that room."

Angela waved her hand for him to give her a minute. She had just taken another bite of the golden-crusted goodness smothered in mushrooms, pancetta, sun-dried tomatoes, ricotta, and fresh mozzarella. Nothing was going to get between her and her pizza. She washed the bite down with some Tattinger Rosé. Although the Italians lived by '*wine, water, or nothing*' when it came to food, their go-to drink for pizza was usually a Morena or Peroni beer. Only Alex would insist the perfect accompaniment to pizza was pink champagne. Angela couldn't agree more. She'd begun to think she possessed an addictive personality because he'd awakened so many cravings in her, one being the way she craved him.

123

"Okay, I'm going to tell you exactly what took place, but I'm only just starting to put the pieces together." She described the room, the furniture, the drapes and the presence of Caravaggio himself. "I didn't exactly see a vision of Caravaggio…" She paused to gather her thoughts. "You took hold of my shoulders and you pulled me into *your* vision. I could see what you were seeing. I could hear Caravaggio's words and sense his thoughts. He was tormented that he'd killed Ranuccio. He was terrified of being exiled with a bounty on his head. And what was even more extraordinary, he realized he cared for Fillide more than he'd known.

"His assistant, Cecco, convinced Caravaggio that he could paint his way out of the death sentence… When you let go of me, the vision disappeared, and the room returned to its present state. Empty. There was nothing there."

Alex sat silent for several moments, his brow furrowed. "You're saying I was somehow channeling something that took place in Caravaggio's life? And because our connection is so strong, I brought you into my vision? But how can that be?" He shook his head. "You're the one with the psychic ability, not me."

She sat up and cupped his scruffy cheeks. "Your eyes changed color. They went from blue and hazel to brown."

Alex cursed under his breath.

"Remember when you told me the portrait of Giuliano Medici spoke to you when you first saw it at the Getty in LA?" She paused. "Our connection to each other is as strong as our connection to our past lives. Honey, you weren't channeling Caravaggio. I'm saying you *were* Caravaggio in a past life."

Angela felt him tremble. She knew he'd suspected he was Caravaggio based on his own actions at the Uffizi, but he'd refused to acknowledge what he didn't want to be true. Now, she'd spoken the words aloud and he couldn't refute them.

He pulled away and pressed his palms over his face. When he looked at her again, she saw the stark awareness in his eyes.

"You know how I feel about this guy," Alex muttered. "Yeah, he was brilliant, so what? He was volatile and vindictive and only cared about himself."

Angela laid her hand on his chest. "Alex, we've both learned so much about reincarnation. We know each life we live is about working out the problems we face and making better choices. We're here in this life to grow, to work out karma, not to judge.

"Caravaggio was all of those things, but I truly believe he was tortured by his actions, and he loved Fillide. There were other outside factors that contributed to his behavior… he wasn't perfect by any means, but none of us are."

Alex's lips curved into a slow smile. "Now just a minute, what do you mean I'm not perfect?"

Angela took another bite of pizza and washed it down with champagne. "We can discuss that later. Besides, you're not the only one dealing with another past life."

"Really? Do tell."

"I'm pretty sure I was Fillide Melandroni… You pulled me into your arms and called me *amore mio*. You've been doing that for weeks now."

Alex's eyes widened. "I hadn't really thought about it—it just felt right calling you my love."

"I didn't tell you my hunch sooner because I was worried… the PTSD dreams, our parents… Celestine and Spinelli."

"So, you're telling me you were a hooker in a past life?"

She frowned. "Yes."

"A hooker… hmmm." He grinned like the Cheshire Cat. "No wonder you're so skilled in the bedroom." He twirled an imaginary handlebar mustache. "I am correct, am I not, that we retain characteristics from our past lives?"

"Yes, detective, we do." Her lips twitched—she knew what was coming.

Alex burst into laughter and pulled her onto his lap, facing him. "Do you know how much I love you?"

"Yes. But tell me anyway." She touched her forehead to his. "And, may I add, you're taking this rather well. I was worried you'd be really upset."

He nibbled her lip. "You think you have me all figured out, don't you?"

She sucked in a breath. She trusted him, and he trusted her. And that was the key to liberating herself from any awkwardness or shyness she'd had in the past.

She suppressed a chuckle. If she had to, she could live without pizza, but she couldn't live without Alex. This clever man was like a Michelin-star chef, taking raw ingredients and fashioning a feast. Whipping up her hunger…

Well, two can play that game.

The flirtatious games they played with each other kept the magic at a fever pitch. In addition to love and trust, what made their relationship work was the fun they had together—sometimes silly, other times sexy. It got them through the dark moments.

Note to self: Never stop flirting with Alex.

"You're keeping me from my pizza." She shifted, rubbing against him.

"Hmm, how can you think about food at a moment like this?"

"It's easy. I'm still hungry."

He kneaded her shoulders. Her muscles relaxed beneath his powerful fingers. "Don't you like cold pizza?"

"You know I do, hence the midnight refrigerator raids."

"I've been meaning to talk to you about that." His lips slipped down her neck to her collarbone. She closed her eyes and leaned back to give him better access.

"What? Are you going to forbid me from eating in bed?"

"Hah, noooo, I'm more likely to encourage it. But it does depend on what you eat." The heat from his lips had every inch of her tingling with desire.

"So, what are you implying Mr. Caine? I am a nice lady after all."

He threw his head back and laughed.

She loved his laugh. But she loved something else even more. She shifted again, rubbing harder against him.

He pushed her back against the pillows on the sofa and lay on top of her. She wrapped her legs around his waist, locking him in place.

"You're such a tease. What am I going to do with you?"

"The same thing you usually do. Whatever you want." She thrust her chin up defiantly as if she might thwart his best efforts.

"When I was in Afghanistan, I never dreamed I'd be having conversations like this with any woman. I'm not sure what I like more, your tantalizing teasing or the actual feel of your body against me."

"Isn't it nice, the little surprises life gives you."

He was grinding against her. "Yeah, it sure is."

CHAPTER 13

London, England
Present day

Anastasia stared at the five Blackberry phones on her desk. She picked up the one that was ringing. "*Da*, where are they, Victor?"

The man answered in Russian. "Rome. At the Hassler."

She smiled. "Alexie has good taste, like his father. Tell me what you've learned."

"They spent most of the day at the TCP. When they left, Alex was carrying a shoulder bag that he didn't have when they arrived. Then the two lovebirds had lunch, which I watched jealously."

Anastasia chuckled. "Ah, yes, the long-suffering deprivation of an operative in the field. Victor, spare me the tears. You could have grabbed a panini somewhere while they ate, which I'm confident you did."

"You're a slave driver, Tashenka. After lunch—many hours later, I might add— their driver took them to the Palazzo Colonna. They spent about an hour at the palazzo and then their driver returned them to the Hassler. I hacked into Alex's phone and found he booked a flight back to Florence for tomorrow morning."

Anastasia drummed her red, manicured fingernails on the modern glass desk in her chic office in The Shard building. From her perch, she could see The London Eye, Europe's tallest Ferris wheel, and Tower Bridge. Alex and Angela were working on a case; that much was clear.

"Stay with them Victor. Bring in some backup. I want a 24/7 tail. Keep them safe, I have a feeling this is going to get ugly. And, please, you need to keep up your strength and get a proper meal. I can't have you wasting away, old friend." Her deep sensual laugh brought a chuckle from the man on the other end of the call.

"*Do svidanija*, Tashenka."

"Goodbye, Victor."

My daughter.

When she left Oliver in Lake Bluff twenty-seven years ago and disappeared, she'd never expected to see her child again. Natalia Rozanova had belonged to the SVR, Russia's counterpart to the CIA, since she was a teenager. She never expected to fall in love with an American. Nor did she expect what followed. Naïve, foolish girl that she was.

When she became pregnant and disappeared to Lake Bluff with Oliver, she'd prayed the SVR would forget about her. She believed the man she loved when he convinced her they could build a life together and shed their pasts. But the SVR had no intention of letting such a valuable asset go. They found her and blackmailed her, threatening to eliminate both Oliver and Angela. There was no way out for her, and she did the only thing she could do. She abandoned the man she loved and the baby she adored.

She left with a broken heart, knowing her dream of happiness was lost to her forever. But she made a promise to get even, and to free herself from the SVR's control. It took her years, but her enemies had finally been politically destroyed or eliminated, and she was able to remove herself for good.

Out of nothing except her determination she built a thriving business, buying and selling art around the world. It was her passion, but it was also a cover. She'd formed a vast underground network on the black market and the dark web, buying and selling arms. When an opportunity presented itself, she never failed to take advantage of making a hefty profit. She'd made hundreds of millions of dollars and lived a life few only dreamed of.

Unfortunately, her alias Madame X, owed a few favors to the Mafia, and that's how she became entangled with Enrico Fortuna and his weasel of a cousin, Alberto Scordato. Owing a favor, she helped them retrieve the lost da Vinci. But she planned on double-crossing them. She had no idea she was endangering the lives of Angela and her boyfriend, Alex, in the process. Had she known of their plans to kill Alex and Angela she'd have eliminated Scordato and Fortuna herself.

She regretted her actions, but now fate had given her a second chance.

What were the odds that Lancelot, her dashing lover, was the father of Alex Caine? Angela's Alex? When she left all those years ago, she had only one option open to her—forget her husband and forget her daughter. She never looked back. She couldn't. It was the only way to survive. But now, seeing her daughter all grown up, meeting her after so many years, had awakened long-ago memories… and feelings she was loath to let go of.

My darling, Angela.

The girl was so much like her.

For the first time in years she felt the stirring of maternal love. Like the high from a drug, the pleasure was so great, she couldn't wait to feel it again. Eventually she'd have to end it, nothing good would come from meddling in her daughter's life, and if Angela discovered who she really was, she'd hate her.

And then there was Oliver, the only man she'd ever loved. The man she'd harmed more than any other. He didn't deserve to be exposed as a liar to the daughter he'd devoted his life to. So many lies. Like the web of a spider—so fine, you don't notice it until you're truly trapped.

Anastasia picked up her cell phone and opened the photo app. She thumbed through dozens of photos of Angela snapped by her agents. It was like looking at herself when she was in her twenties. Had her face not been altered by plastic surgeons to change her identity, the resemblance between them would have been impossible not to see. She longed to know her child better, but she was treading on a thin sheet of ice. If she wasn't careful, that ice could crack and she'd fall through, taking both Angela and Oliver down with her.

Anastasia stood and strolled across the room. She gazed at her most prized possession, a Picasso, one of his early abstracts.

What are you searching for, my darling daughter?

Anastasia couldn't help but be intrigued… Before severing all ties, she had to find out.

CHAPTER 14

Tuscany, Italy
Present day

The Testarossa Ferrari flew past the other vehicles down the main highway through Tuscany, the Strada Regionale 222 Chiantigiana.

Angela had her usual, white-knuckled grip on the door handle. "Alex, please slow down, I'd like to live long enough to marry you."

He glanced at her and downshifted. "Sorry, baby, my mind was elsewhere."

"Elsewhere? For God's sake, you need to focus on driving this speed demon."

He laughed. "Honey, I can chew gum and walk at the same time."

"If you fall while chewing gum and walking, there's little chance of you dying or ending up with every bone in your body broken. Not the same outcome if you crash this expensive sardine can."

"What's that?" Alex cocked his ear to the steering wheel. "'Rosa is quite upset you called her an expensive sardine can."

Angela rolled her eyes. "Rosa? It's a she? I'm not surprised."

"Tut-tut, no need for jealousy. There is room in my heart for two females."

"Well, I am honored that you have such a wide capacity for love."

"But of course, and to show you how much I care, I have slowed down. Notice the speedometer is hovering at a respectable 100 mph, way off the previous 170 mark."

"Thank you. Notice my heart is no longer bursting out of my chest cavity."

"And a fine chest cavity, it is. Mind if I caress it?"

"Keep your hands on the wheel, hotshot."

Alex grinned at her playful rejection. Their sexy banter was a distraction from the message he'd received that morning. Oliver's text had exploded onto his screen with all the subtlety of a nuclear bomb—

ARE YOU KIDDING ME? WHAT THE HELL ARE YOU DOING WITH NATALIA? ANGELA'S MOTHER!!!! CALL ME! WE NEED TO TALK!!!!

Alex had texted back—he understood the state Oliver was in, but it would have to wait until he could find a moment of privacy. They were on their way to Montefioralle, and a phone call was impossible. Once at the vineyard, Alex would reach out.

Alex pulled through the gate of Casa del Sole and drove up the gravel drive to the red-tile roofed house. Most of the flowering plants and trees were bare due to the coming winter, but even so, the house looked warm and welcoming. When Alex opened the driver side door, he was immediately surrounded by whines of joy and wagging tails. Zaba, Ama, and Misu bumped Alex's legs and pressed their noses into his crotch.

"Hey, buddies, how you been? I've got your favorite toy in the car." He sauntered around to the passenger side and opened the door. The dogs crowded each other in a frantic push to reach Angela. Alex grabbed Zaba's collar, pulling the big Spinone hunting dog back so Angela could get out. The dogs were so excited to see her, nothing could prevent them from getting to her. Exasperated, he commanded, "*Seduti!*" but the canine trio ignored him. "Well, it's happened." He laughed. "When it comes to you, all of the money I spent on dog training is out the window."

Angela knelt and cuddled the undisciplined pack. Their rumps waggled in harmony. All that was missing was a Brazilian Samba band. "They're just happy to see us."

"Us? Baby, they've got their favorite toy back. I'm just window dressing."

"You called me, *baby*," she said rubbing Zaba's fur.

He angled his head at her statement. "So, I did."

"Does that mean you're feeling better about Caravaggio?"

He shrugged, squatting down to pet Ama and Misu. "I guess, I've come to terms with it. Do you miss me calling you '*amore mio?*'"

"*Amore mio*… you can call me anything you want. Even if you called me *buddy*, I'd know it would be said with love."

"Okay, *buddy*." He leaned in to kiss her as the dogs squirmed between them, wagging their tails, vying for their attention.

The front door opened, Maria and Joseph joined the greeting committee. The housekeeper ran down the steps and flipped her apron at the misbehaved dogs. "*Fate attenzione. Seduti!*" Three rumps hit the dirt. Their gazes shifted nervously from Maria to Angela.

"Finally," said Alex, "the real power at Casa del Sole has spoken." He patted each dog's head. "Not one of you is brave enough to argue with the keeper of the biscuits, are you?"

"*Benvenuti a casa, signorina.*" Maria grabbed Angela in a bear hug and kissed her on both cheeks.

"What am I, chopped liver?" Alex laughed.

Maria waved away his teasing and hugged him, too. Joseph shook hands with Alex and bussed Angela on both cheeks. "Welcome home, boss. I'll get the luggage. Take the *signorina* inside, Maria has been cooking up a storm for your arrival."

Alex heaped praise on the red-cheeked Maria. "I've been dreaming of meatballs, don't ask me why, but I hope you made some?"

"I've got a big pot on the stove," Maria said, clapping her hands.

Alex put his arm around Maria and Angela's shoulders, leading them into the house. "Maria, did I tell you the story of how Angela and I fell in love over a plate of meatballs?"

Maria fed them until they were ready to burst.

"I'm going upstairs to unpack and snag a nap, not necessarily in that order," Angela announced.

"Tempting, but I need to walk off those meatballs. Besides, I should check on a few things around the property."

"Good luck with that. You'll need a twenty-mile hike up those Tuscan hills to shed that meal." She kissed him and walked up the stairs with the dogs in hot pursuit.

"Angela," Alex called.

She turned. "Yes?"

"No dogs in the bed, please. I refuse to share you with those affection hogs."

She waved him away, giggling. "Don't be long or you may have to forfeit your spot."

"We'll see about that," he tossed over his shoulder.

The weather had cooled, and dark clouds filled the sky. The scent of rain was heavy in the air and the wind had picked up. It wouldn't be long before the storm hit.

Good for the vines.

Alex walked to the wine cellar and unlocked the door. Sophia Caro, the previous owner of the vineyard, had built it years ago. A pregnant Sophia and her lover Gerhard had stolen da Vinci's wedding portrait of Giuliano Medici and Fioretta Gorini from the Uffizi and hid it in a secret cave at the vineyard. The same vineyard that Alex had fatefully purchased.

Angela's visions and dreams had led to the painting's discovery, and the revelation of their past lives. Now there was another past life to contend with, Caravaggio and Fillide. How many lives had they lived intertwined? He shook his head at the strangeness of it all. What had been almost absurd was now something he accepted.

In her sorrow after Gerhard was murdered, Sophia had become a recluse until the day she died. But she would have the last laugh… Alex intended to gift Casa del Sole to Angela as a wedding gift. It seemed fitting to him that Sophia, Angela's past incarnation, would own her beloved vineyard once more. It was a gift he knew Angela would treasure.

The wine cellar's shelves were lined with vintages that dated back one hundred years. He loved the circular stone cellar and the way the racks lined the walls to the ceiling. He pulled a bottle and opened it. Pouring a glass for himself, he sat at the high-top table in the center of the cellar and pulled his phone from his pocket. It was 9:40 a.m. in Lake Bluff and he wasn't in the least surprised when Oliver picked up on the first ring.

"Alex, I've been going crazy. How the hell did this happen? How in tarnation—of all the people in the world how did you come to meet Natalia?"

Alex's heart went out to Oliver. To see a photo of Natalia after twenty-seven years had to be shocking. The threat of the past destroying his relationship with his daughter must have hit Oliver like a bullet between the eyes.

Alex explained in detail how everything had come to pass. He left nothing out, not even the fact that Anastasia, or whatever her name was, was in a relationship with Lance. Oliver listened without interruption, which was what a former CIA operative would do. When he finished, Alex took a sip of wine and waited for Oliver to absorb everything.

"Does Angela suspect anything?" Oliver said, his voice seeming to carry the weight of the world.

"Absolutely not. Although, she seems unusually drawn to Anastasia. But I'm positive Anastasia knows who Angela is. The giveaway was Lake Bluff. It was easy for her to put two and two together."

"Natalia has to know that if Angela finds out the truth, she'll hate her. For God's sake, she'll hate me for lying to her all these years."

Oliver wasn't wrong. Angela's pain would be unbearable. "Anastasia's smart enough to have calculated the consequences. I think she just can't resist wanting to have some kind of relationship with her daughter. I don't think she'd be foolish enough to blow the chance of friendship. I have to be honest with you Oliver, Angela's invited Lance and Anastasia for Christmas to Montefioralle."

Oliver's laugh sounded a bit unhinged. "This is rich. Christmas? You have to stop that Alex— it would be a disaster."

"Why? I don't know if I can."

"Because she's invited me too."

"Holy shit! Wouldn't that be a shit storm?"

"I'm sorry, son. I've put you in a pretty rotten position."

"What do you want me to do, Oliver? I guess I could convince her we have to go to San Francisco because my mother is having a meltdown."

"I don't want you to do a thing, yet. This may require my intervention. Did you say Natalia is living in London?"

"Yes, she lives and works in London. She has an art consulting business of some kind."

"It looks like the past is coming back to haunt me. A conversation between Natalia and me is long overdue."

"I know it's none of my business, but do you still love her?"

"I never stopped loving her. But that train left the station a long time ago. I'm sure there's little left of the young woman I was crazy about."

"I'm sorry, Oliver. But you're probably right. People change and sometimes it's not for the better. I only know that if Angela ever left me, I'd never love again."

"Don't even think it. She's not going anywhere. I know my daughter, and she feels the same way about you, son. Hold on to each other. Don't let anything come between you."

"I won't." He almost wished he could tell Oliver how deep that connection went.

"Okay, Alex, I need to give this some thought. Text me Anastasia's cell number, please."

"Oliver, don't do anything rash. Let me do a little investigating through my connections. You've been out of the game for a long time, but maybe she hasn't. What if she's still SVR? If she is, then my dad could be in trouble. His career and more could be on the line. She could be dangerous."

"I'll wait to hear from you."

"Angela and I are on a case. We're off to Naples on Monday, so give me a little time. Angela won't be out of my sight for the next couple of weeks so there's no chance of any mother-daughter interaction."

"That eases my worries a bit. Take care of her."

"With my life, sir."

Alex hung up and finished his glass of wine. He was tempted to elope with Angela and take her on an extended trip around the world. Screw the Caravaggio case and the past-life issues. Oliver could deal with the "Russian Octopussy." But even as he contemplated running away from it all he knew Angela would never agree. When she got something in her head, she pursued it no matter what, and she was determined to find the stolen Caravaggio.

The best thing to do was stick to the plan. Fly to Naples and then to Malta. After Angela had given him their itinerary, he'd investigated the logistics and realized this was going to be a grueling enterprise. There were no direct flights from Florence to Naples and the thought of checking in and out of short flights and extended layovers wasn't something he was going to subject himself to. Driving would take them forever, it was seven hours to Naples and seventeen hours to Malta, and then the return through Sicily back to Naples—the whole trip promised to be a nightmare.

There was only one way to do this—Angela would throw a fit at the extravagance—but she could scream to the heavens as far as he was concerned. He booked a private jet to be at their disposal. It would be easier for him to carry his weapon and ammo. If the Mafia was involved, he needed to be armed.

Traveling in comfort wasn't going to change him, and it would never change Angela. He was through pretending he didn't have money. He did it in the military, he did it most of his life. He wasn't going to do it anymore. Besides, Angela needed to get used to the lifestyle she was marrying into.

Brave words from a man who can't say no to a woman. Correction—one woman in particular.

Angela rolled over and reached for Alex, her hand landing on the pillow, instead. The clock read 6:30 a.m.

Loverboy is an early riser today.

Getting up, she dressed and made her way down to the kitchen, filling a mug with freshly brewed coffee. The house was quiet, Maria and Joseph had left early to go to the farmer's market. Alex had requested *osso buco* and *risotto Milanese* for dinner.

The door to Alex's office was ajar. Pushing it open, she found him glued to the computer, a spiral notepad open beside him. He was so absorbed he didn't look up. She walked around the large desk and kissed him on the cheek. His jaw was stubbled, and his chestnut hair was disheveled. "Somebody's got a bee in their bonnet. You look like you came straight from bed to the office," she said.

He leaned back in his chair, stretched, and gave a loud yawn. "Hi, baby. I guess it's a good thing you've seen me at my best, or you might run for the hills."

"No worries there." She tousled his hair. "I kind of like how cute you look when you're a mess." Her gaze drifted to the computer. It was the secure laptop they'd received from Lieutenant Spinelli; the flash drive was inserted. "Did you learn anything?"

"Sure did." He pulled up a chair. "I'll fill you in."

Her bottom had barely hit the chair when he pressed his face into her hair, inhaling. "Hmm. I had every intention of making love to you this morning. Damn, you smell good."

"You might get another chance if you play your cards right."

"Trust me, it's in my plans." He returned his gaze to the computer screen and the playful flirt disappeared, replaced by the serious detective. "Most of what the TPC has discovered is based on the confessions of a Gaetano Grado. Grado was a linchpin who ran the Sicilian Cosa Nostra, Palermo operation. When the police arrested him, they offered him a deal if he turned on his Mafia bosses."

"Is that reliable evidence?" Angela asked.

"Depends. In this case I think a lot of it is bullshit. According to Grado, the heist of the *Nativity* was performed by amateurs, petty thugs who tried to make a few bucks and gain prestige with the Mafia biggies.

"On a rainy night in October, these supposed amateurs broke into the Oratorio San Lorenzo in Palermo and cut the Caravaggio from its frame above the altar. The two thieves not only got away with the painting, but they stole gilded-wood choir stalls and pews inlaid with precious mother of pearl, not to mention a solid-gold crucifix." He whistled. "Pretty nice heist, don't you think?"

"Two guys took all of that? By themselves?"

"Yeah, that's exactly the way I see it. Not possible. Anyway, the uproar from the theft was immense and there was no way for these fools to unload the painting, it was too hot. Once word of the theft reached the current Mafia boss, Gaetano Badalamenti, he told his informant Grado to find the painting. Badalamenti must have made Grado a member of the Santa Maria di Gesù family, an offer he couldn't refuse. Badalamenti was the Sicilian Capo di Tutti of the Cosa Nostra, we're talking the head honcho at the time.

"This is where things get fuzzy. Grado supposedly found out the identity of the thieves and they told him they'd passed the painting on to another Mafia chief, who in turn passed it on to another, and on and on. Hence, no one knows where the fuck it is. I might add, during all of this there was a Mafia war going on and a whole lot of dead bodies.

"So, begins the string of tales of what happened to the painting after that," he said, counting down the stories with his fingers. "The painting was burned in a fire and destroyed. The painting was hidden in an outhouse on a farm and eaten by mice. The painting was hidden in a pigpen and eaten by pigs. The painting was hidden by a crime syndicate boss and was only taken out on the occasion of important summits of the families. Oh, did I mention it was used as a bedroom rug by some Mafia Don. But in the end, magically, due to Grado's efforts, it ended up in Badalamenti's hands. Apparently, this boss of bosses with three years of education had a soft spot for religious Baroque art. So, our priceless Caravaggio hung above the bed of Badalamenti until he was arrested and convicted in the Pizza Conspiracy, a Mafia drug smuggling operation. He ended up in a U.S. prison for seventeen years before dying there of lung failure in 2004."

"Wow. It sounds like the Godfather movie."

"Oh, it's way better. This is where the story goes off the rails. During that prolonged prison sentence, Badalamenti wanted to unload the Caravaggio and he made it available to be seen by a very old Swiss art dealer who purportedly 'cried and cried his eyes out' upon seeing the painting. Rumor has it, the art dealer suggested cutting it up into pieces and selling it off piece by piece, because it was too hot to be sold otherwise. Let's hope that didn't happen. But, whatever the Swiss art dealer's role, he died before anyone could interview him. Talk about chutzpah."

Angela crossed her arms over her chest. "Is that it? That's all they've got?"

"Next comes the naysayers' accounts and their repudiation of Grado's tale. According to the experts at the Anice dei Museo in Palermo the theft could never have been accomplished by two thieves. They insist the theft was premeditated, well-organized, and required a crew abetted by an insider. The thieves cut the painting from its frame so precisely, and I quote, 'without leaving a millimeter of paint behind'. You can imagine how impossible that is. The art experts at the museum claim the painting was cut from its frame with 'surgical precision', which meant an art expert was on hand directing the operation. We know the painting has never been offered in any shape or form on the black market, that nixes the-cut-into-pieces story. Also, a daughter of one of the custodians of the Oratory in 1969 says she has never been interviewed or questioned, which leads to the speculation that the theft was commissioned by a family so powerful they are above the investigative power of law enforcement."

"So where does that leave us?" Angela asked.

"Basically, on our own. Now I know why the TPC wasn't opposed to sharing their data with us, they've got nothing but a bunch of moldy old leads going nowhere. We're Spinelli's best hope."

A knot had begun to twist in Angela's stomach. "Alex, is the Mafia still that powerful?"

"It's more powerful than ever. It's just morphed into a savvier, less conspicuous force. It's much more insinuated into government, politics, and the banking industry."

"Do you think the painting is in Mafia hands?"

"If it is, we're going to be in significantly more danger."

"And Naples, is it a Mafia fiefdom?"

"Big-time."

"It's going to be tricky, won't it?"

"Yeah, but I promise I'll guard you with my life."

"But who'll guard you?"

CHAPTER 15

Naples, Italy
Present day

Alex found Angela's protests about the private jet to be muted, at best. After he'd explained the logistics of crisscrossing Italy and flying commercial, she'd understood that stubbornly rejecting the private jet would just delay the investigation.

Angela gasped when Mount Vesuvius came into view, rising above the Bay of Naples. Seeing the world through her eyes was like seeing it for the first time. For Alex, it reawakened the curious child he'd once been and made him aware of just how lucky he was.

They checked into their suite at the Grand Hotel Vesuvio. Their room, with its sweeping view of Mount Vesuvius and the Mediterranean Sea, overlooked the Castel Nuovo where the Spanish viceroy once lived.

"We should have gone to see *David With the Head of Goliath* at the Borghese Museum in Rome, but your reaction to *Medusa* was so extreme, I didn't want to put you through that again," Angela said.

"Another painting of a beheading. I'm glad we skipped it."

They were sitting in bed, surrounded by notes, their laptops, and books. Angela had suggested they bypass the Alban Hills where Caravaggio and Cecco first fled. The Duke Marzio Colonna, Costanza Colonna's brother's palazzo at Zagarolo, was a hunting fortress set in a rugged landscape amid dense woods. Angela told Alex she suspected Caravaggio had spent time there healing from his wounds in the duel.

"The only surviving paintings from Zagarolo were *Supper at Emmaus*, now in the Pinacoteca di Brera in Milan, and *David With the Head of Goliath*. Caravaggio gifted it to Scipione Borghese as a plea for help and mercy."

She picked up one of the books and opened it to a yellow-tagged page. "Since we didn't go see it in person, take a look at the picture. It's important to our investigation to understand Caravaggio's state of mind."

"If anyone can understand Caravaggio's state of mind, it's me," he snorted.

"Okay, Mr. Sarcasm, but let's get serious," she said, rolling her eyes. "Once again, Cecco modeled for Caravaggio. No longer the erotic little sprite of earlier paintings, Cecco is David. His face reflecting both anger and empathy. Caravaggio is Goliath, his face is etched with torture and agony. His art reflects his own self-image—a man who has lost everything, including his head. A man with no way of escaping his fate."

"*Si, Professoressa*, I get it, and I appreciate you didn't make me see it up close and personal. It's definitely nightmare material. It still creeps me out to think I was Caravaggio. So now we're on the trail of a fugitive. What happened in Naples?"

Angela gave him a sweet kiss and then flipped through her notes. "In late September, under the Colonna family's protection, Caravaggio arrived in Naples. A teeming port city under Spanish rule, filled with chiaroscuro, where darkness and light fought for dominance. The discrepancy between the wealth of a few and the poverty of many couldn't have been more extreme. Caravaggio's arrival coincided with a fervor to remedy the appalling conditions of the poor. New churches were being built and he was immediately inundated with commissions..." Angela turned to Alex. "We need to see that first commissioned painting."

Alex glanced with regret at the beckoning granite jacuzzi surrounded by candles. There was no way in hell he wasn't going to avail himself of that sexy tub with Angela.

She followed his gaze and smiled. "It does look inviting." She snuggled onto his lap and looked into his eyes. "How about room service and a bath later." She kissed his neck and ran her tongue to his ear, breathing. "I promise to make it worth your while. I might even channel a little of Fillide."

He closed his eyes, enjoying the jolt that traveled from her lips to his groin. "You know I'm going to hold you to that promise."

"If you don't, I'll be terribly disappointed. Especially since I have a surprise for you."

His eyes flew open. "What kind of surprise?"

She rubbed her bottom on his lap. He sucked in his breath. "Are you channeling Fillide now?" he rasped.

She licked her lips and fluttered her eyelashes at him. "Maybe. It seems possible that Fillide could be finding a way to express herself through me." She got up, leaving him aching with desire. "But you'll have to wait to find out. Work before pleasure..."

An hour later, Alex and Angela made their way down the Via dei Tribunali, a street in the ancient Greek part of the city. Their destination— the Chiesa del Pio Monte della Misericordia. The cobblestoned street, more like an alley, was so narrow they found themselves brushing elbows with locals and tourists. Churches, restaurants, and shops huddled the length of the street, with barely enough room for pedestrians to pass, let alone cars and Vespas. Naples was, indeed, a city of darkness and light. The buildings rising over the narrow streets blocked the sun and cast dark shadows, even in the light of day.

Alex dragged Angela to a small tchotchke shop. "Hey, isn't that a Picasso drawing in the window? It's only twenty Euros."

"What are you talking about?" As Angela pressed her nose against the glass, Alex saw the reflection of a tall man in a baseball cap, standing at a street vendor's stall, stuffing a sausage panini into his mouth. He'd seen him before...

This guy's a tail.

Turning to face the street, Alex bent to tie his shoe, and snuck a better look. The man pulled the brim of his cap down over his brow, paid for another panini and hurried away. Alex's eyes narrowed as he watched the retreating figure.

Rome! I saw him in Rome... but where? One of Spinelli's guys?

It was more likely they had lit up somebody's radar...

"That is not a real Picasso. It's a copy, and a bad one." Angela turned to him, her hands on her hips.

"My bad. Come on." He ushered her down the street to the Baroque church. He didn't want to alarm her when she was in art-history mode, so he kept his silence about the tail.

They walked through the five-arched loggia of the Pio Monte Della Misericordia, a portico where the poor could be welcomed inside. Alex followed Angela toward the main altar. She threaded her fingers through his and led him down the central aisle through the rows of pews.

She whispered, "Seven wealthy young noblemen founded a confraternity to help the poor of Naples and built this church for their benefit. It was a new church when Caravaggio was commissioned to paint an altarpiece reflective of their charitable cause. These altruistic young men wanted to make a difference in the lives of the destitute. They were determined to enlist the greatest painter in Naples and advanced Caravaggio three times his normal commission.

"He was supposed to paint seven paintings of the Christian acts of mercy, but Caravaggio must have convinced them he could include all seven elements in one painting. It was a daring enterprise and nearly impossible to execute, for anyone but Caravaggio. The result is one of the most iconographic masterpieces in the history of art. A painting, I might add, Caravaggio must have created as if possessed, because he finished it in under seven weeks."

At the end of the aisle was a heptagon, a seven-sided polygon, with a soaring dome and arched side chapels that rose to the ceiling. Each chapel displayed monumental paintings, but it was the center artwork above the altar that commanded their attention.

"Do you feel anything?" Angela asked.

"Nothing out of the normal." He knew she'd been watching him closely for any signs of stress. "But at least I like this painting. It's amazing how much he condensed into one canvas. I see multiple stories going on. Break down what I'm looking at."

"The seven acts of Christian mercy include burying the dead, visiting the imprisoned, feeding the hungry, sheltering the homeless, clothing the naked, visiting the sick, and giving water to the thirsty."

"Okay, point them out to me."

"In the center background you can see the feet of a dead man being lifted and presumably on his way to be buried. On the right, a woman breast feeds an imprisoned man, so that takes care of two in one, she's visiting the imprisoned and serving him a drink."

"It's amazing how he managed to combine a gritty street scene with a biblical lesson. She could just as easily have been a whore in the streets being paid for her breast milk."

"That is exactly what Caravaggio captured, time after time, in his paintings. His models were from the streets. The downtrodden, the poor, the misfits, and outcasts became the saints and heroes of biblical legend. It's why his iconography is so often described as 'the sacred and the profane'."

"His own life seemed torn between those two opposites as well. Okay, continue, *Professoressa*."

"The man with the red beard is a pilgrim and might even be Christ in disguise. The pilgrim asks an innkeeper for shelter, hence shelter the homeless. The man with the feather in his cap has torn his robe in half and given it to the crippled naked beggar in the street. Clothing the poor. In the left corner he painted Samson, drinking from the jawbone of an ass, 'I was thirsty, and you gave me drink'.

"The entire tableau seems to be happening on the dimly lit streets of nighttime Naples. Mary and the Christ child accompanied by two angels are present to bless the merciful acts of charity and in turn the confraternity of young noblemen who founded the Pio Monte Della Misericordia."

"Was the painting a success?"

"It certainly was. It changed and influenced Neapolitan art overnight and gave birth to a school of copycats who embraced his style of painting. But remember, Naples was a Spanish holding—Caravaggio's influence would have lasting effects on Italian painters *and* Spanish painters. It would spread beyond to the rest of the Hapsburg Empire including Flanders. His dramatic chiaroscuro style was embraced by artists far and wide, including Rembrandt."

"Okay, you've convinced me, Caravaggio was a genius. So where do we go next?" He leaned in close and ran his tongue around the curve of her ear. "I keep thinking about you, naked in that jacuzzi, surrounded by bubbles... and me."

"Talk about the sacred and the profane. We're in a church, Alex."

"Hey, aren't I Caravaggio? He had no trouble mixing the two."

She laughed, giving him a little pat on the cheek. "Okay, hotshot, you're right about that."

"Are you warming to the idea?"

"Two more paintings and I'll be hot for the idea."

"Hmm. Let's go. We can grab a taxi and save some time."

Victor sat at a café down the street from the Pio Monte della Misericordia. He'd grabbed an espresso and a plate of cannoli, devouring them as he kept his eyes peeled on the doors of the church. He licked his fingers and picked up his cell phone.

"Victor, how's Naples?" It was Anastasia.

He wiped his lips with a napkin. "Much better now that I just enjoyed three cannoli and a shot of Italian nectar."

"And our friends?" She chuckled.

"Alex picked up my tail and recognized me. Peter's on his way to take over. I'll keep my head down for now and supervise."

"How did that happen? Never mind, it doesn't matter. Alex is a pro, so it was probably inevitable he'd nail one of you. I got your text. They're looking for the *Nativity*. We need to keep a step ahead of them. Have you ordered a team to Malta?"

"Yes. But I don't think I'm the only one watching them."

"Really. Who else?"

"At first I thought it was the carabinieri, but I suspect it's the Mafia."

"That will complicate things. I'm sure someone from the police tipped them off. There's a reason this painting has never been found. Watch over them. Keep me posted."

Alex relaxed against the pulsating jets of the jacuzzi and contemplated one of the most erotic lovemaking sessions he'd ever experienced. Angela might deny the link, but in his mind, she was without a doubt channeling Fillide. Holding off an orgasm was unlike her, but damned if she hadn't made him earn his reward.

She said it was all about the water and bubbles, but he knew otherwise. He swore he'd burned off five pounds working to please her. The challenge had brought out the warrior in him, the man who'd trained to engage and conquer. And conquering her felt like climbing Mount Everest. When he tipped her over the edge, her flushed cheeks and moans of pleasure, made him want to beat his chest and do it over again.

Maybe after some room service.

If he knew his woman, and he did, she was already contemplating her next meal. God, he loved pleasing her. He tried not to think about the case but inevitably his mind switched to business. With a sigh of regret, he turned off the frothing jacuzzi jets. He took the opportunity to make a call while Angela was grabbing a shower.

"Lieutenant Spinelli."

"Salvatore, it's Alex."

"I trust everything is progressing."

"Yes. Tomorrow night we leave for Malta. But I have a couple of concerns I need to run by you. I picked up a tail today outside of the Pio Monte della Misericordia, a guy's face I remember from Rome. Are you surveilling us?"

"No. We have the tracking device on your phones. I saw no reason to interfere. I would have told you if I thought it was necessary for your safety. But until now it didn't seem necessary."

"I have to assume there's been a leak somewhere." Alex stopped short of accusing Spinelli, but the possibility hovered in his mind.

"If you have an accusation to make, then make it."

"Look, I don't know. You tell me."

Spinelli grumbled something under his breath. "Naples has quite a few police surveillance cameras in the area. We keep a close watch on the comings and goings of tourists and locals wherever there are high-target artworks. Caravaggio's paintings are at the top of our list. I'm sure there's footage of the church and the surrounding streets. I'll have it delivered here, and we'll check for anything suspicious. I'll also notify the Malta authorities to closely monitor any unusual traffic going into Malta."

"Good idea. Can you also check out Enrico Fortuna? He's serving a life sentence."

"Fortuna? He was the guy who murdered the billionaire Max Jaegar."

"Yes. He was working with Alberto Scordato, the art director from the Getty Museum, who nearly killed Angela and me over the Leonardo. He's a low-level Mafia thug. But low-level or not, he has direct ties to the Cosa Nostra. It would be to his benefit to show himself useful to them. Not to mention, there's a serious revenge factor here. Fortuna would like nothing more than to destroy Angela and me."

"I'll look into it. We'll find out if he's had any interesting visitors at the prison, or if he's receiving any preferential treatment. There's always an element of corruption and payouts in the prison system."

"Thank you. That would go a long way to easing my mind. The closer Angela and I get to the painting, the more dangerous it's going to be."

"I'm in complete agreement. By the way, most hoodlums don't have access to a private jet. You must be giving whoever is tailing you a real run for their money."

"Yeah, I guess you can see I'm not in this for the money."

"Lucky man."

"Either that or I'm a foolish one. I'll touch base with you from Malta, unless I hear from you sooner. *Ciao.*"

"*Arrivederci.*"

Alex hung up, satisfied that Spinelli would deliver. He picked up the hotel phone and called the front desk. His scholarly fiancée was about to experience a food-gasm like no other. Angela considered herself a pizza aficionado, but she was about to experience pizza Heaven. Alex requested the desk to arrange for the delivery of the best pizza in the world. L'Antica Pizzeria da Michele, a hundred-and-fifty-year-old restaurant in the old city, was so popular customers stood in line for hours to get in. Alex wasn't about to put up with a terminal wait amid crowds of hungry patrons. He knew the hotel would pull strings and deliver the pizza right to their suite. He made sure to let the concierge know there was a large tip in it for him. He ordered the only two pies on the menu, a classic Margherita, consisting of cheese, tomato sauce, and decorated with a single basil leaf, and a pizza sans cheese, topped with a traditional Marinara tomato sauce, made with authentic San Marzano tomatoes and flavored with garlic and oregano. For pizza lovers world-wide this was the Holy Grail of pizzas. He laughed when he got off the phone. The pizzas—ten bucks. The tips—two-hundred smackers. Angela's moans of pleasure, after the first bite—*priceless*.

CHAPTER 16

Island of Gorgona, Italy
Gorgona Prison

Enrico Fortuna lifted a cigarette to his lips and took a puff, releasing a smoke ring as he watched his fellow inmates kicking a soccer ball around the prison yard.

He had nothing but time on his hands to contemplate his revenge. There was only one thing he wanted—nail that bitch, Angela's ass to the wall and fuck her until she begged for mercy, while her boyfriend watched. Just imagining her begging for mercy as his dick pummeled her was enough to make him hard. As for soldier boy, he dreamed of taking that cocksucker apart, limb by limb, while she watched.

Family and blood were points of honor, and the murder of his cousin Alberto, required *occhio per occhio*, an eye for an eye, the ultimate revenge being death, *morte*. Death, and only death, would absolve the debt.

Prison wasn't so bad. He'd stuck to his oath of *omertà*—he'd sworn his allegiance in a ritual dating back hundreds of years. For this, he received certain perks and dispensations. Through a fellow inmate connected with the bosses, Enrico had sent a plea for *vendetta*, his right as a *cugine*, a soldier, soon to be a 'made man'. In consideration of his plea for *vendetta*, his *capo* had placed a tail on Angela and Alex.

Enrico bided his time. An old Italian proverb was his comfort. *Chi ha pazienza vede la sua vendetta.* Who has patience realizes his revenge.

He flicked his cigarette to the ground and squashed it beneath his shoe. Soon he would do the same to that *cazzo*-detective Alex Caine, and his *puttana*, Angela Renatus.

CHAPTER 17

Angela's nose pressed to the window as the jet approached Malta. The view was spectacular. The Mediterranean Sea surrounding the island reflected turquoise and aquamarine in the bright sunshine. The domed Cathedral of Saint John rose above the golden stone and brick-faced buildings of the ancient city. On the flight, Angela had brushed up on the island's storied history.

It looked much the same as it had five hundred years ago when seven hundred knights and eight thousand soldiers defended it against an Ottoman invasion of forty thousand men sent by the Sultan Suleiman to lay siege to the island. In the siege, barely eighty knights would live to tell of the victory that saved Christendom from the Turks.

The weather was a perfect seventy-five degrees, but you'd never know it by looking at Alex. As they disembarked, his face had turned a ruddy red and rivulets of sweat formed on his brow. She'd hoped if he accepted that he'd lived before as Caravaggio, it would put an end to these physical reactions, but she was dead wrong.

"Are you okay? You look positively green, Alex," Angela asked as they walked into the air-conditioned private jet terminal in Luqa.

"I wish I was, babe, but the minute we touched down my body went on red alert. It's the same feeling all over again, just like at the Uffizi, and in Rome at the Colonna Palazzo. I'll be okay. I just need to remain rational— what I'm feeling has nothing to do with the present."

She took his hand, her gaze filled with empathy. "And the worst part is even if your brain understands what's happening, your body is processing those past-life memories and reacting to them. Those memories, locked in your subconscious, aren't supposed to be revealed in this life."

"I know, baby, it's not dissimilar to what you experienced with the Leonardo, except in my case I'm not aware of the memories, but I'm feeling them."

She linked her arm through his as they strolled to the front of the terminal and their waiting car. "You need a break, Alex. Hey, how about we take the day off? It's Sunday, and we've been running full tilt. The weather's fantastic and it's so beautiful here, why don't we rest up today, so I can work on my tan?"

Alex kissed her temple. "Have I told you today how much I love you?"

"Only ninety-nine times, instead of your usual hundred." Her bottom lip thrust out in protest.

He chuckled. "I love you, Angela Renatus, and I can't wait to make you my wife." His crooked smile filled her with warmth. "P.S. I can't wait to see your body golden and tanned. And, I might add, I can't wait to kiss every luscious inch of it."

"What a great idea, Mr. Caine. Maybe what you need is a good workout. You might as well earn your sweat."

The five-mile drive from the airport to The Phoenicia Hotel had them settled in their room in less than an hour. Angela stepped out on the terrace and gazed at the bird's eye view of Grand Harbour, dotted with sailing and motor yachts. Alex joined her, slipping his arms around her waist and pulling her in for a hug. "Penny for your thoughts?"

"I was just wondering what Caravaggio thought when he first arrived here. Do you think he finally felt safe?"

"Yeah, he probably did. I was reading on the plane about the military order of the knights. They were nicknamed the 'Friars of War' because they swore their lives to defend Christianity. They wore a bold, eight-point white cross as a symbol of their fealty. They were a pretty formidable group of guys. I think he joined them as part of his atonement."

"That's what I think, as well. Costanza and her son Fabrizio must have suggested it was the best way to exorcise the death sentence hanging over his head. Being knighted would make the death sentence null and void."

"It was certainly up his alley, sword fighting, chivalry, and honor. The only thing lacking was temperament. Caravaggio was a hot-head."

"His volatility was always his undoing, I agree," said Angela with a sigh.

"Hey, you promised me a day free of Caravaggio and I'm holding you to it."

They hit the hotel boutique shop and bought swimsuits and hats. Alex got to indulge his shopping habit and picked out a bathing suit for her. She looked dazzling, lying on a lounge chair next to him, wearing a black, high-cut, one-piece suit that paid tribute to her curvy figure. This was what he imagined their life would be like together. A little work and a little play. Today, he was determined to focus on the play part of the equation.

He ordered Sex on the Beach—a cocktail made with vodka, peach schnapps, cranberry, and pineapple juice. A specialty of the bar.

He took a drink and smacked his lips with pleasure. "Sooooo, what do you think?"

She turned her head and he couldn't help but note the Sophia Loren resemblance. Big sunglasses, floppy straw hat, and that body, already beginning to burnish to gold. He, on the other hand, had slathered sunblock everywhere to prevent the burn he'd get if he weren't careful.

Angela sighed. "I think I'm in heaven, and this drink should be illegal."

"That about sums it up. Let's order lunch, I'm starving." He picked up the menu. "Man, a burger and fries sounds good to me. What about you?"

"If I want to look good in this bathing suit, I'd better stick to salad." She scanned the menu—her lips turned down in an exaggerated mock-sulk.

He bit back a chuckle. Deciding what to eat was something Angela took seriously.

"The grilled and marinated zucchini with mint, basil, feta cheese and quinoa salad sounds healthy. But the Dover sole sounds exquisite, and there's no way I'm not having dessert."

He grinned. "Just order it all. Why choose?"

She matched his grin. "Good idea. Why choose?" She flipped the menu closed and lay back with a contented sigh.

Alex couldn't stifle his laugh. "So, you think my burger and fries is more fattening than your three-course feast?"

"Probably not but think of all the exciting flavors I get to sample."

"All I can think about is sampling all of your exciting flavors."

"Keep your mind on food, Detective Hotshot, 'cause I'm not moving from this lounge for love or money."

"You're such a sybarite. Do you know this is the first time we've really taken a day off and just hung out? I think I could get used to this."

She stretched like a cat on a fur rug. "Anything for you, baby."

Seeing Alex relaxed imbued Angela with a sense of calm and peacefulness. The world fell away and her ability to see beyond the here and now opened the door of her extra sensory perception...

As always, the feeling of leaving her body frightened her, but then the incredible lightness took over and allowed it to carry her like a feather on a breeze, drifting on the air currents of time.

She found herself in Fillide's bedroom. At a small desk sat the famous courtesan. The ghostlike semblance of herself touched Fillide's shoulder, and she floated into the woman's body. She found herself seeing through Fillide's eyes. With trembling fingers, Fillide opened the rag-paper pages of the letter addressed to her.

It was unusual for someone from her class to be literate, but her father, who died when she was a young girl, had left her with one gift she cherished—he taught her to read and write. The letter had been delivered by a courier of the Colonna family. Many days had passed since it was written, but to know the painter thought of her enough to send it meant everything to her.

Caravaggio's penmanship was as artistic as his paintings. She delicately ran her finger down the page and read...

15 July, 1607

Dearest Fillide,

I have wanted to write to you for so long, but I was afraid my desperation and state of mind would only serve to alarm you. Cecco and I made our way safely to the Alban Hills under the protection of the blessed Colonna family, where we remained for a time at the Duke Marzio Colonna's palazzo.

In haste, I painted several paintings and stumbled upon a way to express my visions more succinctly and with greater impact by eliminating anything that distracts from the power of the message I want to convey. I painted a picture of the Mary Magdalen and another of the Supper at Emmaus. These are dark works, which I'm sure was a reflection of my state of mind at the time.

I also painted Cecco as David, the hero of biblical lore who slew Goliath. I modeled myself as Goliath's disembodied head, screaming out in agony, which is true to my misery given the state of my life. How I miss Rome and my dearest friend with her feisty fists raised against the injustices of life.

I sold the Supper at Emmaus to the banker Ottavio Costa, and the David and Goliath accompanied it to Rome, a gift to Scipione Borghese, imparting my plea for forgiveness. I pray he heeds my plea and will take up my cause with his uncle, His Holiness, the Pope.

I have always thought I was a brave man, but my fear of assassins has driven me to near-madness. Zagarolo felt too close to Rome and Cecco and I sought a greater distance from the papal edict of death that hangs over my head. In the dead of night, we departed for Naples. Once again, the Colonna family parted the waters for us and made our travel easy. We were given shelter at the Colonna residence near Naples, a large fortress by the sea in Chiaia.

The beauty of God's creations are an inspiration. Naples lies in the shadow of the behemoth hump-backed volcano, Vesuvius. It's quite startling to witness this wonder, which looms large above us, shrouded in clouds. It is a constant reminder to me of how infinitesimal we really are.

Thanks to the Colonna, our arrival was whispered in the ears of those who could most benefit us. It is lucky for me that praise of my work preceded my coming to Naples, because I found myself inundated with commissions.

I received a contract to paint a very prestigious altarpiece for a new church, the Chiesa del Pio Monte Della Misericordia. I am inspired by this confraternity of young aristocrats who are dedicated to doing good works for the poor. These scions of the finest and oldest families of Naples built this church and dedicate themselves to making a difference here in Naples.

Their desire was for seven paintings reflecting the seven acts of Christian mercy. But the idea came to me of painting The Seven Acts of Mercy on one canvas. I convinced these nobles that such a work would be like no other painting before it. They granted my wish and it was a challenge I readily accepted. Although, it brought me no end of trouble, crowding so many figures into one confined space and still giving each their proper contextual theme. It was a puzzle that dared me to break with tradition, and I was so taken with the idea that I worked at breakneck speed and completed it in less than seven weeks. The painting is the talk of Naples and is receiving resounding acclaim.

I wish you could see it, Fillide, it is my finest work, for certain. As I've told you before, I have strived to portray my biblical messages through the context of the world we live in. I cannot sugarcoat the harsh realities or pretend injustice does not exist. Each of the mercies take place amid the squalor of the lowliest streets of Naples, yet even in this darkest of places, hope abides.

Even for a condemned man, such as myself, the possibility of redemption lies within the mercy of God, and that is what I have sought to convey.

The Seven Acts of Mercy has brought me good fortune and after its completion another commission came to me from a Dominican Monastery in Naples. This painting I undertook was the Flagellation of Christ, painted in a dynamic contrast of darkness and light. My work grows ever more confident and powerful with simplification and less superfluous embellishment. Again, I am most satisfied with the result.

The machinations of my mind have been much relieved by the overwhelming demand for my work. There is little time to wallow in the torment of self-pity. Because of this windfall of commissions, I have found renewed focus and two more have been offered to me. The first commission, The Crucifixion of St Andrew, was offered by the Spanish Viceroy to Naples, himself, Don Juan Alonso de Pimentel y Herrera, the Count de Benavente. It is a dark work that captures what we all will experience at some point—the moment of death—the moment of release from our corporeal body.

The second commission was The Madonna of the Rosary. I would have been most pleased to have painted you, Fillide, as the Madonna, but my promise to you hast kept me from doing so. Pray God, sometime in the not-too-distant future, you will once more be my muse and inspiration. I long to return to Rome and you.

And now I come to the part of the tale which I believe will be of the most interest to you, to us. I have left Naples at the urging of my sponsor and protector, Marchesa Costanza and her son Fabrizio.

We set sail for Malta, where it may be possible for me to end my exile from Rome by receiving a papal pardon. Fabrizio himself found redemption as a Knight of the Order of St John and it may be a possibility for me, as well. It is a chance for me to regain my honor and return to Rome with my head held high. Perhaps this is my calling, to be a warrior of the truth faith, both as a painter and as a soldier of God.

Alas, for Cecco and me, has come a parting of ways, for on this journey I must proceed alone. I left my devoted friend and assistant in Naples, though it was a difficult thing to do. I am now burdened with every aspect of my craft. There is no one to help with the grinding of powder for paint or the preparation of the canvas, but busy hands are less likely to engage in the temptations that have always brought me trouble.

Malta is a wonder to behold, caressed by the rays of the sun, it shimmers like burnished gold. It stands as a bastion of Christendom. The protective walls of the island are impenetrable and rise from the cliffs as if part of the rocky landscape. There is no way to scale or surmount these walls, although many have died, both trying and in their defense.

This fortress city withstood the attack of the Turks and is surrounded by sea. The Knights of St John have stood guard against the infidels and many a brave soldier has given his life in defense of God's kingdom.

As with all things of import, life is not easy here. The Grand Master rules the order with an iron fist, and the monastic life is filled with endless restrictions. It is difficult for a man such as me. I struggle daily with my tendencies toward vice and dissolution, and there is plenty of both here to go around.

But, after a small adjustment I have thrown myself into painting once more. The sooner I gain favor here and come to the attention of the Grand Master Wignacourt, the sooner I will receive the kinds of commissions that challenge me and the closer I will get to returning to you.

Imagine, Fillide, one day you will be lady to a knight.

I pray for you daily, with every beat of my heart,

Your painter,
Michelangelo M. C.

P.S. Amore mio, for your safety, burn this letter when you have read it.

A single tear slipped down Fillide's cheek, but she was disinclined to wipe it away. Crying was a weakness she rarely indulged in, but as a testament of her love for the painter, she welcomed it.

The messenger for the Colonna would return for her response letter in a fortnight. She prayed her response would be worthy. Caravaggio had opened his heart to her, and it filled her with an emotion she found hard to equate with herself. She pressed her cheek to the letter in hopes of inspiration, or maybe it was to seek closeness to the man who had written it.

She opened a bottle of ink and picked up her quill. After she finished writing her own letter, she sealed it with wax and set it aside. She picked up Caravaggio's missive once more, and re-read his beautiful words, imparting them to memory. Postponing the burning of the letter for a few precious minutes more.

From the other side of time Angela felt the press of lips on hers. The elastic band of light between the past and the present pulled tight and released with a snap, hurling her back into her body.

Like Sleeping Beauty awakened by Prince Charming from a hundred years of slumber, her lips tingled from the warmth of the kiss. Angela seemed to be straddling two worlds, the past and the present, and the pull of one over the other fought to take precedence.

The lips that touched hers whispered, "Angela, baby, wake up."

"*Carava*—" Her eyes flew open and the name froze on her lips. She was looking into those unique eyes once more.

"Hey, Earth to Angela? Where did you go?"

"I… I was dreaming, I think."

"You called me Caravaggio. Was he kissing you, too?"

"No, silly. I must have been dreaming, but it felt so real. I was back in time—in Rome." Her hands cupped his face as if by the mere touch she could make him see what she'd seen. She searched his eyes for a sign he understood, but she found only concern.

"Are you saying you time-traveled?"

"It was more like astral projection. I traveled, but I was still tied to my body." Visions from the dream sped across her mind. "I visited Fillide. Caravaggio sent her a letter from Malta." In her growing awareness, the words began to tumble forth. "This is like discovering a Dead Sea Scroll, a page out of time. My spirit entered Fillide and I was able to read the letter with her. I can't tell you how bizarre it was to read the true historical record.

"I know I've told you before how distressing it is for a historian to see that we are often so wrong about history. In Caravaggio's case, what we know leads to the conclusion that he was a terribly flawed man, but what we are missing is the intent. We've been all wrong on that front." Angela read the confusion on Alex's face. "I'm having trouble making myself clear. I can see it in your eyes. I tell you, Alex, he wasn't a monster. He was misunderstood, and a set of unfortunate circumstances set his life reeling out of his control."

"Baby, slow down. Do you think the letter still exists? Is it possible?"

"No, no, she destroyed it."

"Fillide did? But why?"

"Caravaggio instructed her to burn it. He made it very clear, the letter could be dangerous to both of them. Remember, he was a marked man and she could have been condemned as a co-conspirator. I didn't see her burn it, but she planned on doing so once she memorized it. She loved him."

"Really?"

"Yes, she did. She was heartbroken…"

"I'm sorry baby," he said, tucking a strand of hair behind her ear.

"Your kiss pulled me back."

"I'm glad it did," he grinned. "I don't like you time-traveling without me. The toll it takes on you tears me up inside. What if that elastic cord you told me about was accidently severed? How would you be able to get back? Just the thought of that scares the hell out of me."

"Then don't think about it." She rubbed his shoulders. "Look, I don't have any control over it. When I'm meant to go back, I go back. It usually happens when I'm in a relaxed state, but I can't stop it from happening. It's a calling."

"Calling? Strange way of describing it. You're not a nun—thank God!"

"I've given this a lot of thought and I believe I'm being called by some universal consciousness to set the record straight. Repair a tear in the fabric of time. And it has to do with us."

He tapped the tip of her nose. "Honey, please don't tell anyone you're receiving your orders from God. They'll run us out of town."

Despite his jokes, she knew their conversation was causing him distress; it was in his eyes. She planted a gentle kiss on his lips. "Don't worry, Alex, I'll keep my mission a secret."

"Damn, I thought today was going to be just about us and not about Caravaggio, and just like that, the bugger finds a way of crashing the party."

"Not gonna happen. We're spending the rest of the day and tonight having fun. Why don't we get a couples' massage? I've never had one, and I read about it in the spa brochure."

"Now you're thinking. Forget the spa. I'll have two masseurs sent up to our suite, and we can drink pink champagne—before, during, and after." He arched a brow, like a hero in a Regency romance. "When we're properly oiled and relaxed, I'll give you my very own, personal massage."

Her arms looped around his neck. "Tell me lover boy, how long have you been suffering from this heightened sex drive of yours. I wonder, how many women were targets of your insatiable lust?"

"I'm not divulging my pre-Angela sex life secrets. Let's just say, my sex drive got a rocket launch when you showed up, and now, I'm at warp speed, babe."

"Liar."

His hand covered his heart. "You wound me. You know this conversation goes both ways. Maybe you'd like to confess where your sex-goddess skills were acquired."

"Me? Skilled? I defer to your argument. It seems any talent I may exhibit, I owe to osmosis."

"Osmosis, my ass." He removed her sunglasses and tossed her hat aside. "Hey, what are you doing?"

He swept her up into his arms and in less than three strides he jumped into the pool with her. Streams of bubbles from their laughter broke the surface of the water.

Angela came up gasping for breath. "I can't believe you just did that," she sputtered.

Alex was laughing too hard to answer. She huffed and swam to the steps and sat. Dunking her head backwards she swept her hair back, reclaiming her dignity.

Alex swam to her, joining her on the step. "Are you angry over a little water?"

"No, of course not. The water is very refreshing." She glanced around and noticed there was no one else in the pool area. Taking advantage of the moment she slid onto Alex's lap facing him, hooking her legs around his hips. Rocking her body against him she murmured, "I think it's time for a little payback." He hardened against her. "I've got you just where I want you."

His strong hands grasped her waist and yanked her tight against his chest. "Mmm, you know what it does to me when you take control. I'm frickin' putty in your hands."

"Just as it should be. When all else fails, the sex-goddess wins." She claimed his lips in a fiery kiss. Then, kissing her way to his ear, she nibbled on his lobe.

"Baby, you're making me so crazy I want to rip that bathing suit off you."

"Do you?" She felt his heart beat thrumming against her breasts. "Then why don't you? There's no one here."

He glanced around the pool area, and grinned.

Uh oh. She jumped off his lap and scrambled out of the pool. "I wouldn't come out of there just yet if I were you. It could be embarrassing." She dried off and packed up her things.

Alex took a couple of deep breaths and eased out of the pool. He grabbed a towel. "You think that's payback? Just wait until I get you back in the room." His muscles rippled as he dried his hair.

She couldn't help but stare. He was way too sexy with beads of water running down his chiseled body. She'd thought to tease him and scamper off, but who was she kidding, every time she looked at him, she melted. "I want to go up to the room and get ready for the massage you promised me."

"Wait for me."

"If you count all five hundred years that we've been in love and then lost each other, I think I have been waiting for you forever," she reminded him.

He walked to her, his hands wrapping around her waist. "Now that we've found each other again, I think forever works for me."

"Then forever it shall be."

CHAPTER 18

St John's Co-Cathedral
Valletta, Malta
Present day

Angela stood spellbound in front of the largest altarpiece Caravaggio ever painted. Her gaze strayed to Alex who stood beside her in silence with a grim look on his face.

"It's horrifying and morbid," he observed. "Because the figures are life-sized it's even more gruesome."

"Many art historians consider it to be his greatest painting."

"I don't see it. In his other works, I saw the possibility of redemption. Here I see nothing but cold-blooded cruelty."

"Do you see the signature written in the Saint's blood?"

"Yeah, I see it."

"It says F. Michelangelo, which stands for 'Fra Michelangelo'. That's the title he was invested with when the Grand Master anointed him as a Knight of Magistral Obedience on the fourteenth of July 1608. It's likely he added this signature to the painting following the knighting. In blood, he declares for the world to see that not only is St John reborn by his martyrdom and given eternal life, but Caravaggio, through his acceptance into the Knights Hospitaller, is granted forgiveness of his sins and reborn. In other words, this painting symbolically represents his redemption."

"And then a few weeks later he goes and fucks it up again by attacking another knight and they lock him up. What a crazy nut."

Angela shook her head. "When Caravaggio added his signature, he believed he would be a free man and be allowed to return to Rome and Fillide. It only took a few weeks for him to realize he'd been duped. The greatest painter in the world could not leave the island without the Grand Master's permission—and Wignacourt had no intention of letting his prized catch get away."

Angela sensed Caravaggio's heartbreak emanating from the painting. *His depression must have been dark and deep.*

Alex slipped an arm around her waist and drew her close. "You okay?"

"Yeah, I'm fine. Just thinking about how desolate he must have become when he realized the truth."

Alex nodded. "That would have been a hell of a bummer." He kissed her temple. "Tell me about the painting and what Caravaggio wanted us to see. Tell me why it's so acclaimed."

"Okay." She wiped away the tears and cleared her throat. "At the bottom of the painting he depicted St John. He's alive and suffering the worst imaginable death, his head partially severed and his lifeblood draining from him. The mismanaged blow of the executioner denies him the benevolence of a clean cut and a swift death.

"Holding him down is the central figure, the figure Caravaggio chose to make prominent, the executioner who has botched the execution." She pointed. "See, he's laid down his sword and just pulled a fresh knife from his scabbard behind him. The soldier who supervises the execution is dressed in the attire of a Turk, a symbolic reference to the Knights of St John and their mandate of guarding against the infidels. Notice the impassive face of the infidel soldier. He's not a believer in Christ and as such he's indifferent to the plight of humanity. He shows no remorse. There is also a subliminal message that to become a knight is to pledge yourself to the ultimate sacrifice. It's a warning that only the bravest should apply because you might be called upon to suffer the most terrible of deaths in defense of Christendom."

"Do you think Caravaggio was afraid and that's why he made the painting so macabre?"

"I don't know. What we do know is that he was driven by a fear of beheading. He returned to the same theme in many paintings. After he accidentally killed Ranuccio, his life was no longer his own. Until he found forgiveness from the Pope, he would be on the run for the rest of his life."

"He definitely was paranoid. Go on, tell me about the rest of the cast of characters."

"On the left side of the painting is a servant girl bending to receive the head of the martyred saint on a golden tray. She can't bring herself to witness the killing and looks down. Is she indifferent to the tragedy of a man being subjected to a torturous death? Notice that's not the case for the two prisoners in the background, who eagerly watch.

"What is Caravaggio saying about the morality of mankind? Are we no better than beasts?" Angela paused as she considered the final actor on the stage. "Only the old woman shows regret. She has realized the enormity of the crime. She doesn't turn away or cover her eyes in the face of evil. She is the witness to the unspeakable evils of man's deeds. It's as if she's just discovered there is no redemption in this life and realized our only salvation is in the next world with God."

"From your description, I'm beginning to understand how much symbolism and philosophical thought Caravaggio put into his paintings. His work is so much more than paint on canvas. His commentary on the inequities of the times he lived holds no punches. The viewer is forced to confront the disparity between the haves and the have-nots. It's hard to imagine that kind of intellectual depth of vision in a man who came from such humble beginnings. I wish we knew more about his early life and his education."

Angela squeezed his hand. "I wish we did know more. But what is really amazing, he stayed true to his beliefs and didn't back down. He didn't care if his message or the way he painted was popular or not. He painted for those without a voice. Incredibly brave of him."

Alex touched his head to hers. "You know, I find myself actually admiring the guy… I think it's more about how you describe him than anything else."

"When I lose myself in his paintings, I feel the same way." Angela observed the painting in silence. "We're learning a lot Alex, and I know it's going to help us find the stolen painting. **Are** you up for visiting where Caravaggio spent his last days in Malta?"

"The Castel St Angelo—from what I've read it was a pretty frightening place."

She tilted her head up and caressed his cheek. "Don't worry, Alex, I'll protect you."

He laughed. "I'm counting on that sweetheart."

Cavallo Island
Strait of Bonafacio
Present day

Antonio Greco's hulking shoulders slumped as he ran his finger down the numbers in his account's ledger. Blessed with a mathematician's mind, he accurately tallied up the numbers in his head. On his desk was a gold-framed photograph of his father, dapperly dressed in a suit, tie, and fedora with his arm around Antonio's shoulders, his smile bursting with pride. Antonio wore a cap and gown. The photograph had been taken on the day of his graduation from the University of Bologna.

Over the years, Antonio studied the photo, trying to recall why he stared at the camera with such intensity. Shouldn't he have been smiling? He couldn't remember who'd taken the photo. It could not have been his blessed mother—she'd passed away his first year in college. Perhaps a random stranger had snapped the candid shot.

Time had blurred his memory and now he wondered what the younger version of himself had been thinking. Had he sensed his destiny, and stared into the camera as though seeing into the future? His father had also passed away, so it was unlikely Antonio would ever solve the mystery.

Antonio never forgot his father's words. "Tony, you will be an anomaly in the world of Cosa Nostra, a man who will rise through the ranks not based solely on his brawn but based on his brain. *Un uomo di storia.* A man of history."

In the end, it had taken more than brains to remove the forces opposed to his rise to the top. It had taken rivers of blood. He'd had to wage war in order to capture and retain the prize of Capo Familia, the title given to the boss of a family in the Mafia.

Had it been worth it? Forty years later he still asked himself that question every day of his life. Some days, yes, and some days, no. He'd achieved great wealth and comfort, which were nothing to sneeze at. And keeping his family protected from the avarice of outsiders was another reason for satisfaction. He answered to no one and the decisions he made affected many. Even with the best consigliere in the world, the final word rested with him. With great power, came great loneliness. He often rued the isolation of being the man at the top.

Dressed in black mourning, Antonio's eyes filled with tears. Since his niece's death a few weeks ago, an overwhelming sorrow seized him at any given moment. Clarissa had died of breast cancer. He brushed away a tear.

I guess you're not as tough as you thought, Antonio.

Antonio had never married and after Clarissa's husband had been killed in a feud, she and her two children had moved in and she'd run his household. Antonio's beloved older sister, Beatrice, and her husband had died in a car bomb attack during one of the Mafia wars. And so, he'd always watched over Clarissa, even walking her down the aisle on her wedding day. He'd often joked that Clarissa was an angel among demons, but in truth, she was…

He fell in love with her. His own niece.

No other woman held a candle to Clarissa, but he'd hidden his forbidden love for her beneath the pretense of a favorite uncle's devotion.

When Clarissa became ill with the cancer, he'd moved heaven and hell to save her, but in the end the Devil had won. On her deathbed he confessed his love and she forgave him, admitting she felt the same. They were star-crossed and their love for each other would never have been morally sanctioned.

In Clarissa's estimation, death was a merciful release from a love condemned by God. And so, the angel who'd walked the Earth had found peace when Antonio swore an oath that he would care for the two children she'd left behind.

With his heart weighted down with sorrow, Antonio rose from his desk and walked to the shuttered windows. He partially opened the shutters, giving him a view of the private beach. The cove was naturally protected by granite outcroppings rising from the crystal-clear sea. Over the millennia, Cavallo's granite stones had been polished smooth by an endless cycle of sun, sand, and waves. The midday sunlight cast golden rays on sand as white as sugar where small ripples of waves caressed the shore.

Luna and Stefano were playing on the beach, running in and out of the turquoise water with Plutarch, their mastiff, chasing protectively behind. Even with a broken heart he couldn't help but smile. No tragedy could diminish the joys of youth. No matter what the sorrow, *la dolce vita* could not be ignored.

The phone on his desk rang and he closed the shutters, casting his office back into gloom. He picked up the receiver, "*Sì, Arturo, come va?*" Antonio picked up a cats-eye marble from the silver bowl he kept on his desk and maneuvered it through his fingers. It was a habit that helped him concentrate and relieve whatever stress he was operating under.

"Don Greco, my apologies for disturbing you during your time of grief."

"No apology necessary. I'm curious to know what you've learned about the detective and his girlfriend."

"They arrived in Malta and I put our local friends on them. I have to admit I don't understand why we're surveilling those two. They seem like a couple on their honeymoon. But, of course, you know better, Don Greco."

"I have my reasons, Arturo. Please continue."

167

"Just like in Naples, they visited the St John Co-Cathedral and viewed a painting by that same artist."

"Caravaggio. The artist's name is Caravaggio. One of the greatest artists to have ever lived. An Italian. Go on."

"Yeah, whatever. My men just checked in—the detective hired a private boat to take them across Grand Harbour to the Castel St Angelo. It's some kind of prison, or it used to be. I'm sure we could arrange an accident for them that would not draw too much suspicion. Just say the word and it shall be done."

Antonio continued to weave the marble through his fingers with adroit precision. His curiosity was piqued. Ever since he'd received the plea for the vendetta from Fortuna, the petty thug in prison, he'd been intrigued. He'd done his research and discovered the detective and the girl had somehow found a missing da Vinci painting, lost for five hundred years.

It seemed incongruous and impossible. How had they done it? The mystery of this alone played through his mind like a record needle stuck in a groove. It was the reason why he hadn't ordered the hit. It was the reason why he kept surveillance on them and watched their progress with fascination. "Arturo, my orders are for you to keep a tail on them. Under no circumstance are you to harm them, at least not yet. I have my reasons. Your job is to do exactly what I tell you to do. *Capito*? Let me know when they make their next move. I need to know where they go next."

"*Si*, as you wish, Don Greco."

"*Eccellente*. Call me when you have anything new to report. Don't worry about disturbing me. *Ciao*." Antonio rolled the marble back and forth on the desk, wondering what the detective and the woman hoped to gain by following the final years of the doomed artist's life.

What do they seek?

If it was the *Nativity* painting they were searching for, why follow the thread of the artist's final years, like some kind of pilgrimage? Antonio had long ago learned that sometimes what you think you know has no connection to the truth. He tossed the marble back in the bowl and got up, flicking on the overhead lights.

The room lit with a soft glow. He sat on the couch across from his desk and stared at the painting that hung on the wall behind the desk. When he looked at the painting, he was filled with a sense of peace. This room was Tony's private sanctuary, his chapel, and few were ever allowed entrance. He'd long ago lost his belief in God and Church... The painting had become his religion and he meditated before it daily.

A gift for sparing a life, the painting had indeed changed *his* life. Law enforcement agencies around the world had sought the work of art, but a few well-placed bribes, along with a sprinkling of false leads and rumors over the years, had kept the painting off the radar. Until now.

This art detective and his partner seemed to have a different approach. One that had proven successful in recovering the da Vinci. If they were successful again... He would be forced to eliminate them. In the meantime, he was enjoying this cat and mouse game. He flipped through the photos he'd received of the young couple. The woman was a beauty... An idea began to form in his mind, an idea that just might give him what he most desired.

He contemplated the painting once more, his eyes filling with tears.

Birgu, Malta
Present day

The speed boat raced across Grand Harbour from Valletta toward the towering fortress of Castel St Angelo in Birgu. The fortress loomed large and forbidding at the head of a promontory of land that jutted into the harbor. A blustery wind blew from the west, pushing the clouds eastward at an accelerated pace. Angela held onto the brim of her straw hat with one hand, the other hand rested on Alex's knee.

Alex grabbed her hand, his jaw clenched, his body tensing beside her, as if anticipating bad news. She wished she could calm his anxiety. This was going to be a tough one.

Five minutes was all it took to navigate across the harbor. Not enough time for Angela to determine what she would do if Alex was again swept backward in time. Lieutenant Spinelli had arranged for the curator of the fortress to meet them.

Standing on the dock, a slender, youngish man in a cream-colored linen suit, waved his fedora—his beaming smile in stark contrast to Alex's stiff-upper-lip.

"*Buongiorno!* I'm Rodrigo Bologna, the curator of the Castel St Angelo and I will be your guide today."

Alex and Angela shook hands with the curator and exchanged greetings.

"The Lieutenant told me you'd like to see Caravaggio's prison cell."

"That's why we're here, Rodrigo. We appreciate you taking the time to escort us. Let's get this over with." The tone of Alex's voice made her turn her head. His words were stilted and abrupt—he was fighting for control.

Rodrigo, however, paid no mind and kept up a steady stream of facts about the castle and its history as he lead them through a gate and began to climb the stone steps, progressing in and out of light and shadow.

Angela tried to focus on what Rodrigo was saying but she found it hard to concentrate when Alex held her hand in a death grip. He was displaying signs of a PTSD attack—shortness of breath, sweaty palms, tense muscles—she felt his pulse drumming against her hand as they entered a tunnel and wound their way to the upper battlements.

Rodrigo informed them the Castel had recently undergone a restoration, but the *guva*, the underground cell where Caravaggio had been kept in isolation, remained in its original state. They climbed nearly to the top and emerged from the tunnel to an open courtyard where a row of Roman arches enclosed an arcade that ran the length of a water-stained stone wall. The courtyard sported an abundance of wild bushes, growing haphazardly wherever a patch of dirt could be found.

Rodrigo stopped before a rusty-hinged metal plate on the ground. "This is the *guva* where they kept Caravaggio. They cut this chamber from solid rock and used it only for those knights who'd committed the worst crimes against the order. The cell is narrower at the top and wider at the bottom and it's about eleven feet down to the dirt floor."

With a grunt, he shifted the metal cover to the side, revealing a hole. He pointed to the thick cords of rope attached to metal hooks. "You'll have to climb down this rope ladder to access it. I warn you, it's pretty claustrophobic down there. Caravaggio must have gone crazy, he spent nearly a month held captive with no windows and very little light. Are you sure you want to climb down, there's not much to see?"

Angela looked at Alex, his face was damp and flushed. "Alex, I can do this myself if you're having second thoughts."

His gaze pierced through her like an arrow released from a bow. "Don't even think about it. We do this together or we don't do it at all."

This wasn't how Alex spoke to her, not ever, but she knew why, and it worried her. Her instincts told her they had to walk in Caravaggio's footsteps together if they wanted to find the *Nativity*. She took his hand. "We're in this together, Alex, I just want you safe."

He sucked in a ragged breath. "Sorry, baby, I'm not myself… I don't mean to sound abrupt or angry. Be patient with me, okay? I can do anything with you by my side."

Rodrigo silently observed their exchange. He tapped Alex on the shoulder. "Do you want me to go down with you?"

"No. We'd rather do this alone, but thanks for the offer." Alex forced a smile.

"No problem. I'll be here should you need me." He pulled a flashlight out of the back of his pants. "Here, take this. When Caravaggio was imprisoned, they probably lowered a ladder daily to provide water and food. However, the night of his escape, someone must have called off the night watch. Six months later, *in abstentia*, he was expelled as a 'foul and rotten member' of the Order."

"Typical Caravaggio," Alex scoffed. "I'll go first." He descended into the blackness. When he reached the floor of the cell he called up to Angela, his voice echoing through the bottle necked chamber. "Okay, baby, your turn." He shone the flashlight upward to light her way. "Just take your time."

Angela carefully placed one foot below the other and lowered herself down the ladder. When she felt Alex's hands around her waist, she sighed with relief. The air was stale and reminded her of the pungent scent of an unwashed body. Alex shone the flashlight around the stone-walls of the cell—she shuddered at how small the space was. Rodrigo was right, she couldn't imagine spending an hour in this tomb let alone a month.

"There are some carvings etched into the rock. It looks like the names of knights and a coat of arms." Alex ran his fingers over the words. "'Imprisoned forever, victim of evil triumphing over good—so much for friendship.'" Alex turned to her. "I wonder how many languished in this shithole."

"Caravaggio must have been going mad down here. No conversation, no paints, nothing to do but stare into darkness. Horrible. Torture." She walked closer to the wall to examine the name of the prisoner. A giant cockroach crawled up the wall—she screamed and stumbled. Alex dropped the flashlight as he caught her, and the two of them fell backward and hit the ground with a thud. Flashes of light bounced against the walls, blinding her… she felt herself spinning into the center of a vortex, sucking the air from her lungs. She could hear the pounding of Alex's pulse, or was it hers? The air was fetid as she finally drew a breath. Her head throbbed, she must have hit it when she fell. When she opened her eyes she stared into the abyss of madness… Red-rimmed eyes, bulging from a gaunt face, struck her to her soul.

"Fillide, *amore mio*, you've come to me." Caravaggio buried his face in her hair.

She didn't answer, she didn't want to break the spell. The dimensions of time had altered. Alex's past-life vision had taken hold and dragged her backward in time. Even though Fillide had never visited Caravaggio in the *guva*, his desperate longing had summoned her there. His anguish and agony were entombed in the very walls.

The painter hugged her but she felt nothing because she wasn't corporeal, she was a figment of his desire. Nothing was real, yet everything was so real – she could smell the filth and taste the bile that rose in her throat.

"Fillide, it's all ruined. I've destroyed my chances of knighthood and freedom. Wignacourt will never forgive me or set me free." He let go of her, stood, and began to pace the confined space. He tore at his greasy hair and pounded his chest with frustration. "I was such a fool to think I'd ever be allowed to leave this godforsaken island. I gave in to my worst impulses and went drinking with some fellow knights. I got drunk and was filled with fury and resentment at what I perceived my bad luck. I'd done everything right, Fillide, everything required of me. I painted with such passion, several portraits of high-ranking knights including Wignacourt, and none of it changed a single thing. I fear I am cursed, Fillide." His eyes burned with a feverish gleam. His remorse and regret was distressing to see. Rising, she took his hand.

"I allowed them to coax me into a fight—of all the knights to have an altercation with—I ended up confronting a Knight of Justice, the highest-ranking of them all. Things got out of hand and a *sclopo ad rotas*, a small pistol went off and this knight, Giovanni Rodomonte Roero, the Conte della Vezza, was badly injured. He was shot several times."

Caravaggio's laughter bordered on hysteria, "It's doubtful that gun could kill a grouse let alone that *bastardo*. It's certain he'll live. It wasn't me, Fillide, that fired the gun, I swear it. But I was the lowest-ranking knight of the group and the worst fell to me. I'm to be defrocked and will lose my knighthood. The punishment will be severe — I will not survive it."

He turned to her, his hands resting on her waist as he searched her eyes. "I'll never see you again, Fillide, if I don't get out of this hellhole. Sometimes, just to keep my sanity, I think of you, of the first time I painted you. Do you remember, Fillide? You were only fifteen years old, barely a woman. So beautiful and so full of fire, you were a match for any man and more than a match for me." For a moment laughter lifted his spirits, and then just as suddenly it disappeared from his face as if it had never been there.

"I've been rotting in this stinking cell for a month." He let go of her and resumed his nervous pacing. "There is a slim chance, a possibility of freedom, and I have decided to try, even if it means my death. Fabrizio Colonna came to me and offered me a way out. He wanted to do more as did others in the order, but their hands are tied by ridiculous ordinances that can't be ignored. The best I can hope for is a small window of time to escape. It is very dangerous and my chances of survival are slim. But, with Fabrizio's help tonight, I will run to freedom or die trying...

"Now that you've come to me, I know I can do it. I can do anything with you by my side. You, Fillide, will be my guardian angel." He crushed her to his chest and once more the room spun around her and darkness fell like a curtain over them.

She closed her eyes to stop the dizziness, and when she opened them again, she felt time shift. She was standing in a corner of the dank cell, watching events unfold. In the distance, the cathedral bells tolled the midnight hour. Caravaggio rose from a pile of straw and stared up at the heavy iron trap door in the ceiling. It opened, squeaking on its hinges. A rope ladder dropped down and Caravaggio began to climb.

Spinning once more, Angela closed her eyes. When she opened them, she was outside, standing on the cobblestoned path, watching from a distance. Caravaggio emerged from the cell, climbing out of the hole. He was out of breath and took a moment to inhale the sweetness, after a month of rank, stale air. Resting his hands on his thighs a groan of joy escaped him.

The full moon slipped behind a cloud and he crossed the courtyard in swift strides. He needed to climb the ramparts of the castle to the highest point, to the parapet. He whispered a prayer aloud. "Fillide, no one has ever escaped from the *guva* or this island, but you are my angel and with you by my side, anything is possible."

Angela found herself floating above him, following along as he ran along the path, winding around the tower. She watched him and yet she could also feel what he was feeling, know what he was thinking.

Caravaggio clung to the shadows, stopping only when a sentry passed. He made it to the top of the castle and looked down. Two hundred feet below was a small stretch of beach on the bank of the Grand Harbour. He searched the parapet and found a crenel where a rope had been tied. Adrenaline pumped through his body, giving him a strength he'd never thought he possessed. Even the fact that he'd never done anything like this before didn't give him pause. He was frantic to get away and even with the odds against him, he was determined to risk life and limb to gain freedom.

The walls of the castle bowed outward which allowed him the ability to hold the rope and brace his legs against the stone and walk down the two hundred feet. A breeze fingered his hair, he found it invigorating. That is until the rope ran out perhaps twenty feet above the ground. He murmured a silent prayer to God, pushed away from the wall, and let go, trusting that God and his angel would watch over him. He landed with a thud and rolled until he came to a stop. A groan escaped him from the impact. He gripped his shoulder, his hand massaging the pain. He'd no doubt sustained a bruise, but nothing was broken. With shaky knees, he stood and brushed the dirt off.

Walking away from the cliff toward the small waves breaking on the sand, he knelt and swished his fingers through the water. It was warmer than he'd imagined. He removed his tattered clothes, except his shirt, and flung them aside. Taking a deep breath, he dived into the water, and emerged, newly baptized. The water washed away his filth and his doubts—he was clean. A strong swimmer, his arms sliced through the water, propelling him forward. With nothing to do in the cell he'd spent hours each day exercising. He'd shed nearly ten kilos and his body had grown fit.

Fabrizio had explained there was no way to reach the open sea from Grand Harbour. The narrow opening at the mouth of the harbor was heavily patrolled. No knight was allowed to leave Malta without written permission from the Grand Master, so he had to go a different way.

He would have to swim around the Castel St Angelo promontory to a bay where the captain of a small schooner awaited him. The captain had been bribed and would take a circuitous route to Sicily, a sixteen-hour journey at best.

After the first week of languishing in the *guva*, he'd fretted that the Colonna family were so angry with him, they'd let him rot in the cell until he drew his last breath. But their influence was far-reaching, and the Marchesa was a master at manipulating those in power. Her devotion to him had never wavered and Caravaggio often recalled when she told Fillide she would never abandon him.

The tide was against him and he swam for an hour before spying the marker that had been left for him. He dragged himself out of the water, exhausted, and found a package under a tree. In the package was a change of clothes and a map. He dressed and studied the map. His destination was at least nine kilometers away.

Ignoring his exhaustion, he jogged down the beach to the inlet where the boat awaited him. An hour-and-a-half later, he found the beached skiff in the sand. He dragged it into the water and rowed out to the schooner, anchored a hundred yards offshore. The captain offered his hand and Caravaggio climbed aboard.

The compact crew immediately pulled anchor, and the vessel sailed smoothly out to sea. Caravaggio watched the island grow distant and ate the simple meal given to him. He knew the Grand Master would send men to recapture him and bring him to trial, but he had a dear friend in Sicily who he hoped would offer him refuge. He smiled, finally at ease.

We did it Fillide. Nothing is impossible when love exists. I will find my way back to Rome, back to you.

He lay back and stared at the millions of stars in the heavens and then closed his eyes and thought of her. Fillide... Fillide... Fillide...

"Angela... Angela... Angela..."

Alex was calling to her and she needed him now more than she ever had before. Seeing Caravaggio broken by his own madness, yearning to reclaim his life, yearning for Fillide, made her realize how fragile love was. It had taken four lifetimes and possibly more for her and Alex to finally get it right.

Her psychic gift had given her the chance to see her past lives with Alex as a saga, a journey to enlightenment filled with obstacles to be overcome. When the visions had begun and she'd discovered her ability to weave through time, she'd been afraid, but now, she understood the full measure of this power. There was a universal order and she was meant to see beyond the past. It was her destiny.

She relaxed, letting the winds of time carry her back to the present, to Alex.

"Baby, let me see that smile that turns my world upside down. Please come back to me."

She opened her eyes and blinked. The sad dark eyes of the painter were gone. The beguiling dual-colored eyes of Alex, surrounded by worry lines, smiled at her. She caressed the roughness of his cheek. "Hi, I'm back, and there is nothing in this world that could ever keep me from you."

He lifted her hand and pressed his lips into her palm. "I think we both hit our heads and were knocked out."

"No, Alex, we were together. Here. You had a past life remembrance," she said with a giggle, "and I went along for the ride."

"What? How? What happened? I don't remember anything."

"It was the night of Caravaggio's escape from here. Out of his fear and desperation came madness and in order to function, he hallucinated. He imagined Fillide was here with him and she would protect him. He needed to believe he could surmount the impossible and avoid certain death so he conjured up his muse." Angela smiled triumphantly at him. "And you know what? It worked. Against all odds, he escaped."

"You saw the whole thing?"

"Everything. It was one of the most daring exploits I've ever witnessed. I saw it all through your eyes—his eyes—my eyes. We're done here, Alex. We need to get to Sicily."

"Lady, traveling with you is a non-stop adventure. I'll put the pilots on standby and tell them we're leaving first thing in the morning. I want to hear every detail of what happened, but for now, let's get the hell out of this dungeon before something else happens." He stood and yanked her to her feet.

"Alex?"

"Yes." He brushed off his clothes and rubbed the back of his head frowning. "I'm definitely feeling a headache coming on."

"Alex, maybe it's because I know we've loved before in other lives and I've seen what losing that love did to us, but I want you to know you mean everything to me. I love you so much and I don't want to ever take your love for granted. I will treasure it all the days of my life."

He pulled her into his arms. "I wish you'd picked a more romantic place to confess your love." He chuckled. "Like in a hot tub or between silk sheets."

"Alex, you can't choose when you feel something."

He pressed his forehead to hers. "I suppose not. Could I get you to repeat those words when I get you back to our room?"

She shook her head and laughed. "You're so cheeky. I'm serious about this. I love you, Alex Caine, and I always will."

He bent to kiss her. "I love you Angela Renatus and every day I thank my lucky stars I found you. Now, can we please get the hell out of this dungeon?"

CHAPTER 19

Oliver sat in a pub near The Shard building drinking a Guinness draught beer. He wiped the foam from his upper lip with his napkin. He hadn't realized how much he missed London. It had been one of his favorite places to be stationed. Although time had wrought plenty of changes in the dynamic city, he still felt comfortable walking around. He felt that old swagger in his gait.

When he'd first transferred from Germany, to the London station of the CIA in 1988, he'd really hit his stride and was considered a rising star on his way to station chief. But meeting Natalia had changed everything. In no time, she'd carved a place into his bachelor existence, and carved out an even greater place in his heart.

Given the chance he'd do it all again. Angela was worth any sacrifice he'd had to make. But there was no way Natalia was going to waltz in after all these years and destroy everything he'd sacrificed so much for.

He'd been going crazy back in Lake Bluff, waiting for Alex to get back to him. Instead of twiddling his thumbs, he'd decided to take a long over-due vacation. He'd rented an apartment at the Cheval Three Quays with spectacular views of the River Thames and City Hall. The Quays guaranteed privacy and discretion and was only a ten-minute walk to the financial center of London and The Shard building. Oliver liked it so much, he'd made a few inquiries about availability. If Angela and Alex were going to live in Italy after their marriage, London was a lot closer than Lake Bluff.

He picked up his cell phone and began texting. *Hi Alex, I know I promised to wait for you to get back to me, but sorry, I was going crazy. I needed to act. I'm in London. I contacted some well-connected friends and they know where I can find Anastasia. They've arranged a cover for me and I have an appointment with her in about thirty minutes. She has no idea it's me, so I have the element of surprise. I can't let her destroy Angela. I will do anything to stop that. Wish me luck!*

Palermo, Sicily
Present day

Alex stared at his phone. "Shit."

"What is it?" Angela was unpacking, something she'd become very adept at.

He gave her his best poker face. "Huh? Did I say something?"

She rolled her eyes. "Yes. You looked at your phone and out came an expletive. What's going on?"

"Oh... nothing. Just a stock. It's down."

"Really? What is it?"

"What's what?"

"The stock, Alex. What stock is down?"

"Crawford Oil."

"Your family's oil company? That's not nothing."

"Oil companies have a lot of volatility. They go up and down depending on the futures. Nothing to worry about."

"Then why the potty mouth?"

"Sorry, *Professoressa*."

"Do you want a time out?"

"Only if you join me."

"Just hang up your clothes, hotshot."

He chuckled and glanced around the room—white and beige with a draped, four-poster bed. The only splash of color was a vase of orange sunflowers on the desk. "Are you happy with this room? I can change it, if you're not."

"I like this room, it's charming, and the location's great. Besides, we won't be here long. Are you okay, you seem distracted?"

"I'm fine." He set his suitcase on the luggage rack and opened it. "I might as well unpack mine too."

"Good idea, because I'm tired of folding your jockeys," she said with a smirk. "When we're done, why don't we take a walk and get our bearings? The weather is beautiful, and we're close to the Ballarò Market. I was reading about it and it sounds like it's right up Chef Alex's alley." She wiggled her eyebrows, imitating him when he tried to entice her into something.

"Sounds great, baby." Alex hung up his clothes in the walk-in closet. Their companionable silence gave him a few moments to think about the text he'd received from Angela's father. Oliver was actually going to confront Anastasia.

Holy Shit! I don't envy him.

Alex had spent his childhood as a pawn in the cold war between his own parents, but Angela was a grown woman. She was strong. And she had him.

I love you so much and I don't want to ever take your love for granted. I will treasure it all the days of my life… Her words resonated down to his soul. After the da Vinci case, they vowed never to hold things back. Oliver had placed him in a precarious position. If Angela discovered the truth, would it shatter her?

Alex stared at the rack of clothes with unseeing eyes, completely unaware of the sports jacket crumpled on the floor at his feet.

"Alex? What are you doing?" Angela leaned against the door jamb, her arms folded across her chest.

He turned, her eyes were laced with worry. Noticing the jacket, he picked it up and hung it on the rack. "Just finishing up. You ready for that walk?"

London, England
The Shard building
Present day

The London Eye Ferris wheel completed another full circle. Staring out of her office window, Anastasia waited for her next appointment. An art dealer from New York with some pieces for sale. As a courtesy to some mutual friends, she'd agreed to see him.

Her phone beeped, and she checked the screen—it was Victor. Before she could read his texts, Gwen, her assistant, knocked on her door. She knew it was Gwen. Her gatekeeper.

"Come in," she said, scrolling through her messages.

"Mr. Edwards, is here," announced the petite brunette as she marched in.

Anastasia waved her hand indicating the chairs in front of her desk. "Yes, yes, thank you Gwen. Mr. Edwards, please sit down. I'll just be a moment."

A moment passed and then another. Anastasia scanned Victor's texts informing her that Alex and Angela were in Palermo.

"What should I call you, Anastasia or Natalia?" said a deep, masculine voice.

Her head shot up. She was still facing the window, the Ferris wheel making yet another spin. Her heart stopped.

Everything stopped.

She turned as though in slow motion and beheld the face of the only man she had ever loved.

"What's the matter sweetheart? You look like you've just seen a ghost." He was smiling, but his jaw clenched, and his hands gripped the arms of the chair.

Almost twenty-seven years had passed since the last time she'd seen him. She'd left on some errand—she couldn't even remember what it was…

She'd never returned.

Angela had been napping. Her baby. Desperate, and without thinking of the consequences, she'd abandoned her new-born daughter and new husband. And now those consequences had come home to haunt her.

She blinked back tears.

"Oliver… H-how did you find me?" Her voice sounded odd to her own ears, faraway, youthful, from another time. A place of hope, and love, and light.

His head tilted, his gaze assessing. "You really don't know how I found you."

Not a question. Just a statement.

"Alex. It had to be Alex… I didn't think…" Her shoulders slumped. She was losing her touch, if she wasn't careful, she could blunder again, and the consequences could be catastrophic.

Regaining her composure, she gave a little shrug and strolled to her desk. Although, it offered no protection against the intensity of Oliver's stare. "I should have known he'd figure it out by his questions and his attitude. It never occurred to me you would confide in him."

"Why wouldn't I? I trust him to take care of *my* daughter. He loves her. I needed to warn him about you. He needed to know the truth."

"You wanted to protect her from me…?" she whispered brokenly. "I understand."

"Do you?" Oliver looked around her office and his gaze settled on the Picasso behind her desk. "I see life's been good to you, financially."

Anastasia took the chance to study him while his attention was focused on the painting. His dark hair was liberally threaded with gray, and deep lines had formed around his steel-blue eyes, but he was still a handsome devil, no loose jowls, his jaw was still strong, square, cut from granite. And his physique could rival a man half his age.

Oliver had always been meticulous about his health, always kept a rigorous regimen—five miles every morning, thirty minutes of weights. She was the opposite—curvy, hated exercise, loved chocolate. But he'd adored every curve and wouldn't hear of her going on a diet. She was much slimmer now, had learned over the years to keep her figure taut and fit with the help of her trainer, chef, and cosmetic surgeon. All the perks that money could buy.

Oliver unfolded his tall frame from the chair and walked to the window, staring out over the Thames.

Looking at him more closely, she noticed his suit was a few years out of fashion, but it didn't matter. He still looked good. Too good. She swallowed the lump in her throat.

She'd taken his love and thrown it away like a piece of trash.

That he didn't rant and rave at her was a miracle, but then again, he didn't love her anymore… Did he? He probably didn't care enough to throw a fuss.

"Quite an aerie in the sky you have here. Life's been good to you, but then you were always a resourceful woman." He turned back to her—those azure eyes couldn't mask the pain. "What are you doing, Natalia? Haven't you caused enough damage?"

"I didn't seek her out. It just happened. I have no intention of hurting her. I know it will have to end… but I can't help it. She's lovely, Oliver. You did a wonderful job… she's so like you—"

"Cut the bullshit, Natalia. She looks just like you. Smart like you. Stubborn like you. She even chose to study art, even though I did my best to dissuade her." His eyes scanned her features. "Why the face change?"

A bitter laugh escaped her. "You don't want to know where the dead bodies are, Oliver, or what it took to free myself from the SVR. When Natalia died, Anastasia was born. A new identity and a new face."

His eyes narrowed a fraction. "Was it bad?"

"Very."

"I'm sorry."

"You're still the good guy, Oliver. If I could do it again, I'd still have chosen you to be the father of my child." Oliver was a good man. That was one of the things she loved best about him. He was wrong about one thing though, Angela was more like him than he thought—she was a good person like her father. Kind and trusting… Which was why Anastasia was worried.

Angela and Alex were in more danger than they knew. Victor had snapped photos of the men tailing them and had run the photos through high-security police databases he'd hacked into. The thugs were Sicilian soldiers from one of the most powerful Cosa Nostra crime families.

"And good guys finish last, don't they, Natalia? I want to know what your intentions are, because if Angela figures out you're her mother, not only will she hate you, but she'll hate me for lying to her all these years. Don't you understand what this will do to her? And what about Alex? Confiding in him made him an accomplice to my lies. You nearly destroyed my life once. I can't let you destroy my daughter's life and the life of the man she loves."

"What do you want me to do, Oliver?"

"I want you to disappear just like you did twenty-seven years ago. You have the means to go anywhere. I know it's a lot to ask, but you owe me. Nothing good can come of you connecting to Angela now. She's going to get married in a few months and begin a new life. You can't be a part of her future. I know you have some kind of relationship with Alex's father, but let's be realistic, you need to end that too. I doubt he'd be too keen on knowing the truth about you."

"You're not blackmailing me, are you Oliver?"

"Don't twist this around. I don't have to blackmail you. If Angela finds out who you really are, everything about you will be out. There are some secrets that should never see the light of day. Don't you agree?"

A tear escaped, and she brushed it away.

He groaned. "Please, don't cry. It's better this way and you know it."

"Do you have regrets about the past?"

"I do, Natalia, I regret a lot of things. I've spent the last three decades looking backward, it's time for me to look forward. You and I made a beautiful child who's grown up into a remarkable woman. Let's leave it at that."

After all these years, it was time to tell him the truth. To wipe the slate clean. It wouldn't change anything between them, but at least it might give them a sense of closure. "I want you to know the hardest thing I ever did was leaving you and Angela. But the truth is, I had no choice. I did it to protect you both. They—the SVR—found me, found us… they threatened to kill you and Angela. I couldn't allow that."

"You could have told me," he whispered. "I could have gone to the CIA, asked for protection—"

"Protection," she interrupted him. "You know how the SVR worked. How they still work. I had to go back. I bided my time and I dealt with them, one by one."

"Is my daughter in danger because of you?"

"Not from the SVR, not anymore." There was no way she could tell him that Angela *was* in danger.

I may be the only one who can keep her safe.

CHAPTER 20

Palermo, Sicily
Ballaro Mercato
Present day

Angela and Alex walked from the hotel to the Albergheria district, one of the five Norman quarters of Palermo, Sicily's capital. They wandered the Mercato Ballaro, drawn to different stalls decorated with brightly colored awnings and the booming calls of the colorful sellers. The art of yelling to attract perspective customers had been in practice since the tenth century and added to the vibrant chaos of the market.

Alex held tight to Angela's hand as he led her past stands bursting with the sweet smell of chickpea fritters mingled with fresh herbs, along with the pungent aroma of aged cheese, cured meats, and fresh fish.

"Are you hungry yet?" Alex asked. They'd stopped at a table, covered in baskets of dark, purple eggplants with skins so shiny you could almost see your reflection, and large, purple artichokes that appeared more floral than vegetable.

"How could you not get hungry surrounded by all this temptation?" She grinned.

"I wish our room had a kitchen," Alex said, picking up a huge, poppy-red pepper. "Look at this beauty. Chop this up and throw it in with some onion, garlic, sausage, and potatoes and I promise you'll be *mmm-ing* every time you take a bite. I don't have to think twice about why I ended up living in Italy." Alex gestured to the grizzled, gray-haired vendor, and spoke to him in Italian. The old man replied in a flourish of words and broad hand gesticulations. He finished with a kiss to his fingers, his eyes and hands directed to the sky. Alex turned to Angela and translated. "He says, I should consider myself one of the luckiest men in the world to have the privilege of walking in your radiant glow."

The color rose in Angela's cheeks from the vendor's compliment. "*Sei troppo gentile, grazie.*" She thanked him and told him he was too kind and was rewarded with the street seller's toothless grin.

"You'll be fluent in no time, baby. You won his heart with your modest reply." Waving goodbye, he led Angela past vendors vying for their attention. They brushed past tourists with digital cameras and iPhones, snapping pictures and selfies, and young mothers pushing strollers with slumbering toddlers, heavy cloth bags hanging from the handles, until a delicious aroma filled the air and Alex made an abrupt stop. "Mmm, that's the scent I've been waiting for."

Angela sniffed and oohed. "What is it?"

"It's heaven, baby. Two different kinds of arancini, *al ragu* and *al sugo.* Come on."

They stepped into a crowded, enclosed seating area with round tables and chairs. Alex commandeered a spot for them and told her he'd be right back. A few minutes later, he returned with a tray bearing steaming plates, setting them down on the table. Angela looked at the golden-crusted globes of perfection, each dressed in a different sauce. "Looks yummy. I've never tried this before."

Alex loaded two plates with a sampling of each dish. "So, my arancini virgin, let me deflower you." He cut one of the steaming balls in half and skewered it with the fork and blew on it. "Open up."

There was something so sexy about the look of expectation in his eyes when he fed her, she loved it. This was their private world, the pleasure they received when they gave to each other. She moaned with delight, knowing it would send a tingle down his spine. "I'm waiting for your description of what this delightful morsel is."

"It's a Sicilian specialty—balls of cooked rice, coated with bread crumbs and deep fried. That one," he pointed, "is filled with meat, slow-cooked in tomato sauce and spices. This one," he cut another in half and milky white cheese oozed out, "is filled with mozzarella and cacio cavallo cheeses. There are dozens of versions of this golden street food. Some are stuffed with peas or other vegetables." He repeated the process of feeding her. Another moan escaped her, and he smiled. "Sicily is particularly famous for its street food and now you know why."

"Oh, Alex, this is sinful."

He nodded, digging in.

He'd also bought a carafe of local Sicilian red wine and poured them each a glass. "*A salute nostra!* To our health!"

"*Salute.*" She touched her glass to his.

In the distance came the rumble of thunder. Angela spied dark clouds rolling across the sky. "It's going to rain, Alex."

"Probably—*un po' di pioggia, poi un po' di sole.* A little rain, later a little sunshine. After lunch we might as well get out of the rain and visit the Oratory of San Lorenzo. I'm glad we're fortifying ourselves before heading over there. This is it, right? The church where the *Nativity* was stolen."

"Yes. Caravaggio spent a year in Sicily, on the run. His dear friend, Mario Minniti lived in Syracuse. He was Caravaggio's model in many of his early works. Remember—*Boy Bitten by a Lizard*?"

"How can I forget that homoerotic creation. Not my cup of tea, but fortunately my past-life persona was quite prolific. It's pretty odd to think I was a painter."

"You have other talents in *this* life," she said, arching a brow and making him grin. "Anyway, Mario had become a successful painter in his own right—and he was delighted to have his mentor, the greatest painter in Italy, with him. He secured Caravaggio many commissions with the blessings of the officials in each town he visited.

"Caravaggio painted frenetically as much as he could, from Syracuse to Messina, and finally sailing to Palermo. He must have needed money and as usual he painted his way out of dire straits. He also must have been going out of his mind—by all accounts, he was deranged by that point. Supposedly, he slept in his clothes, his sword and dagger at his side. As long as he painted, he was protected from the Knights of Malta by the Sicilian Senate, but he must have felt the noose tightening around his neck. He couldn't stay in one place too long. He was always running, in fear of being captured."

"And from here he went to Naples again, right?" Alex said, around another mouthful of arancini.

"Yes, and things only got worse."

Alex wiped his mouth with a napkin. "How about dessert, and then we'll head over to the church before the rain starts?"

"What do you have in mind?" She leaned forward seductively and stole a kiss. "For dessert that is."

"Hmmm, you're on the dessert menu for tonight. But right now, I was thinking of cannoli, Palermo's gift to the world. The classic recipe originated here. Divine fried pastry tubes filled with ricotta cheese, sweetened with cinnamon, chocolate chips, almonds, pistachios, and sugar. How does that sound?"

"Orgasmic."

"No way, all orgasms belong to me."

Palermo, Sicily
Oratory of San Lorenzo

The rain came in a deluge at the exact moment the taxi dropped them off at the Oratory of San Lorenzo in the dilapidated old Kalsa quarter of Palermo. The street was narrow, and the oratory sat catty-corner to the Basilica San Francesco d'Assisi. Drawing Angela close under his arm, Alex opened the umbrella he'd bought at the market.

A flash of lightning struck the bell tower, turning the sky white. The crash of thunder that followed was deafening. Angela trembled, looking up at the sky. "The night the *Nativity* was stolen, there was a storm like this…"

"It's okay, we can wait out the storm inside."

The oratory was empty, and they glanced around to get their bearings.

"Pretty elaborate church decor, wouldn't you say?" Alex whistled.

"This is a perfect representation of the Sicilian Baroque style. Sicily was a Spanish possession during Caravaggio's year here, but her power was waning. In order to draw attention away from the extreme poverty of the people and the heavy taxation the Spanish levied on them, they built these ornately decorated churches. It's one of the reasons Caravaggio was so busy when he arrived in Sicily. City and Church officials clamored to engage his talent and paid several times more than he normally got for a commission."

They made their way up the aisle. "I've never seen so much white stucco work," Alex said. "Somebody had a definite fixation on putti, there's an awful lot of little naked fellows blowing bubbles and cavorting about. Quite a contrast to the expressive martyrdom of that saint over there."

Angela scrutinized the three-dimensional wall-painting. "That's the martyrdom of San Lorenzo. This stucco work is considered a masterpiece and was created by Giacomo Serpotta. Art historians have described these interiors as 'a cave of white coral.'"

"That describes it perfectly." They crossed an inlaid marble and stone floor to the altarpiece. "It looks like a ghost of a painting," Alex observed.

"It's a facsimile, a reproduction from black-and-white photographs. They based the colors on Caravaggio's other works from the same period. It couldn't possibly hold a candle to the original."

"But the size must be right. It's big, probably nine feet tall and eight feet in width."

A blaze of white light lit the church, followed by an ear-shattering crash of what sounded like cymbals clashing together. Stunned, Angela stumbled back. An atmospheric charge bounced off the walls and surrounded them. The fine hairs on the back of her neck stood on end and her chest constricted, making it hard to fill her lungs. Dizzy, disoriented, her legs wobbled. Firm hands kept her from falling.

A hoarse voice filled her ear. "Fillide, I wanted you to see it. Do you like it?"

She opened her mouth to reply, but no words came forth.

"I had you in mind when I painted it. The Virgin is not as beautiful as you, *amore mio.*" She turned toward the gravelly voice and saw him standing there. *Caravaggio!*

His smile was impossibly sad, his pain lanced through her, like it was her own.

"My paintings have been so morbid of late." He angled his head and studied his work, his brows raised in critical appraisal. "I tried to strike a more hopeful balance, but I'm not sure I achieved that. I worked even more quickly than usual. When I'm immersed in the act of painting, it's the only time I am able to forget the reality of my life.

"Each time I start a project, I live in constant fear that I won't be able to finish it. The terror is driving me to madness. Every day I look to the harbor and see their fleet—the tall sailing masts and flags of the Knights of St John. I'm hounded by the knowledge that any minute they will fulfill their grisly wish to kidnap me and take me back to the *guva,* or perhaps slit my throat and toss me into the sea. I don't know how much longer I can live like this. You have no idea how much I wish to return to Rome and to you, Fillide."

She turned away from him, unable to bear the sorrow etched into his face. Her gaze landed on the shadowy replica of Caravaggio's painting, and the air grew misty once more as a fog appeared in front of the work of art. And then, after a few moments, it cleared, and the copy was no longer pale and milky but warm and rich with earthy colors. The Virgin Mother's jumper displayed Caravaggio's signature red. The Madonna sat on the ground amid a few strands of straw in a stable. The exhausted mother had just given birth. Wearily she stared down at the baby whose eyes were focused on her face.

It seemed to Angela by Mary's expression that she already knew what was to come, that one day she'd lose him, her beautiful boy. Surrounding the mother and child were two men, San Francesco d'Assisi and San Lorenzo. A young man sat on a low stool across from her and the baby, his bare foot just touching the infant's hand. The young man's body was leaning forward, his hand and finger pointing at the baby. He seemed to be conversing with a haloed Joseph. A cow looked on while an angel hovered above, announcing the miraculous birth and pointing to Heaven.

There was something so incredibly sad about the painting. The Virgin was alone and forlorn, and the men who surrounded her could do nothing for her. It reminded Angela that Caravaggio was reliving his own painful childhood. Like the infant Jesus in the painting, there was no one who could help him on *his* journey. Caravaggio, too, had been an extraordinary child, left to fend for himself without male support. His father, uncle, and grandfather had been taken by the plague and he was left with only his mother.

Angela turned back and stared into the dark eyes of Caravaggio. "The painting is beautiful, a masterpiece, but it's been stolen and taken from the world. Do you know who took it and where it is?"

With sorrowful eyes he nodded. He reached for her hand and led her to an upstairs balcony. The front doors of the church opened with a squeak as another flash of lightning illuminated the nave. Four men dressed in black and wearing gloves followed a woman up the aisle. They carried a ladder and tool boxes. Oddly, no one spoke, and the scene played out like a black and white silent movie. All that was missing were the mournful chords of an organ.

The men seemed to be arguing over how best to remove the painting. Finally, the one man who appeared to be directing the operation angrily stalked off. Did he wash his hands of the situation? Was he waiting outside? Was he upset they were going to cut the painting from its frame? A wave of nausea washed over Angela as she observed one of the thieves slice the *Nativity* from its frame with a razor blade, while the other man cut the inlaid mother of pearl from the mahogany pews.

This was an organized theft, carefully planned by professionals, not random thugs. All the while, the female co-conspirator's attention wavered from the door of the church to the thieves as she kept watch. *She must have been paid handsomely for her help.*

Angela recalled Alex telling her there was a woman custodian of the Oratory at that time, and she'd never been questioned by the authorities. How badly had they boggled the investigation? Someone must have had the power to pull strings and send the investigators spinning in the wrong direction. Every testimony of what had happened to the painting must have been fabricated. Somewhere, a puppeteer had manipulated law enforcement, the government, and the world.

When the painting was finally cut free, only a gaping hole remained in the frame. Tears welled in Angela's eyes as she watched the thieves fold the priceless painting and stuff it in a suitcase. The last thing to be taken was a beautiful, golden crucifix. The door opened, and Angela was blinded by a burst of light and a roar of thunder. She squeezed her eyes shut and covered her ears, as strong arms wrapped around her from behind. "I will always love you, Fillide," the craggy voice whispered. A moment later the church was quiet once more. Angela opened her eyes and beheld the fac-simile of the *Nativity*. She didn't have to turn her head to know that Alex's arms were around her and he was calling her back.

"Did you see it?" she asked.

His sigh of relief cast the last of the vision from her. "See what?"

"I watched them steal the painting. They were pros, Alex. Caravaggio watched with me. He wants me to find it. I was certain he was going to tell me where it is, but he disappeared." She glanced around. "How did I get up here?"

"I carried you." He kissed her forehead. "You begged me to take you upstairs."

"You mean, you were aware the entire time?" she asked, her eyes wide. "You didn't black out?"

"No, not this time. You were having one of your visions. I was so worried about you. You started shaking. You kept going on about a horse in the sea."

"I said what?"

"*Cavallo nel mare.* Horse in the sea. You must have said it four or five times."

Her brows knit together. "I don't remember anything about that. I don't understand, my visions are usually clearer. What could it possibly mean?"

"It's all right, baby. We'll figure it out. I hate what this is doing to you. You scared the life out of me."

Fatigue gripped her. "I don't feel very well—can we go back to the hotel?"

He helped her to her feet. "This is what I'm talking about. I have a good mind to drop the case. The damn painting has been missing fifty years, I don't care if it stays missing another fifty. I only care about you, and my patience is running thin."

The thought of not continuing the search made her sick to her stomach. "Alex, we can't stop. Your past life is reaching out to me. Why else would Caravaggio be helping me? Please, I beg of you."

"He isn't helping you, Angela. It's Fillide. He's going mad and he thinks you're Fillide. He's a ghost whose soul has never found peace."

She couldn't argue with him, because he was right. "Please take me back to our hotel room, I need to lie down. I need to feel your arms around me."

"You never have to worry about that, because I'm all about holding you." He led her to the front of the church. "Wait here while I grab a taxi." Alex opened the door. All that was left of the storm was a light drizzle. He ran down the steps. Angela turned around to take one last look at the painting facsimile and was stunned. A shadowy figure stood with his back to her staring up at the painting.

Alex opened, the door. "Come on, the taxi's waiting."

She glanced over her shoulder for a last look at the ghostly figure, but he was gone.

CHAPTER 21

"What happened inside the church?" Antonio rolled two cat's-eye marbles between his fingers, staring at the *Nativity*. His cellphone sat on the coffee table on speaker mode.

"We couldn't follow them inside without being made. The place was empty. Plus, there was a big storm."

"Interesting... There was a storm in '69 the night the painting was stolen. What happened after they left?"

"They just caught a cab and are on their way back to the hotel. We're tailing them. So, they went to see the fake painting, what do you figure comes next?"

"If my calculations are right, they'll head back to Naples. That's the last place Caravaggio lived and painted."

"Okay, so I guess it's back to Napoli."

Antonio rubbed his unshaven face. "I think it's time we put the fear of God in them."

"What do you have in mind?"

He considered the options. "Something that throws their whole game plan out of whack. A little roughing up. A few cuts and bruises. Nothing serious. Just enough to slow them down and maybe think twice. Make it look like a robbery, but maybe not. The detective will get the picture."

"How do we do that?"

"Caravaggio was attacked when he returned to Naples. He spent the evening in a tavern called Locanda del Cerriglio. He was ambushed after he left the tavern. He was beaten and his face badly slashed. I think they're going to retrace Caravaggio's steps."

193

"Are you saying three-hundred-fifty years later the tavern is still there?"

"It's a restaurant now, but, it's still there."

"And you want history to repeat itself."

"Not exactly." Antonio squeezed his palm around the marbles. "Don't deform him, just something he can carry forever to remind him of who he's dealing with."

"Your wish is my command."

"Arturo, don't touch the girl. I don't condone violence against women. This woman in particular, intrigues me. Understand?"

"Whatever you say, Don. Do you want us to bring her to you?"

"Not yet. Sometimes you learn more by sitting back and watching. I want a full report. Keep it clean and don't get caught."

"You can count on it, Don Greco."

Antonio pressed end. Shutting off his phone, he leaned back on the sofa. He held a cat's eye marble up to the light... turning it, the yellows and greens reflecting his swirling thoughts... He had to meet her. The art historian. An idea had taken root—an idea he couldn't get out of his head. It was blasphemy, it was insanity, it was his yearning.

She must be a seer.

Over the past few weeks, he'd investigated several individuals who claimed to have the second sight, but they were all scam artists. And yet, his instincts told him that Angela Renatus had the gift.

He strode to his desk and picked up the landline. His assistant answered. "Giorgio, I want you to look into Angela Renatus and Alex Caine. I need to know everything about them. They're both American, but Caine resides in Florence. Talk to our police friends in Rome and Florence. I want a copy of the case file on the Leonardo da Vinci painting they found. Also, the court records and transcripts of Enrico Fortuna's trial."

"Okay, boss. I just received a call from *Signore* Carillo. He's been trying to get a hold of you about the meeting coming up in Sicily."

"Postpone them for a week. Call him and tell him I'm still in mourning, I need a little more time. Then notify the other families and make the arrangements. I'm not going anywhere until this other issue is resolved. *Grazie. Andare subito!*

"Yes, sir. Right away. Consider it done."

London, England
The Shard building
Present day

Anastasia paced her office amid packing boxes that littered the floor. The industrial-sized shredder droned in the next room, eating page after page of documents that needed to be destroyed. Gwen was busy feeding them into the hungry machine.

The Ferris wheel drew her attention once more. The Thames was shrouded in a cloak of gray mist and the London Eye appeared to float above the fog. She would miss the view, but her estate in Kusnacht, Zurich overlooking Lake Zurich offered the kind of privacy not possible in London. She would need that protection, if everything went according to plan. Besides, she'd made a promise to Oliver. Fortunately, disappearing was something she was good at.

She regretted her relationship with Lance would have to end. She enjoyed his company, although love was never a factor in the equation. Contrary to what Alex had jokingly insinuated at dinner, Lance had never been a target for intel. Too bad she had to give him up. But Oliver was right. Lance had to go.

She sighed and picked up one of the satellite cells on her desk and connected to Victor.

"Madame, what can I do for you?"

"Victor assemble the spetsnaz team, I'm coming to Naples. Have the Blackhawk readied for a black-ops operation, and see *The Delilah* is ready to sail."

"Where are we going?"

"I'm not sure yet, but I'll know soon. Move quickly, we don't have much time. Tell the men everyone will be paid double."

"Finally! Our Russian special forces team has been itching to go on a mission. And I'm tired of tailing the lovebirds and watching them eat their way across Italy."

"Ha-ha, Victor, nail this mission and soon you'll be eating your fill of zurcher geschnetzeltes with rösti."

"Ah, my favorite Swiss dish." Anastasia found it amusing when Victor rhapsodized over food. She heard him smack his lips in anticipation. As if reciting a prayer, he listed the ingredients, "Medallions of veal cooked with mushrooms, cream, onions, and wine, and paired with potatoes. A meal fit for a king. Does this mean we'll be laying low in Zurich for a while?"

"*Da*, your biggest problem will be trying not to gain ten kilos."

"Fear not, Madam X, jogging Lake Zurich in the dead of winter will keep a man fit. Your safety is always my first priority."

"I'll text you all the details as per my arrival. Be ready to move when I get there."

"We'll be ready."

"Victor stick close to the lovebirds."

"Of course, Tashenka."

Palermo, Sicily
Palazzo Brunaccini Hotel
Present day

Dark circles rimmed her eyes, and her face was pale with exhaustion. Alex insisted Angela take a nap after they got back to the hotel. He was Caravaggio'd-out.

They were leaving first thing in the morning for Naples, so tonight was pizza night. He preferred just hanging out in the room, making love to his woman, inhaling pizza, and watching movies, instead of going out.

He peeked into the bedroom and heard Angela's even breaths. He closed the door and returned to the sofa. Pulling out his phone, he punched in a number. "How'd your meeting go?"

Oliver's heavy sigh told him everything. "Sorry, Alex, I was out, just got back. I handled the situation. Natalia isn't going to be a factor in our lives going forward."

"Just like that? What about my father?"

"She's going to disappear from our lives and that includes your father."

"Wow. I'm shocked she agreed. It must have been hard seeing her again."

"It was surreal. I couldn't help but feel sorry for her. Even with her success she's lost so much." The silence that followed spoke louder than his words.

"How's London? Are you enjoying your visit?"

"Yes, I am," he chuckled. "Renewing old friendships. Time is a funny thing, it's easy to erase the years in between. You find yourself picking up right where you left off. How's Angela?"

"She's good. Wearing herself a bit thin. I'll be happy when this case is closed."

"You'll have to temper her predilections, her habit of keeping her nose to the grindstone."

"I have every intention of taming the shrew, or in her case satiating the goddess."

Oliver groaned. "Not good imagery for a dad, Alex."

"Sorry, sir. Your girl keeps me on the edge of my seat. Sometimes I don't know if I'm coming or going."

"Hold tight to the wheel, son. Make sure you hold tight to the wheel."

"I can assure you, I have no intention of letting go. By the way, how long are you planning to stay in London?"

"I'm enjoying myself so much that I've started looking for a more permanent residence. I'm tired of living alone in the middle of nowhere. Putting things to rest with Natalia made me realize it's time to move on and build a new life."

"That's great, I know Angela will be thrilled. Even though—she let the cat out of the bag, she's excited about your visit for Christmas."

"I can't tell you how much I'm looking forward to visiting now that I know Natalia won't be joining us. Angela's told me so much about Montefioralle and I can't wait to see it, especially that pizza oven of yours."

"I suppose you know your daughter is a pizza addict."

"The apple doesn't fall far from the tree. Alex, take care of her, keep her safe."

"My first priority, sir. Have a good evening."

"You too. I'm heading out again to have dinner with my former station head, now happily retired."

"I would love to be a fly on the wall for that meal. Enjoy yourself, sir. Speak to you soon."

CHAPTER 22

Naples, Italy
Grand Hotel Vesuvio
Present day

Her glasses were perched on the edge of her nose as she scrolled through pages of research on her laptop. Angela had cleared the desk in the hotel room and set up a makeshift office. Now and again, she glanced through the sliding glass door at Alex who was on the balcony sipping espresso and talking on his cell. He was shirtless, and his sweats hung low on his hips, an immense distraction. He turned and smiled at her, she sucked in her breath. His six-pack abs and his 'I want you' smile made her heart do backflips. Would she ever be able to look at him and not quiver like a bow string after an arrow's release? Not likely.

Love does strange things to you.

Just thinking about the joy Alex had brought to her life reminded her of the stark contrast between their bright future and Caravaggio and Fillide's doomed love.

She blew Alex a kiss and forced her attention back to the screen. She'd been racking her brain all day trying to find a key to unlock the meaning of *Cavallo nel mare*. "Horse in the sea. Horse in the sea." It didn't make any sense. At least not yet. If she cracked the code, the door would swing open.

Horses in the sea?

She ruled out seahorses, which made no sense. Several islands around the world were populated with horses. Assateague Island in Maryland had a thriving wild horse population, but why would the *Nativity* be in a national park in the U.S.? The same was true for the Newfoundland and Sable Island horse populations of Canada. No, this reference was more abstract. She chewed the end of her pen with frustration.

The sliding door swished open. "You've been on that laptop since we got here this morning. It's nearly five. I'm up-to-here with Caravaggio." His hand wrapped around his throat. "It's time to take a break before dinner. I'm expecting we'll be drudging up our favorite painter again tonight, when we eat at his favorite whorehouse tavern. Every time he makes an appearance my love life takes a dramatic step backward."

Alex's penetrating gaze made her shiver with desire. From his cocky grin, he knew she'd been checking him out. Before she could answer, he'd closed the gap between them, and his mouth claimed hers hungrily. He broke the kiss and his hands cupped her ass, pressing her firmly against his hardness. His eyes gleamed, playfully. "How about some rocking hard sex in the shower? I feel like Vesuvius ready to explode." The imagery of a volcano exploding and filling her with hot lava made her laugh.

"I see you find this amusing." Despite his grin, his intensity took her breath away.

She pressed deeper into his embrace and trailed her nails down his back. "Have I been working you too hard, Alex?" she purred.

"Depends what kind of work you're talking about. There's a few parts of me that could use more of a workout."

"You're saying I've been shirking my duties."

"The day it becomes a duty there's going to be hell to pay," he snarled.

"Has it occurred to you I might like you to bring me to my knees?"

His lips curved. "I like knees."

"But, do you like knees in the shower?" She ran her lips up his neck to his ear and whispered, "Me on my knees, hot water streaming down our bodies, your hands in my hair…"

He blew out a breath. "Jeez, baby, you certainly know how to ring my bell."

"Then you better hurry or you're going to be late for class. And I don't think you want to miss this lesson."

He laughed and swooped her up in his arms. "Touché, *Professoressa*-tease. Let's see if the class is as good as the preview."

"Oh, I bet you a massage it will be."

"You're on."

"By the way, how are your knees?"

His pupils dilated. "What do you have in mind?"

"In the eyes of the law, I'm entitled to reciprocity."

He howled with laughter. "I love you, Angela. My knees love you, too."

Naples, Italy
Locanda d'el Cerriglio
Present day

Alex was still smiling from their shower. On a scale of one to ten, it ranked a fifteen. He was convinced she was channeling her past-life minx, Fillide, which had its positives. Fillide must have been a femme fatale considering all the men's hearts she'd laid waste to. Angela knew how to drive him crazy, but she'd gotten even better as of late. His brainy girl had figured out flirting and teasing kept him on his toes. She had him wrapped around her little finger. She had to know he'd jump through hoops for her— hell, he'd probably jump off the London Bridge if she asked him.

And then she'd emerged from the bathroom, wearing tight black jeans that hugged her curves in all the right places, and a red cashmere sweater with a low vee neck. The purple pashmina was an odd contrast, but Angela had a way of carrying off a look few other women would attempt. They'd just had earth shaking sex, yet the sight of her had him wanting to order in room service.

Yeah, you're head over heels for sure.

Angela had been right when she'd described their first meeting. At least, for him, it had been *coup de foudre*, love at first sight. But, if you believed the reincarnation thing, it was love at first life, and second, and third, and fourth. He'd lost her tragically in every previous life, but he wasn't going to let that happen in this one. As far as he was concerned, they'd broken the cycle and claimed the right to be together.

Thirty minutes later, Angela studied him from across the table. "That's quite a smile you're wearing. What are you thinking about?"

"As if you don't know." He covered her hand with his. "I was thinking about a song that reminds me of you."

She cocked her head and smiled. "What song?"

"I can't sing it, or I'll send you running for the hills. It's a country and western song by Billy Currington, *She's Got A Way With Me.* I guess I don't have to say more than that, do I?"

She leaned across the table and kissed him as if there was no one else in the room. "Oh, Alex, don't ever stop looking at me the way you are now. I love that song, it's so romantic." She settled back in her chair, and applause rang out. Everyone in the restaurant was looking at them and smiling. She stood and gave a little curtsy.

"Your cheeks are as bright red as your sweater," he laughed.

"I get nervous when I attract attention."

"You handled it perfectly, baby. As the Italians say "*l'amore è tutto quello che c'è*", love is all there is. You can kiss me anywhere, anytime."

She picked up the menu and studied it. "If you want more kisses, you'd better feed me, I'm starving." The menu was written in Italian with no English. "I don't want to miss out on anything special. You order for the two of us, please."

"Leave it to me, Angel. The grilled octopus is a must have."

The waiter wrote down their order. Angela may not have followed every word, but from Alex's hand-speak and the waiter's nodding, Alex had made himself clear.

"Okay, back to the man of the hour," Alex said. "Caravaggio spends one year in Sicily, two of those months in Palermo. Then returns to Naples, what happens next?"

"He must have sensed the Knights closing in on him in Palermo, because by September 1609 he was back in Naples staying at the Colonna Palazzo at Chiaia." When Angela shared her art history knowledge with Alex, their discussions often led to fresh observations.

"Chiaia was a fortress palace with towering walls. He must have felt safe," she mused. "The Marchesa Costanza came to his rescue, yet again. She must have finagled some kind of pardon or letters of support from Rome, or else she wouldn't have been allowed to protect Caravaggio from Grand Master Wignacourt."

"That guy had nine freakin' lives. But the paranoia… I bet it got to him."

"I'm sure it did," Angela replied. "But his saving grace was painting. Within days of his arrival, he began working on *The Resurrection of Christ* for the Sant'Anna Church of Lombardi. Unfortunately, the large altarpiece is no more, most likely destroyed during an earthquake in the early twentieth century. Just like in Sicily, Caravaggio was painting with such skill and at such a pace that he could turn out a painting in a month or less, which he did with *The Resurrection*.

"According to an eyewitness account by a French art critic traveling at the time, *The Resurrection* was extraordinary. A masterpiece. He described it as a dark, dramatic work that depicted Christ escaping his guards at the Holy Sepulcher. The art critic likened Christ to a criminal on the run, and not the idolized vision normally depicted of His ascension, accompanied by a chorus of angels. Perhaps the painting was inspired by Caravaggio's own escape from the *guva* on Malta.

"The critic wrote about the painting in detail. He was there one hundred and fifty years after Caravaggio painted it, and the altarpiece was darkened with age, and unsigned. He had no idea it was the work of the master. Remember, this was the period when Caravaggio had been all but forgotten. But the painting left a great impression on the critic."

"If only he hadn't left the safety of the palazzo to come here, to this place." Alex said, jutting his chin, indicating the dining room.

"His papal pardon case had been reopened. He might have felt hopeful and let down his caution. He must have been terribly lonely."

Alex laughed. "What you mean to say is he was terribly horny and risked it all to get laid."

"I suppose you're right," she frowned. "Maybe he just wanted to celebrate his pending freedom and return to Rome and Fillide."

"Honey, he may have loved Fillide, but neither he or she would have been faithful to the other. He came here to get his rocks off and was attacked when he left. The question is, who did it? Was it Ranuccio's family taking revenge, or Wignacourt's knights exacting punishment for his escape from Malta, or was it the Knight of Justice, the guy Caravaggio attacked on Malta, seeking his own vendetta?"

"Given the nature of the wound he sustained, it had to be the Knight of Justice from Malta," Angela answered. "The vicious punishment fits the bill of a classic vendetta. Knights weren't known for forgiveness, and Rodomonte Roero must have tracked Caravaggio from Malta to Sicily, and finally to Naples. *Sfregiato*, according to the honor code of the day, was vengeance for an insult to one's honor. He'd dishonored the name of the Conte della Vezza, and the Conte exacted equal justice by scarring Caravaggio's face."

Their food arrived, and Caravaggio took a back seat for a moment. Alex served the first course of grilled octopus. "Here you go, my lovely. It's not every day you eat in a restaurant that's three hundred and fifty years old and maintained its quality. That's one for the record books."

"Hmmm, how do they get it so tender? I've had octopus before and it was like chewing rubber."

"They pound it against the sink, and then simmer it in water for a couple of hours with some red wine corks, herbs and seasoning. Then you can do anything you want with it, barbeque it, or toss it in a salad."

"What do the corks do?"

"No one knows exactly, but it helps the octopus keep its color—most chefs swear the tannin in the wine cork acts as a tenderizer."

"That's crazy."

"It's all in the prep." He took a bite. "Man, this is good. Food's great and there's no sign of the painter. All good."

She glanced around. The room was filled with reproductions of Caravaggio's paintings, including one of the *Nativity*. Across the room she spied Ottavio Leoni's chalk portrait of Caravaggio. "It's odd, given the traumatic event that occurred here, neither of us has had any premonitions or physical signs of the past intruding on the present."

"I'm all for keeping it that way. Any luck with the "horse in the sea" angle?"

"Nothing yet. I keep coming up against a brick wall."

"Maybe you're looking at it wrong."

"Maybe you're right. Maybe I'm making it more complicated than it needs to be." She popped another piece of octopus in her mouth. "Alex how do you say horse in Italian?"

He looked at her as if she were crazy. "Cavallo."

She attacked the cell keyboard on her phone.

"What are you doing?"

"Just a second." When she looked up, she beamed triumphantly.

"What did you find?"

"A tiny island between Corsica and Sardinia. It's what Caravaggio wanted me to know. The 'horse in the sea' is Cavallo, an island in the Mediterranean Sea. It has to be it. That's where the painting is." She scrolled down the screen on her phone. "It's a private island. The houses are owned by super wealthy celebrities, aristocrats, royals, and various Fortune-500 CEOs. Princess Caroline of Monaco has a house there." She looked up. "Alex, there's a hotel. We have to go there."

"Slow down, baby. Let's take this one step at a time. We're dealing with a powerful adversary. Someone who's capable of keeping the most sought-af-ter art theft in history from being found. You're not going to just show up and have them hand over the painting."

She frowned. "Alex, we have to find the painting."

"Yes, but we have to proceed with caution. We need back-up."

"Then call Spinelli and we can meet him on Cavallo. Tell him we've found the painting."

"All right, let's finish up and head back to the hotel. Tomorrow I'll call him. Tonight, you're mine."

The attack came out of nowhere.

Out of the darkness, an arm snaked around Angela's waist, dragging her away. Two black-clad figures leapt out and surrounded Alex. Before Angela could scream, the attacker sealed her mouth shut with duct tape. She flailed and kicked but he held her in an iron grip.

They hadn't seen it coming.

Angela and Alex had been waiting outside Locanda del Cerriglio, on the cobblestoned street. The taxi had never shown up, so Alex had suggested walking to the main road.

Her worst nightmare was coming true.

Terrified, her gaze flew to Alex. The attackers had flanked him on either side. Alex pulled his gun, but a third figure leaped from a shadowy corner and kicked it out of his hand.

The tape made it hard to breathe, let alone scream for help. It was claustrophobic. Angela fought against a wave of dizziness. A rush of wind drowned out the sounds of grunts and punches. She closed her eyes to regain her equilibrium. When she opened them again, everything before her had shifted.

Time had decelerated like a slow-motion replay.

A ghostly apparition of Caravaggio emerged beside Alex.

It seemed impossible, and yet she was witnessing Alex fighting with the thugs in the present and Caravaggio battling his attackers in the past.

Both Alex and Caravaggio were powerful fighters, but they were outnumbered, and when Angela saw the glint of knife blades, bile rose in her throat.

History is repeating itself. Please, God, save him.

Panic seized her. She struggled to break free from the thug holding her. Caravaggio had sustained horrifying wounds when he was ambushed outside of Osteria de Cerriglio. His face had been completely disfigured, and it took him six months to recover. He may have been blinded in one eye. He only produced two paintings after the attack. Both were shadows of his former brilliance…

Alex!

The blades sliced through the air and cut the flesh on Alex and Caravaggio's faces. Angela's scream was muffled by the tape. Blood gushed from their wounds, their yells of pain reverberated off the stone walls.

Waves of nausea gripped Angela.

Alex and Caravaggio hit the ground, their arms raised defensively against the onslaught of kicks that followed. The thugs were merciless, beating Alex and Caravaggio brutally, until they were curled up in fetal positions on the blood-soaked cobblestones.

With a mighty heave, Angela finally broke away from her attacker, throwing herself over Alex's motionless body. Using herself as a shield, she braced for the coming kicks that were sure to land on her.

Alex, I'm here. I'm here. Don't leave me…

Like a mantra, she repeated her thoughts over and over again. One single thought possessed her—protect Alex.

Caravaggio was lying beside him.

The tear in the fabric of time closed once more, Caravaggio faded into the past.

Time sped up again.

Singing voices floated out to her. Drunken, singing voices. Bewildered, she glanced up and saw two men staggering into the alley with their arms around each other's shoulders. They were tipsy, stumbling forward, completely unaware of what lay ahead.

The attackers scattered and Angela's muffled sobs echoed in the alley.

Alex, moaned her name, clutching his ribcage, twisting in agony. The painter was gone. She was alone with Alex.

Footsteps pounded toward them.

Naples, Italy
Ospedale Loreto Mare
Present day

Angela fought to keep her eyes open.

Beside her, Alex was sleeping, thanks to the painkillers the nurse had given him. Resting her head on his hand, dozing off and on, jumping awake whenever he stirred.

Everything after the attack in the alley was a blur. The drunken singers, two men who spoke very little English with an accent that she couldn't identify, had run back to the restaurant to get help. In the confusion, they disappeared before she could thank them. Minutes later an ambulance arrived. She and Alex were rushed to the hospital. Since her Italian wasn't up to par, she'd called the Vesuvio hotel, and they were kind enough to send an interpreter to help her.

Alex's fingers moved. Angela raised her head and whispered, "Alex, come back to me."

He smiled through cracked, swollen lips. He tried to speak, but all that came out was an unintelligible rasp.

"Let me get you some water, baby." She filled a cup from the pitcher on the bedside table, adding a straw, raising it to his lips so he could sip without undo strain.

"Angela," he croaked. "You need to rest."

Tears welled in her eyes. Of course, that would be his first thought. He was worried about her and not himself. "I'm fine, Alex. Right now, the only thing that matters is you. Don't worry about me."

"That's my girl." His smile turned into a wince. He raised his fingers to touch the bandage on his face. "What's the verdict?"

"You have a concussion and a hairline fractured rib, which they tell me will be painful for the next week."

"Only when I laugh." He laughed and groaned.

"You have a doozy of a bump on the back of your noggin. I had them bring in a plastic surgeon to stitch the laceration on your face from the knife attack. Another millimeter and—." Her hand flew to her mouth, muffling a sob that threatened to bubble up.

"Hey, hey, it's okay, baby." He squeezed her other hand.

"I'm s-sorry. But I was so s-scared I was going to lose you."

"As you can see, it's gonna take a lot more than a few assholes to get rid of me."

She gave him a watery smile.

"Shit. Did I land any punches at least? I can't remember a thing."

"I think you broke one of their noses and another guy's male plumbing is probably out of commission."

"That makes it hurt a little less." Alex lifted her hand and kissed it. "How are you, sweetheart? That bastard didn't hurt you, did he?"

"No, I'm fine. A couple of guys came along and scared them off. Both you and Caravaggio were down for the count."

"Caravaggio?" he groaned.

"I had a vision during the attack. It was the eeriest thing…"

"That's saying something. What happened?"

"There were two fights in that alley, you in the present and Caravaggio in the past. You both took a beating and were slashed with a knife at the same time."

"Except, it wasn't at the same time."

"No. Thank God, you weren't wounded as badly as Caravaggio. He never recovered."

"There's another difference," Alex said. "We know who attacked Caravaggio, but we have no idea who got to me or what they wanted. They didn't kill me, and they could have. This was a warning. If this is about the painting, we need to reconsider what we're doing and how we're doing it."

"I know. I'm done with all of this. I don't care about the painting. I care about you."

"Angela, you need to get some rest. Call the hotel and have them send a car for you. Tomorrow we'll figure everything out. I'm not staying in this hospital. We'll fly back to Rome. I want to talk with Spinelli."

"I'm not leaving you."

"I insist you go back to the hotel or I'm getting out of this bed right now and taking you back myself."

"Alex, you can't. You're all wired up." She pointed to the drip and monitors. "Besides, what if you have another PTSD attack? You need to rest."

"Angela, I'm not going to have another PTSD attack. I know you're worried, and I'm sorry I haven't exactly been an open book when it comes to my PTSD. If you go back to the hotel, you can be my Mother Theresa and hear all my confessions, forever and ever. Just promise me you'll always forgive my sins."

"This is no time for jokes. I'm scared to leave you alone."

"Please, go back to the hotel and rest," he said, kissing her hand again. "I'll survive until morning. I promise. We'll both get a better night's sleep. Okay?"

She sighed. "Okay, but I'll be back here first thing in the morning, *capeesh?*"

"*Capeesh.*"

CHAPTER 23

Cavallo Island
Strait of Bonafacio
Present day

"Bring her to me."

"The girl, you want the art girl?" Arturo's voice echoed through the speaker.

"Yes. Do it fast and cover your tracks," Antonio replied, rolling the marbles over his knuckles. He'd spent the last few hours reviewing a dossier on the detective and the art historian. What he discovered only intensified his desire to meet Angela Renatus. He couldn't stop thinking about her. He had to act now, while the macho detective was in the hospital.

"As you wish, Don Antonio."

"And don't harm a hair on her head. The yacht is waiting for you in the port. Don't waste time, like the Roman job."

"Waste time? We had car trouble."

"Car trouble," Antonio snorted. "You and Vincenzo picked up a couple of whores."

"Did Vincenzo tell you that?"

"Yes, he bragged about it."

"That *cazzo* has a big fucking mouth."

"Well, make sure he keeps his dick in his pants. It'll take you eight hours to cross on the boat. Any longer and I'll cut off both your dicks."

Vesuvio Hotel
Present day

Angela checked her watch. Visiting hours at the hospital would start soon. She'd spent a miserable night without Alex, tossing and turning. She'd woken up twice in a cold sweat, her hair matted and pasted to her head, unable to fill her lungs and catch her breath. She kept reliving over and over again the nightmarish attack in the alleyway.

Even the hot shower hadn't relieved her anxiety.

One night apart and I miss him so much.

He'd recover, but it was her fault he'd bear a scar. He'd warned her it was dangerous to tangle with the Mafia. And she had insisted. Her need to put the past to rest, her need to recover the painting, and her need to correct history. How could she have been so selfish?

But if we don't solve this mystery, Alex might be plagued by nightmares the rest of his life.

There'd been no way to avoid the Cosa Nostra. They were behind the theft. Mafia families have always existed under a thin veil of legality, enabling them to maintain their hold on all sectors of society, even the police. Especially the police. They owed allegiance to their own and had an army of trained assassins at their beck and call. One of those powerful families had the *Nativity* and they weren't going to give it up. Eliminating her and Alex would be nothing to them, and it would dissuade others from trying to retrieve it.

No more!

She had a fiancé to love, three rambunctious dogs to spoil, a gazillion more meals to savor, and a wedding to avoid planning. The best thing to do was turn their research over to Lieutenant Spinelli. Let *him* figure out how to get the painting back. Because of their investigative work, Spinelli now knew the painting was on the Island of Cavallo. It was up to the authorities to retrieve it. Even Celestine, who was desperate for the masterpiece to be returned to the world, wouldn't want Angela and Alex to risk their lives any more than they already had.

A cab pulled up the second she stepped out the door of the hotel.

No sense waiting for the hotel car to drive me.

She jumped in and the taxi sped away. Her sense of direction was topsy-turvy, getting around Naples was confusing to say the least. It was several minutes before she realized the cab wasn't headed for the hospital.

She tapped on the plastic divider.

"*Scusa, dove andiamo?* Take me to the *l'ospedale!*" The driver's silence was her only reply as he nodded at her in the rear-view mirror.

What's going on here?

The cab screeched to a halt and she flew forward against the plastic partition, hitting her head. Before she regained her senses, two men jumped in on either side of her. She fought, scratching one brute's face. He reacted ruthlessly, slapping her so hard her head snapped back, and her cheekbone struck the other man's shoulder. She cried out, her hand covering her cheek. Suddenly, the muzzle of a gun pressed against her ribcage.

I'm in big trouble, now.

"Sit back, *signorina*, and behave yourself, or I'm going to teach you a lesson you'll never forget."

She tried to mask her fear by lowering her voice. "You need to let me go."

"Sit back, bitch. My orders are to deliver you in one piece to the boss. A few bruises won't make a difference to him. *Capisci?*"

Angela shrank into the seat and looked out the window of the cab. She was trying to hold it together. The windows were rolled up, and if she screamed, who'd hear? If they wanted to kill her, they'd have done it already. Alex would go crazy when he realized she'd gone missing. Nothing in the world would stop him from finding her.

Breathe in. Breathe out. Keep your wits about you.

She thought she was done with the painting, but the painting wasn't done with her. A premonition sent a chill through her...

They're taking me to the painting, and the man who has it.

Where the hell is she?

Angela never showed up. Alex tried calling her cell many times, it went to voice mail.

Something's dead wrong.

Frantic with worry, he called the hotel. They checked their security cameras and reported her last sighting. She'd gotten into a taxi outside the hotel. The hotel was less than ten minutes from the hospital, and yet she never made it.

She's been kidnapped.

There was no question in his mind—first the attack in the alley and then Angela suddenly goes missing.

Fuck! The attack was a set-up to get me out of the way.

He called the police, but they were of no help. A missing person needed to be missing for twenty-four hours before they could open an investigation. He called Salvatore Spinelli in Rome and he agreed something was amiss.

211

Alex told the Lieutenant he and Angela suspected the *Nativity* was on the island of Cavallo. "Are there any Mafioso on the island?"

"Cavallo is a French protectorate, I'll make some calls. We'll get their cooperation."

"I'm checking out of this hospital, now. I'm going after her, but I could use some help."

"Let me make some arrangements. I'll call you back."

Alex hung up and made the call he dreaded. "I can't explain everything right now, but Angela is missing."

"What the hell happened to my daughter?"

"We were assaulted last night. Angela was unharmed, but I was beaten up pretty good. They held me overnight at the hospital and she went back to the hotel to sleep. This morning she was on her way to me when she disappeared. We have to assume she's been kidnapped. I've already got the police working on it, but this is going to take some time. I promise you I'm going to find her. I'm sorry. It's my fault."

"What are you talking about, son?" Oliver barked out. "Why is it your fault? And where the hell are you?"

"Naples, we're in Naples. I was out of it last night and she was exhausted. I made her go back to the hotel to get some rest. A hotel car picked her up last night and I assumed she'd have them bring her back here in the morning. I saw the video footage, she jumped in a cab that pulled up the second she stepped out of the hotel. Security cameras caught the whole thing on video."

"Oh, my God. Who the hell would kidnap her, and for what?"

"The Mafia."

"The Mafia! Why?"

"We've been on the trail of a painting. A painting stolen by the Cosa Nostra. Last night at dinner we figured out the painting is on a small island in the Mediterranean. It's a haven for the super-wealthy, an island called Cavallo—"

"I'm going to get to you as fast as I can," Oliver interrupted.

"There are only two ways to get to Cavallo. Either by helicopter or boat. The island is about two hundred and fifty nautical miles off the coast of Naples. That's about an eight-hour crossing. The good news is, the kidnappers can't get there much faster than we can."

"Can we fly?"

"The closest airports are in Sardinia and Corsica. It would take too long, we'd have to charter a boat from one of those two locations."

"I'm going to enlist Natalia's help. She has connections, underworld connections. We're going to need all the help we can get."

"Agreed. I've already called the TPC, Italy's art police. Angela and I have been working with them." Alex dragged his fingers through his hair. "I'm so sorry, Oliver. I swore to you I'd keep her safe and I failed. I don't deserve her."

"Alex, pull yourself together. It's not your fault. The only thing that matters is finding her and getting her back."

"Yeah, you're right. Let me get the hell out of this fucking hospital. Call me as soon as you speak to Russian Octopussy."

Global Bombardier 6 500
Present day

Where is she?

Oliver gazed out the window of Natalia's private jet, his fingers gripped the armrest. Natalia sat in the forward cabin, admonishing someone on the phone in Russian. She hung up and a slew of Russian curses filled the air. She got up and joined him in the mid-cabin. The plane was luxurious, and definitely not a rental. Whatever Natalia did, it was extremely lucrative and most likely illegal.

Natalia laid her hand over his. "You did the right thing, Oliver, calling me. I will do whatever it takes to rescue Angela. My yacht is ready to sail, and we'll leave as soon as we're aboard. I might as well tell you, I have a Russian spetsnaz team that work for me. They're skilled in high-risk military operations and experts in extractions. They'll get Angela out, I promise you."

Oliver's gaze strayed to Natalia's hand on his. Her touch awakened memories he'd thought he'd buried. He pulled his hand away. "I just hope we're not too late."

"Call it a mother's intuition, but I know she is alive."

"When she was a little girl, she asked me all about you," Oliver whispered. "I told her you were a Russian princess whose family had cast her out when you decided to marry me. She started to cry when I told her that. Such a tender-hearted girl. She'd ask me if you were sad after you left your family. I told her you were so happy, every day you would rub your belly and smile and say, 'All I need is you and Angela.'" He looked away, pretending not to see the tears in Natalia's eyes. "I told her you'd died giving birth to her, that you loved her more than anything in this world. I filled her head with lies and now everything's come full circle."

"You didn't lie completely. You and Angela were all I needed."

Oliver's laugh was laced with bitterness. "Not hardly. You wouldn't have had all of this." His chin jutted out, pointing at the dark, plush leather and rare wood interior of the cabin. "What do you really do for a living?" The question had been eating at him ever since they boarded the jet.

"I deal in art... and other things. Leave it at that, Oliver. The less you know the better. I'm not ashamed of what I've done. I'm good at it." She paused, studying him. "Things were very hard for me when I left you. I've told you already, even though you don't believe me, I left to protect you and Angela. The SVR made me pay for my insubordination." Her eyes became hard and flinty. "It took me years, but I made *them* pay."

He nodded, drumming his fingers on the side table. Now was not the time to argue with Natalia or probe into things long dead. What good would it do to tell her they could have fought the SVR together and found a way to elude them. She left because she didn't believe he could protect her. It gnawed at him, but he had to let it go. He hadn't expected the rush of emotion her touch evoked in him. It angered him that he still had feelings for her. What was even worse was the realization that she had power over him after all this time.

"Oliver, we left so quickly, did you call Alex and tell him where to meet us?"

"Shit!" He grabbed his cell from his jacket and punched in Alex's number. "Alex? I have you on speaker with Natalia. We're on our way to Naples."

"What's your ETA?"

Natalia broke in. "Two hours."

"Natalia—thanks for giving Oliver a lift to Naples. What can you do to help us?"

"I have a fully equipped spetsnaz team on stand-by, experts in rescue and extraction, a yacht fitted with modern weaponry, an inflatable naval dinghy for special ops beach landings, an armory loaded with every firearm imaginable, and a Blackhawk helicopter. Not to mention, the jet Oliver and I are flying in on. What do you have, Alex?"

Her question was greeted with silence.

"Alex, are you there?" Oliver frowned at Natalia. What wasn't needed was dissention between Alex and Natalia. They were all in this together.

"I'm here, Oliver. Natalia, I guess Lance told you I was a Navy SEAL."
"Yes, Alex, I'm well aware."

"Your Russian special forces team isn't going in without me. Do I make myself clear?"

"*Dahrahgohy*, darling, but Oliver told me you were attacked and injured. Perhaps you should leave this to my men."

"I'm not your darling, Natalia. Thank you for your concern, but I'm not going to sit back while others risk their lives to save the woman I love."

"Suit yourself, I have no problem with you joining the team. We both want the same thing, Alex. My daughter."

"It's a little late for the daughter thing. If you really care about Angela, you'll disappear once she's safely back in my arms."

Natalia and Oliver's eyes were locked on one another. "I'm not disappearing because of you, Alex. I'm doing it for Oliver. He's the only one I owe a debt of gratitude. When I know Angela is safe, I'll disappear."

"Good enough. By the way, Angela and I have been working with Lieutenant Salvatore Spinelli at TCP on a case."

"Really, what case?"

"I'm sure you know about the Caravaggio painting that was stolen fifty years ago from a church in Palermo. The authorities have always believed it was the Mafia who took it. Angela figured out it's on Cavallo."

"Do we know which house?"

"Spinelli should have that information for me, shortly. He's checking the property ownership records. A process of elimination should narrow it down. Of course, the Mafia makes it a far riskier enterprise."

"Whether it's Mafia or not makes no difference to my men. They take their orders from me. Go to the port, Alex, and locate the yacht *The Delilah*. I've cleared you to board. Victor, my right hand, will see to whatever you require. Body armor, weapons, whatever you need."

"Thank you, Natalia. If you help me get Angela back, I'll be in your debt."

"I like a man who doesn't mince words, so I won't mince mine. I will disappear once Angela is safe, but you and Oliver will never mention me or my team to the authorities. We don't exist. We were never here."

"And what about how Oliver and I got to Cavallo?"

"You called in a favor and were sworn to secrecy. You're not the enemy, Alex. They won't question your honesty."

"Oliver, you know we're making a deal with the devil. You're good with this?"

"I am. It's the only way, Alex. We'll find Angela and she'll never know her mother is still alive."

Oliver knew it sickened Alex to lie to Angela, not to mention the authorities— but there was no way around it.

"It seems I have no choice." Alex said.

"Good. We'll see you aboard *The Delilah*, Alex."

CHAPTER 24

Cavallo Island
Strait of Bonifacio
Present day

It would be hard for Angela to imagine a place more serene or beautiful than Cavallo. The water was crystal clear, translucent as glass. White sandy beaches glittered, catching the bright sun. The house was perched on a rock promontory above the sand in a secluded cove, where sculptured monoliths of granite rose above the water like sentries, protecting the privacy of the home's dwellers. The manor, with its slate roof and stone face, blended in with the landscape, unobtrusive, almost hidden.

Her captors escorted Angela to shore in a tender. They led her to a side entrance of the house. At the end of a long hallway, they opened a door and pushed her inside.

From their minimal conversation and her minimal Italian, she'd gathered this area was separate from the main house. The room was dark, without windows. Empty, except for a canopied bed, end table, clock, and bathroom. Thick carpeting covered the floor and the walls were lined with wood paneling. Without being able to test her theory, she knew the room was soundproof.

There was nothing for her to do. The kidnappers had taken her phone and smashed it, removing the SIM card before locking her in the room. Her life was in the hands of whomever had ordered her abduction. Exhausted and anxious, she kicked off her shoes and fell onto the bed. She needed a nap to revitalize her strength, before facing whatever came next.

Her eyes fluttered closed, her breathing deepened, and a portal opened. She floated through, a pulse of energy, synapsing between the past and present into another dimension. She settled onto a rich, red velvet coverlet. The scent of burning wax and herbs couldn't hide the pungent odor of rotting flesh. In the bed lay a man she barely recognized. Swollen red welts and crude stitches distorted his face. He reminded Angela of Frankenstein's monster. His eyes were closed, and his chest rose only slightly with each shallow breath. Waves of pity rolled through her and tears pricked her eyes. Above the heavily carved headboard hung a crucifix of gold. From what she could see, it brought no solace to the man suffering beneath it.

Her hand was ghostly and without warmth, but her desire to bring comfort to the painter compelled her to try. She rested her hand on his —he trembled, his eyes fluttered open, and a smile graced his lips. "My prayers have been answered. I didn't want to leave this world without seeing you one last time, Fillide."

"I've come a long way to be with you, Caravaggio. I haven't forgotten you or the promises we made to each other. I hold them within my heart, and they light the darkness of my days," she whispered. "You must try to recover for me. I had a dream, one day we'd be together."

"Look at me, Fillide. I was never a handsome man, but now I'm a monster. I'm half-blind and see the world through a fog. Fillide, look at my hand," he lifted his left hand. "I tremble like an old woman. This would be acceptable for most, but I am a painter. How will I work when I can't see, and my hand can't hold a brush?"

"You will recover enough to paint again. Don't ask me how I know, but I do. Please, Caravaggio, come back to me?"

In his dark eyes she could see a speck of light. She knew more than anything, he wanted to believe. "I've heard rumors, you're to be pardoned by the pope. Think about Rome and me, both of us await your return."

He inhaled the deepest breath and a kernel of hope took root within her. Her heart was breaking for this man, who'd spent his whole life seeking love and respect. His distorted dreams of honor had produced nothing but turmoil in his life.

"Is it possible, after all I have done? All that I've been through, I might be forgiven?"

"I pray you believe. God has a purpose for us all. I believe you have learned your lesson." She chuckled. "You've learned the hard way, but it doesn't matter so long as we learn. We are all equal in the eyes of God."

"If I can still hold a brush and see the canvas, then I can paint."

"Yes, you can. Now you must rest, gather your strength, and fight another day. We will see each other again, if God allows."

"Knowing you are beside me in all that I do, gives me reason enough to live. I believe we will see each other again, Fillide."

How she wanted to comfort him, to tell him it was true. It would take more than 400 years, but Caravaggio would be reborn as Alex, and Fillide as Angela. Knowing the future and what was to come, she held her tongue. For the time being, at least, there was something for the tortured genius to hold on to.

If only you could see what I see, Caravaggio…

He sighed, drifting off to sleep, she hoped he'd find peace from his suffering… The hands of time were already pulling her away, back to the present. Back to her own undetermined fate.

Alex, have we suffered through so many lifetimes only to lose each other once more?

"Angela…" A gruff voice called out to her, and with a whoosh of air, the years roared past her—triumphal and tragic moments of past lives, spinning around her like a falling deck of cards, plummeting her back into her earthly body.

"Finally. You're here," the man's voice said.

She opened her eyes and looked around. The scent of candles was gone. It took her a moment to focus. When her eyes adjusted to the dim light, she saw a man seated on the edge of the bed, observing her.

"I'm amazed, given the circumstances, that you could rest so peacefully," the stranger said.

She sensed no threat from the man. "Sometimes the world slips away from me. Why am I here?"

"I've been impatient to meet you, and now that you're here I don't know where to begin."

Her heartbeat kicked up, sending the blood rushing to her head in a burst of awareness. She sat up. "You have it."

He nodded.

Fear took hold of her and her forehead grew damp. He could easily wipe her off the face of the earth. "What do you want?"

"I want something only you can give me."

Her brows furrowed. "What could I possibly give you, I'm your prisoner."

"I prefer to think of you as my guest. If you answer my questions, it's possible we can come to a satisfying resolution. I have no burning desire to hurt you."

"You're not what I imagined a Mafioso to be like."

219

"Ah, yes, well I've always been an enigma. That's why I'm the boss. I operate differently than most of my predecessors… Would you like to see it?"

"Yes."

"Come with me."

He helped her up and she followed him out the door where one of the thugs stood watch. She shrank back. The boss spoke in rapid Italian and the man stepped away from her. She hadn't thought to ask the boss his name, she was afraid to even know it. She followed the man who held her captive down the hallway.

They entered the main house, the sound of children giggling floated out to her. A young boy and girl lounged on the sofa watching TV. "*Zio* Tony," the dark-haired children shouted in unison.

"Your kids?" Angela asked.

"*Zio* means uncle. My niece, Clarissa's daughter and son." He addressed the children. "Hey, *dove sono le tue buone maniere?* Where are your manners? Say hello to the pretty lady."

The children scampered to their feet and bowed and curtsied. In Italian they greeted Angela.

"*Piacere.*" She smiled.

Zio Tony continued through the room. She glanced out the window to the blazing splash of colors that glittered beyond the panes of glass. The clear-watered sea reflected the yellow, gold, and reds of the setting sun.

"Are they on vacation for the holidays?"

"No, they live with me." His features softened. "My niece died a month ago. I'm raising them now."

"Oh… I'm sorry."

"Sorry for her loss, or sorry that I'm raising them?" he chuckled.

"For you and the children's loss. Your wife must be very kind."

"No wife."

Before she could reply he opened a door and waited for her to enter. Shutting the door behind her, he walked down another hallway and stopped at another door. He punched in a set of numbers on a touchpad and the door unlocked. Keeping her head about her, Angela memorized the code. Again, he waved her through. The room was dark, and she didn't move. *Zio* Tony hit a switch and the room was bathed in a warm, soft light. "Sit down," he commanded.

The sofa faced a large partner desk of heavy mahogany. He clicked a remote on the desk, and an innocuous landscape painting on the wall slowly rose, disappearing into the ceiling.

Angela gasped in awe. Before her was the painting that had eluded authorities for the last fifty years—the *Nativity* in all of its glory hung before her. It was breathtaking and stole her ability to speak. The room was temperature-controlled, and the lighting was professional museum quality. Sunlight is damaging to paint, and yet she sensed the window shutters always remained closed. The painting was in perfect condition. In truth, better than it would have been hanging in the Oratory of San Lorenzo.

"You look surprised, Angela. Did you believe all the myths about rats and pigs dining on the *Nativity*?" He laughed. "Or the story of it being hidden in an outhouse, or used as a rug beside some Don's bed?"

"I'm just speechless. It's so beautiful and I wasn't sure I'd ever see it in person. I'm grateful you've taken such good care of it."

He stared at it with reverence. "It's my most prized possession. "

Her eyes widened at his comment, and laughter rumbled in his chest. "What? You don't think a crime boss can be cultured."

"May I... get closer?"

He nodded. She rose from the sofa and walked around the desk. She studied the brushwork, the faces, the placement of the ensemble, and the message Caravaggio had meant to convey. Once again, she wondered about the blond young man in the painting, his back to the viewer, who questioned Joseph. Art historians had always been puzzled by the unidentified youth.

"Tell me, Angela, do you believe in life after death?"

She was taken aback. "Do you mean as in the Christian belief of heaven and eternal life?" Even as the words slipped from her lips, she knew what his answer would be.

"No. I'm asking about reincarnation. I'm asking about the notion of past lives, present lives, and future lives. The question has plagued me since Clarissa's death."

"Are you hoping to see her again?"

"Yes."

A wave of relief washed over her. He was fishing. He'd loved his niece and wanted to believe there was something more than a final goodbye. "I don't know. I've never given it any thought."

"You're lying. Please, don't lie to me. It insults my intelligence. I know about the da Vinci. I've read Enrico Fortuna's testimony. I've studied you. I need you to be honest with me."

She nodded. It was senseless to lie to him. "I not only believe in past lives, I've seen them in visions and dreams."

The release of his breath hung in the air between them. "I knew you'd understand." His gaze returned to the painting. "She's beautiful, the Madonna, isn't she?"

"Caravaggio painted with great love and respect to women."

"Let me show you something." He walked to his desk and opened a drawer. He removed a tooled, leather-bound album. "Come, sit with me."

She followed him to the sofa and he carefully opened the album. She watched as he turned the pages. The album began with a much younger Tony, his black hair, thick and wavy. He held a beautiful infant with wisps of auburn hair that peeked from beneath her bonnet. It was the baby's Christening and Tony must have been named the infant's godfather. The photos that followed chronicled the little girl's life through her teens.

At her college graduation it was Tony standing and beaming with pride beside her. Photographs marked the passage of years in a series of family events—birthdays, parties, and holiday photos of the girl with Tony. She grew into a beautiful woman.

Clarissa's wedding was an elegant formal affair. She looked dazzling in her white *peau de soie* gown with its pearl encrusted bodice. Tony began to turn the page, but Angela stopped him with her hand. The photo had captured Tony, standing to one side with a crooked smile that didn't reach his eyes. He stood watching as the handsome dark-haired groom made a toast to his bride. What held Angela's interest was the bride.

It wasn't entirely clear, and most people wouldn't have picked up on it, but Angela saw the world through an art historian's lens. To her discerning eye a photo was even easier. In the photograph, Clarissa looked past the groom—her gaze locked on Tony. Clarissa's eyes were filled with love.

He was in love with her... and she with him.

Tony turned the page and Angela froze. A picture of Clarissa gazing down at her newborn son...

Angela's eyes flew to the *Nativity*. There could be no mistaking it. The Madonna in the painting gazing down at her newborn son...

"You see it too, don't you?"

"Yes." Her voice was only a decibel above a whisper.

"You understand, then, what this painting means to me. Why I would do anything to keep it."

She swallowed the lump in her throat. Unable to speak, she nodded.

"*Bene*. Now tell me what you know about reincarnation. I need to understand everything."

CHAPTER 25

The Delilah
Strait of Bonifacio
Cavallo Island
Present day

His only desire was to hold Angela in his arms again.

Alex stared across the bow of *The Delilah* as she plowed through the waves of the Tyrrhenian Sea. He wasn't psychic like Angela, but his connection to her was strong...

I'm on my way, baby.

Lieutenant Spinelli had located a house on Cavallo owned by a Sicilian trust. Salvatore was good, he'd managed to secure the original building permits and architectural plans for the house, which gave them a good working knowledge of the layout. The property had an auxiliary annex off the main building—Alex focused his attention there. If you wanted a secure area to hold a prisoner this was where you'd put them.

It had been several years since Alex had dressed for a special ops' operation, and the memories of those missions were dangerous to recall. He couldn't afford to be drawn into a PTSD attack or let horrifying memories cloud his mind, so he concentrated on Victor, the man leading the rescue mission.

Victor had served in the Russian military in some of the most dangerous places in the world. He was eventually recruited by the SVR as a special agent, meeting Anastasia on a mission. Alex surmised they were lovers— the muscled giant with a blond crew-cut and square jaw was devoted to Anastasia. Victor took Alex under his wing, and Alex felt an immediate kinship to the mercenary.

Victor was a man's man with a cryptic sense of humor, he enjoyed a good story. They'd exchanged a few highlights from their military service. As far as Alex could tell the only thing Anastasia hadn't confided in him was her relationship to Angela. Victor was under the impression that Anastasia owed Oliver a favor and rescuing his kidnapped daughter would cancel the debt.

Alex's reception by the spetsnaz team had been cool to indifferent, but Victor had assured him they'd deliver when things got down and dirty. They were professionals, and Anastasia had made it clear that the point of this operation was to free Angela. They were very well paid to carry out whatever Anastasia asked of them.

The Delilah was a floating arsenal. A sleek, gray mega-yacht outfitted as a warship. Victor showed him around, bragging about all the bells and whistles. From the armory Alex was given his choice of weapons and he opted for a MK-16 assault rifle and a Sig Sauer P226 pistol with suppressor, both of which he'd used as a SEAL.

In the wardrobe room he found everything from camouflage uniforms to black Ninja suits with balaclava helmets. The raid was planned for midnight, so he went with the all black uniform. By the time he'd finished with tactical equipment, arms, and uniform, Victor informed him that Oliver and Anastasia were on board.

He followed Victor to the main deck—Anastasia and Oliver were having a cocktail. Since neither of them were going to shore, a drink was probably in order. Oliver was wound tighter than a drum, a drink might calm his nerves. He'd drink too, if he was in the older man's shoes.

"Alex," Oliver jumped up and shook his hand, then pulled Alex in for a hug. "Good to see you son. If only Angela was here too—" he choked out. "I'm going out of my mind."

Alex wished he could relieve the worry of a father for his child. All he could offer was reassurance. "We'll find her, Oliver, I promise you."

"I know—I know."

Anastasia threaded her fingers through Oliver's. "Alex is right," she said in a comforting voice. "You need to believe and stay positive. We'll find her."

Oliver nodded and squeezed her hand. "You've met Anastasia, of course."

Alex felt the gut-punch of guilt. Angela would never know the joy of seeing her parents together. "Yes, we've had the pleasure. Quite a rig you have here, Anastasia."

"It serves its purpose."

"I bet it does. Where do you keep it in the winter?"

"Normally, I send *The Delilah* to St. Bart's in the Caribbean, however, this year I'm thinking the Maldives. I know what you're thinking, Alex. I'll be gone once Angela is safe. I promise you."

"It has to be this way. For Angela's sake, this is the best outcome."

Victor cut the engine of the inflatable naval dinghy and two members of the spetsnaz team jumped into the water and pulled the boat to shore, beaching it on the sand. They'd chosen a spot behind an outcropping of granite beyond the purview of the stone and glass house, silhouetted against the star-filled sky. They huddled together in silence, each man bent low, leaning forward, their positions a switchblade ready to snap open.

When the moon slipped behind a cloud, Alex and the team ran up the beach. Their faces and hands blackened with camouflage, giving them the appearance of animated shadows. The imprint of their footsteps disappeared in the small waves breaking upon the shore, washing away the proof of their presence. In synchronization, two at a time, the men broke away leaving only Alex and Victor. The well-trained team worked like clockwork together, each man knowing his role.

He and Victor jogged toward an annex off the main house. A guard stood sentry, smoking a cigarette. Victor signaled, pointing to his watch. He opened and closed his hands three times, indicating a count of thirty. Alex ran wide avoiding the guard, bringing him to the sentries' rear. Noting the time, he counted to five, and crept toward the man's back.

Quick as lightning, he brought his arm around the man's neck and applied the carotid choke hold, cutting off his ability to breathe. The guard struggled to break free, but without oxygen traveling to and from the brain, hypoxia kicked in and his body slumped, unconscious. Alex lowered him to the ground and Victor joined him. Together they zip-tied the guard's hands and feet and taped his mouth shut. Victor inserted a tension wrench and a rake into the door lock—with a turn and twist the door opened. They dragged the guard into the entry and left him.

Alex peeked around the corner into a dimly lit hallway. At the end of the hall, another guard sat on a chair, his head resting against the back wall, his eyes closed and his breathing even. Without making a sound, Alex and Victor ran down the hall. The guard's eyes opened and he reached across his chest to pull his gun from his shoulder harness, but he didn't see the glint of the hypodermic. Before the gun could be aimed, Victor stabbed him in his neck. The guard's eyes opened wide and he struggled to catch his breath.

He toppled to the floor. Victor ran ahead to the last door in the hall, his gun drawn, he nodded back at Alex.

Alex aimed his suppressed hand gun and shot the knob off, then threw his weight against the door, flinging it open. Angela sat up, clutching the sheet to her chest, her eyes wide with fear.

"Angela, baby, it's me, Alex."

"Alex!" She was on her feet running to him and he opened his arms to her trembling body. She repeated over and over again, "Oh, Alex, I knew you'd come for me. I've been so frightened."

"You're fine, baby, it will all be over soon. Look at me?" Her big brown eyes looked up at his. "We've got to get out of here, okay?"

"The *Nativity*, Alex, it's here—" before she finished the sentence an explosion rocked the building, followed by an acrid smell of smoke. "Oh my God, what's that?"

"I don't know, but I've got to get you out of here."

"We have to get the painting. It'll be destroyed, if we don't."

"I don't care about the painting."

"Alex, please. I'll take you to it." She slipped on her shoes and ran out the door with Alex on her heels. Angela stumbled when she saw Victor, but Alex whispered, "He's with me."

Victor had already gotten the door open and they passed through into the main house. Angela stopped dead in her tracks. "I smell smoke."

Screams resounded from different directions along with the sputtering of gun fire. "Take us to the painting."

Both Alex and Victor held their guns ready and followed Angela through the living room into another hallway. The smoke was thicker now, and all three covered their noses and mouths, trying to breathe through their fingers.

Angela stopped at a door with a keypad on the jamb. Hissing and crackling emanated from the other side of the door. "I think we're too late," shouted Alex.

"Maybe we can get it out," she cried. She punched in a series of numbers. After a click she wrenched on the door knob and threw open the door. Smoke billowed out. The room was an inferno. The roar of the fire, a tornado whizzing toward them. The heat drove all three back with their arms raised, protecting their faces.

Alex shouted above the conflagration. "Nothing we can do." He held fast to Angela's arm, afraid she might do something crazy.

"The painting's behind the desk," she shouted. But Alex couldn't see anything beyond the wall of smoke that rushed toward them. He grabbed her, dragging her away. Angela struggled against his grip, irrational at this point. Alex figured the painting was never meant to be found.

So be it. Angela's life is the only thing that matters.

Angela's fingers tore into him. "The children, there are children in the house, a girl and a boy. We have to save them."

"Do you know where they are?"

"Second floor, it has to be."

Alex shouted to Victor who'd remained vigilant and had stayed with them. "Take her outside and watch her. I'll find the kids." Alex ran toward the front of the house and spied a staircase. Muffled cries reached his ears. He ran up the stairs and down the hall toward a row of doors. The fire hadn't reached the upper level of the house yet, but the smoke was getting stronger by the minute and it was only a matter of time before the fire would claim the entire house. He opened the first door and found a girl of about ten-years-old, crouching in a corner, clinging to a doll. She was terrified, struggling to breathe through her sobs. Alex swept her up in his arms and soothed her in Italian. He ran out of the bedroom with her and nearly ran into a swarthy man carrying a young boy. For a second, the two men stared at each other. Anger and fear glinted in the man's eyes. His voice was gruff and accusing, "What the hell is going on, for the love of Christ? Who are you?" His anger turned to recognition. "You're the detective, Angela's detective."

Alex wondered at the familiarity in the crime boss's voice when he said Angela's name. "There's no time to explain. Is there anyone else in the house? We need to get out of here!" The children were choking and coughing, burying their faces in each man's chest.

The man's gaze swept from the girl to the boy and he shook his head. "Everyone else ran out."

They rushed down the stairs, Alex's heart pounded in his chest when he glanced toward the living room. The room was completely ablaze, the screeching flames consuming everything in their wake. The two men ran for the front doors.

Outside, Alex spotted multiple figures on the shore and ran toward them. The Mafioso followed him. A helicopter touched down, its rotors still spinning, drowning out everything but the shouting of armed men. Angela ran to him and the young girl reached for her. She took her from Alex and the girl wrapped her arms and legs around Angela's waist and buried her face in her neck.

Lieutenant Spinelli alit from the helicopter and ran to them. "The painting, Angela, did you find it?"

A look passed between her and Antonio. She turned toward the smoldering house. "No. What I saw was an excellent reproduction. Masterful, but unfortunately fake. It seems we were following a false trail of clues. It wasn't the *Nativity*. Not the real one."

The disappointment on the Lieutenant's face was palpable. "I see. At least our hope in finding the real painting still exists." He glanced back at the house, now completely engulfed in flames. The local fire department had arrived and was doing whatever they could to contain it. "Just as well, it would have been lost." Spinelli called to one of his men. "Take *Signore* Greco into custody and see to the children." The little girl reluctantly released her hold on Angela, after she whispered in her ear and kissed her on the cheek.

Before being led away, Antonio nodded to Angela. "*Signorina*, we will meet again, perhaps." Alex watched the mobster and Angela's exchange with interest. There would be time enough for explanations. He looked around, searching for any sign of the spetsnaz team and Victor. But to a man, they'd melted into the night, and most likely were on their way back to *The Delilah*. Oliver ran up the beach calling to Angela. She rushed into her father's arms.

"Dad, how'd you get here?"

"Angela, sweetheart, I'm so glad you're safe. Alex called me in London, and I came as quick as I could." He hugged her, kissing her forehead. After a few moments, he stood back, searching her face. "You have some explaining to do, young lady. Honestly, I don't think I've taken a breath since I found out you were kidnapped."

"I wasn't exactly kidnapped, but I'll explain later."

Spinelli had returned after directing his men. "We'll be flying out of here momentarily. I need to clear this area and get you back to Naples where we can take your statements."

Alex noticed that Angela's attention was riveted on something in the distance. He followed her gaze down the beach but could see nothing noteworthy. He wanted to ask her what she was seeing but didn't want to arouse the curiosity of Spinelli.

"The sooner the better Salvatore. I think I've seen enough of Cavallo for one night."

~~~~

Naples, Italy
Present day

Angela was having trouble concentrating on what Lieutenant Spinelli said to her. All she could think about was what she'd seen on the beach at Cavallo...

Caravaggio had appeared, he still bore the scars from the attack in the alley. His hand reached out to her, his words echoing in her mind. *Someday we will meet again, and I will explain, Fillide.* He turned and walked up the beach and was swallowed by the darkness. Shouts from Spinelli's men broke through her vision, the ghost of the painter had smiled and nodded at her.

"Angela, you mean to tell me, *Signore* Greco contacted you and wanted to know if the painting he'd acquired was real?" the lieutenant repeated. "You went willingly to Cavallo alone to meet with a Cosa Nostra boss?"

"Yes, Lieutenant, he insisted I examine the painting and I agreed. I should have called Alex and told him, but he was in the hospital and I was afraid to upset him. He'd never have agreed to my going, anyway. I know I shouldn't have gone, but I was so excited at the prospect of finding the painting, I threw all caution aside. Mr. Greco behaved courteously and promised he'd bring me back to Naples once we determined whether the painting was real or not. For some reason I trusted him."

"And you're sure the painting was a fake?"

"I'm almost positive, but without doing a technical examination of the paint and the canvas, or infrared analysis I can't be absolutely certain. But there seemed to be less articulation in the painting." Her thoughts returned to the charred mansion. "I hope it was a fake or else Caravaggio's masterpiece is lost forever."

Spinelli's sharp eyes turned to Alex. "And you're telling me you engaged the help of a friend whom you can't reveal. He delivered you and Angela's father to Cavallo, provided you with arms, helped free Angela, and then disappeared like a puff of smoke?"

"That's pretty much how it went down. I regret that my friend must remain anonymous."

"I find both your explanations unsettling."

Angela was having as much trouble as Spinelli swallowing Alex and her father's story. The two were hiding something. Then again, she was hiding something, too. It was eating her up inside that she couldn't reveal the original *Nativity* had been burned in the fire. It was the deal she'd struck with Antonio to protect the children. It made no difference now, since the painting was ash, there was nothing she could do about it. However, lying to Alex was going to be more difficult than lying to Spinelli. "Salvatore, do we have any idea what started the fire?"

"They tell me it was a tragic coincidence. A gas leak ignited by one of *Signore* Greco's bodyguards. A cigarette. But we'll learn more once it is safe for the fire inspector and his team to investigate."

Angela was weary and barely able to hold her head up, but she had to know one more thing. "Salvatore, what will happen to Mr. Greco and the children?"

His eyes raked her with disapproval. "He has been released and so have the children. His lawyers arrived within minutes. Since the painting is a fake, no crime was committed on his part. The children are legally his." The lieutenant shrugged. "Unfortunately, we can't hold him, since in this instance he perpetrated no crime."

Alex took Angela's hand. "Salvatore, if we're done here, I'd like to take Angela back to the hotel. It's been a long night for everyone."

"*Si, si,* I understand. I need you to remain in Naples for a couple of days in case we need to question you further."

"Of course."

Casa del Sole
Montefioralle, Italy
Present day

Even in the depths of winter, the vineyard was magical.

Angela kept pace with Alex's long stride. The glorious greens of summer's vines were bare now. Christmas was a week away and her father and Lance were arriving soon. Angela had tried to contact Anastasia to renew her invitation to spend the holidays at Montefioralle, but the number was no longer in service. At her urging, Alex had asked Lance about it, but he knew nothing. Lance had tried to track her down but came to a dead end.

Anastasia had disappeared from London. Lance was confused and upset, but too busy wrapping up things at the office before he left for Montefioralle. He told them she'd done it before—disappear for a period of time and then come back. Alex greeted the news with indifference.

Since their return from Naples, they'd been busy preparing for the holiday. Maria and Angela cooking up a storm, Giuseppe and Alex decorating the house. A few days before, the men had chopped down a fragrant pine fir, and the four of them had trimmed the tree together.

Alex's mother took the news that they weren't coming to San Francisco for Christmas with aplomb. She was busy planning the wedding and understood that traveling over the holidays was a nightmare.

Nothing had changed between Angela and Alex, and yet everything had. They loved each other beyond reason, and their lovemaking was as fiery as ever, but Alex was keeping something from her, and her own secret was eating her alive.

She'd done her best to let go of the painting. She told herself it was impossible to succeed with every case. She was torn between the loss of the priceless masterpiece and her relief that Antonio would be free to raise Luna and Stefano. In her mind, he'd paid the ultimate price. Having lived through three life times of doomed love, Angela understood that kind of torment. Antonio had lost the woman he loved, the woman he could never be with, not in this lifetime. And to add salt to his wounds, he'd lost the painting. The one thing that connected him to Clarissa.

When Caravaggio walked away from her on the beach in Cavallo, he said they'd meet again… but the dreams and visions had stopped. Both the ghost and she had to accept the truth – the painting was no more.

"You've been running yourself ragged preparing for Oliver and Lance's arrival. Take a nap before we leave for the airport." Alex held tight to her hand and led her up the stairs to the second floor.

"I'm too tired to argue."

He pulled her through the master suite and settled her on the bed. He bent and removed her shoes. "Alex, we need to talk."

"We do, but not until after your nap. I'll wake you in an hour." He kissed her forehead and before she could argue with him, he pulled the door gently shut. She fluffed the pillows and lay back against them, exhaustion claiming her.

Her eyes fluttered beneath warm beams of sunlight.

Didn't I just close my eyes?

A terrible pain shot from her pelvis through her body. Her insides were on fire, the pain was so intense, she cried out, "*Cara Madre di Dio!*" She gasped trying to breathe. Frantic, her eyes searched the room, landing on a mirror by her bedside. She reached for it, raising it to her face.

Fillide!

Her beautiful face was ravaged by an angry, red rash. Fillide was dying.

The room was decorated with antiques, and delicately carved furniture. Brocaded drapes hung on either side of a window and sunshine poured into the room. A bird landed on the windowsill, pecked on the open windowpane and flew away.

Life goes on.

Her teary eyes fell on a portrait, the first painting Caravaggio had painted of her, *Portrait of a Courtesan.* She gritted her teeth through another blinding pain that left her weak. Blood oozed from between her legs, drenching the sheets. She didn't have much time. The doctor and the priest had come and gone. One had given her a medicine to ease the pain—it had done nothing. The other had administered the last rites—but she felt no peace.

You were right, amore mio, Giulio Strozzi was a good patron who's given me a life of ease. A beautiful villa and everything I have ever dreamed of. But none of it has brought me happiness.

"Soon we'll be together, painter," she whispered aloud. She clenched her eyes shut as another pain shot through her, setting off a series of seizures and soaking her body in sweat. In agony, she cried out, "Caravaggio."

A cool hand raised her fingers to his lips and the unbearable pain vanished. "I'm with you now, Fillide, I've come back to you."

Her eyes flew open and her heart pulsed with joy. "Caravaggio, you kept your promise—but I thought you were dead." His smile was benevolent, but he said nothing. "Oh, I see. You're not of this world."

He nodded. "I've come to take you home, *amore mio.*" He laid down beside her and drew her into his embrace. Peace enfolded her for the first time in eight years. She'd shed a million tears since word had arrived of his death. He died on his way back to Rome. On his way back to her. She relaxed against his chest—the man she'd dreamed of every night. "Neither death nor time could keep you from me."

"No, *amore mio.* Rest and let go of this life, so we can begin our next journey."

Her eyes lifted to the window, to the bright world she was leaving. She took her last breath and smiled, closing her eyes.

Angela gasped, struggling to breathe. She bolted upright. Her scream pierced the silence.

The door flew open and Alex raced in the room, gathering her in his arms. "Angela, baby, breathe."

As if she'd just broken the water's surface, her lungs expanded and filled with air. Her shoulders shook from her sobs.

"It's a dream, Angela, you're safe. I've got you."

"Fillide took her last breath and I couldn't breathe," tears streamed down her cheeks. Her hands captured his face. "You came back to her—Caravaggio came back—he held her, easing her passage into death. Fillide died eight years after him, but still he came back."

"Shhh… good, I'm glad. It's a happy ending."

A sense of peace washed over her. She had to heal things with Alex and tell him the truth.

The gnarled grapevines in winter appeared to be dead, but in a few months, they would be green with color and budding with fruit. The dogs raced back and forth, their snouts brushing the ground, searching for a scent, then bounding up the trail, seeking whatever mystery animal had been there.

"We've avoided the subject, but we need to talk." Angela stopped, forcing Alex to look directly at her.

"What's up?"

"I haven't told you the truth, and you haven't asked."

He rubbed his stubbled cheek the way he always did when he was contemplating a decision. She placed her hand over his, her thumb circling. Even when he was angry with her, he never refused her affection.

"The painting wasn't a fake, Alex. It burned in the fire. It's gone forever."

"Why did you lie and say it was a fake? Why would you help that crime boss?"

"Because I promised him I would. I just didn't expect to lose the painting in a fire."

"So, let me get this straight. You were going to let a thief keep the painting. How did that guy get to you? Did he threaten you?"

"No… It's a long story."

"I've got nothing but time."

She tugged on his hand. "Let's walk while I tell you everything…" She started at the beginning and told him all that had transpired from the minute she was picked up by Antonio's soldiers, until Alex busted into the bedroom and freed her. When she was done, she let out a sigh. "Now you understand, why."

"Damn. Poor bastard. I feel sorry for those kids."

"I know… but he loves them like his own. Why bother telling Spinelli, the painting is gone." She lifted his hand to her heart. "It's over, Alex. We know the truth, and that's the important thing. Caravaggio and Fillide are reunited." She kissed his hand. "Now it's your turn to come clean. I've been skeptical of the story you and Dad told me about how you got to Cavallo. Tell me the truth, Alex."

Alex stared straight ahead, his silence seemed to stretch out. "You must be projecting, because everything I told the Lieutenant is true," he said finally.

Angela let go of his hand. She studied his face. He wasn't going to fess up like she did. He was going to stick to his story and most likely, her father would too. She let out a slow breath and came to a decision. She wasn't going to ruin her holiday or her life over it.

Sometimes, it was better not to know the truth…

One day, you'll tell me.

Right now, the only thing that mattered was her first Christmas with Alex. All she wanted was the tension between them to disappear.

"Alex, kiss me."

"Baby, you'll never have to ask twice." His arms encircled her, pulling her in tight. Lowering his head, he kissed her with such passion, he stole her breath.

There was nowhere else in the world she'd rather be.

EPILOGUE

Kusnacht, Zurich
Present day

Anastasia poured two glasses of champagne. She handed one flute to the man sitting at the bar.

The falling snow had begun to blanket the trees. She'd didn't miss London or even Lance—

"When do I get to see your treasure?" Victor asked.

She smiled. What she missed she could never have. Her greatest treasure would have been sharing Christmas with her daughter and Oliver. She'd sworn an oath for Oliver's sake to let sleeping dogs lie, to keep the secret, and remain a memory, but the sorrow was almost too much to bear.

Her former lover was as handsome as ever. In his velvet tuxedo, Victor put *007* to shame. What she needed was to feel alive again, perhaps Victor would not mind holding her through the night and making love to her.

What is that American expression? Friends with benefits.

As if reading her mind, Victor leaned in and pressed his lips to hers. The kiss was chaste, but she knew behind its sweetness was a formidable passion. Victor had the stamina of a long-distance runner and a Tsar-like need to conquer.

"Come on darling, show me the treasure," Victor cajoled.

She rose from the bar and took his hand. "*Da*, your wish is my command."

Victor chuckled. "I think we should pursue that thought into the bedroom."

"Convince me," she teased back. "I might be open to negotiation."

He gifted her with an enigmatic smile. Having opened the door, she knew when the time came, he'd simply sweep her up in his strong arms and take his pleasure with her. For a time, she'd forget about Oliver and Angela.

She led him to a floor-to-ceiling painting of Diana, the Huntress. Dressed in a diaphanous, white sheathe, the goddess was notching an arrow through a bow. Anastasia touched her index finger to the point of the arrow and stood back. A clicking sound resonated, and the painting slid to the side, revealing a carved mahogany door.

Victor followed her down two flights of stairs to another door, this one was armored steel. She laid her hand flat over a screen and the sound of bolts sliding and unlatching followed. The heavy door opened to an underground bunker the length of a large living room with a ceiling that soared to an imposing height. Shelves lined the walls, with row upon row of priceless antiques. Precious works of art covered the walls in the climate-controlled room.

At the far end of the room was a sofa and a coffee table. Anastasia led Victor to the sofa. She set her champagne down on the coffee table and strolled across the room to a special easel built to display large works of art. A massive painting rested on it, covered by a tarp.

She pulled the fabric aside, revealing a masterpiece. "*Voila!*" She watched Victor's reaction. His eyes were wide with astonishment.

"Cat got your tongue, comrade?" she teased.

She sashayed back to him, the thousand Swarovski crystals on her black gown reflected the light, prisms of color danced on the walls like a spinning disco ball. Sitting beside him, his hand encircled her waist, drawing her close. "It's breathtaking." His warm breath filled her ear, and he tenderly nibbled her lobe. "Like you, boss."

Making him wait would only make the sex better. Right now, all she wanted was to immerse herself in the magnificence of Caravaggio's *Nativity*. A rush of heat traveled up her spine. The *Nativity* was hers and no one except Victor and her spetsnaz team knew otherwise.

"You are brilliant, Tashenka."

Anastasia smiled—it had been a brilliant plan. While Victor and Alex had freed Angela, her team had removed the painting and safely brought it on board *The Delilah* with no one the wiser. Everything had gone seamlessly, and now the painting was hers.

The only person who might figure things out was Alex. But Alex would hold his peace, he had no choice. Caravaggio's *Nativity* was the tradeoff for Anastasia disappearing from their lives. For her part, Madame X would keep the masterpiece safe and, as far as the world was concerned, Caravaggio's masterpiece would remain stolen —one of the greatest art thefts in history.

Anastasia snuggled into Victor's shoulder and awaited his kiss.

WHAT DO YOU THINK?

What did you think of *The Girl Who Loved Caravaggio*?
If you'd like to write a review **click here**.
Or email me at **belle@belleamiauthor.com**

ABOUT THE AUTHOR

Belle Ami writes intriguing romantic/suspense/thrillers with a touch of sensual heat. A self-confessed news junky, she loves to create cutting-edge stories about politics, espionage, and redemptive love.

The Girl Who Loved Caravaggio is the second release in Belle's highly acclaimed *Out of Time* thriller series, and a follow up to the #1 Amazon bestseller—*The Girl Who Knew da Vinci*.

Belle is the author of *The Only One* series which includes *The One*, *The One and More*, and *One More Time is Not Enough*.

She is also the author of *The Tip of the Spear* series, a compelling romantic suspense series which includes the highly rated *Escape*, *Vengeance*, and *Ransom*.

She was honored to be included in the RWA-LARA Christmas Anthology *Holiday Ever After*, featuring her short story *The Christmas Encounter*.

Belle is a Kathryn McBride scholar of Bryn Mawr College in Pennsylvania. Her passions include hiking, boxing, skiing, spinning, cooking, and of course, writing.

She lives in Southern California with her husband, two children, a horse named Cindy Crawford, and her brilliant Chihuahua, Giorgio Armani.

Belle loves to hear from readers.

If you are interested in writing an honest review in exchange for a free Belle Ami book, contact Belle at: belle@belleamiauthor.com

Click on the following links to connect with Belle Ami online:
BookBub
Amazon
Twitter: @BelleAmi5
Facebook
Instagram
belleamiauthor.com
Newsletter Signup

Made in the USA
Middletown, DE
12 October 2020

21480214R00149